THE PROFLIGATE

THE PROFLIGATE

THE LEGEND OF ANNE BONNY

D.A. NASH

Library of Congress Control Number:		2012906304
ISBN:	Hardcover	978-1-4691-9654-1
	Softcover	978-1-4691-9653-4
	Ebook	978-1-4691-9655-8

To order additional copies of this book, contact:
Xlibris Corporation
1-888-795-4274
www.Xlibris.com
Orders@Xlibris.com
113733

Dedicated with love to Natalie.

CHAPTER 1

ANNE FELT AS though she were watching a replay of her own youth while observing the turmoil from a second-story window of the plantation mansion. It was a most unusual event to view a young girl in colonial South Carolina engaging in a fistfight with a boy. Anne would have thought to intervene, but her granddaughter, Rebecca, actually had the advantage. So Anne gazed on in wistful silence, having a good idea as to why Rebecca might be behaving in such a feisty manner. The boy was the grandson of Beaufford Johnson, and Beaufford had a lengthy history of being a formidable gossip in Charles Town.

Anne was in her seventy-fifth year. Her body and mind had not succumbed to a feeble condition, so she was able to stand there erectly and recall with clarity the circumstances and motives of her past.

Although Anne was far from an innocent woman, improper imaginations and rumors had skewed the tales of her life to such a degree that she should be punished a horrible death. The mouths that passed those twisted fables were worthy of a much greater determination, because Anne possessed an unadulterated heart. She had a keen ability to appreciate the enduring truth in matters where others were blind, or if they perceived, they kept virtue buried by hushed lips.

It was September of 1775, less than a year before the Declaration of Independence would be signed, and the American Revolution was in its prime. The majority of the British invasion had been concentrated in the northern colonies, which left South Carolina virtually unscathed. Consequently, Charles Town exuded peaceful wealthiness, with its lush leafy acreage of indigo, rice, tea, and tobacco at their peak foliage, ready for the harvest. Sprawling mansions dotted the terrain along the Ashley River, which joined the Cooper and flowed into the Atlantic.

Anne's father, William Cormac, had acquired the four-hundred-acre plantation situated on the west bank when he arrived from Ireland in 1705. After he passed away, it was handed to Anne, his beloved only child. The original mansion on the property had been meticulously maintained; however, Georgian-Palladian architecture had been added to create the illusion of a modern manor.

Anne's dear husband, Joseph, had passed when Anne was only thirty-eight, but she chose to never remarry, and not wanting to live alone in such a grand home, she resided in the South Carolina mansion with her eldest daughter, Johanna, Johanna's husband, Charles, and their three youngest. Johanna's four older sons had already transitioned into adulthood.

As with all of the New World territories, Carolina had turbulent beginnings filled with contention as to its rightful ownership—France, Spain, and England being the contenders of this certain contest. Since agreement as to the first man who set foot on the prize was debatable, ownership was eventually to be defined by the country that settled and developed the land.

The French explored the territory in 1519 but failed to develop it, as their main objective was that of the fur trade. The Spanish attempted a colony in 1526, which soon dissolved, and further exploration was only done for purposes of acquiring gold. England would eventually secure the ownership of Carolina by beginning to settle the land in 1663.

Originally, the land was named Carolana by the French, derived from the Latin root Carolus, meaning Charles, to honor Charles IX, King of France. In 1663, Charles II, King of England, chartered the territory, claiming the right due to the English citizen John Cabot who led an expedition to North America in 1497. As if created by divine providence, King Charles II preserved the name Carolana in honor of his father, King Charles I.

The English charter of Carolana gifted the portion of land from thirty degrees to thirty-six degrees north latitude, as a reward to eight loyal subjects. These men, known as the lords proprietors, had assisted Charles II in overturning Oliver Cromwell, thus placing him on the throne of England that had belonged to his father.

The name Carolana would later be changed to Carolina. And in order to distinguish the vastly different political views, terrain, and attributes of its territories, the terms North Carolina and South Carolina were utilized.

The Carolina land grant to the lords proprietors was paraded as merit for their loyalty. However, the true motive of the king was ulterior. His desire was to see these men and their heirs develop the land in order to generate revenue for the crown. His design would soon prove to be a prosperous enterprise solely due to a single factor, the slave trade.

In 1670, Charles Town was established in South Carolina along the Ashley River but then relocated in 1680 to Oyster Point where it was to remain. It was an impeccable location with its rich soil to be cultivated for cash crops, but it possessed an even more lustrous quality. This piece of paradise had an accessible seaport from which to receive and to ship its merchandise.

Charles Town had become the ninth American colony of the British Empire, and with the prospects of great financial gain, immigrants flooded into the area—the majority being from the English colony of Barbados. Others migrated from Holland, Ireland, Scotland, Germany, and France, but by far fewer numbers.

The promises of wealth did not disappoint; and by the early 1700s, the thriving colonial seaport had perfected into an aristocratic society for the elite, a polite society bountiful with Protestant morality. The population was approximately six thousand, half of which were imported Negro slaves.

Although in its early years Charles Town was able to turn great wealth, it was far from the utopia it so desired to portray. Due to lack of interest and support on the part of the lords proprietors, the patrons of the American colony were left to contend with constant perplexity. There was aggression from the French, who still debated entitlement. From the frontier, the Yamasee Indian raids were common. The southern Spanish-occupied Florida presented an ever-menacing caveat as well.

Plenty of blame was cast upon the lords proprietors; but even more, the citizens of Charles Town believed that the attacks were simply Lucifer's way to attempt in discouraging them from achieving their divine appointment, which was to prosper. Despite their adversity, they overcame, and their abundance flourished.

And only when victory seemed assured, another villain began to surface. This assault would prove to be almost unconquerable, and the threat came by way of Charles Town's seaport. Plaguing the Atlantic Ocean was a growing host of pirates. They seized ships leaving from and arriving to the coast of South Carolina, upsetting an abundance of revenue.

It was in those budding years of Charles Town that Anne had spent her childhood, and reflecting upon them she peered from the window. She could see that Rebecca had only bloodied two knuckles, probably from a swift blow to Thomas Johnson's two front teeth, which left one dangling by a root nerve. Her cotton gown had been slightly soiled, but otherwise, she was completely intact.

Rebecca clenched her jaw. "You take it back or I'll knock 'em clean out."

Thomas staggered a bit but wasn't ready to give up his position. "It's true. My grandfather read it in a book!" Blood spewed from his lips as he emphasized his last words. "Your grandmother was a—"

Rebecca connected a final blow to silence her oppressor, and he fell to the earth clutching his mouth with a scream, crimson fluid seeping through his fingers.

"Rebecca, Rebecca! Stop, you stop!" Millicent, the Negro house slave with a thick Barbados accent, sprinted down the long pathway leading away from the mansion losing her headscarf in the chase.

Millie's eyeballs appeared as if they would bulge from their sockets as she grabbed Thomas by an arm lifting him clean to his feet in one fluid movement.

"Now you go, and you don't come back!"

"Rebecca, what is your mudah ever going to say about dees? Oh, my my my my my my! Dees is not proper!"

Millie had been sent to intervene on Rebecca's behalf by Anne who loved the Negro servant dearly and entreated her not the slightest less precious than her own family. The devotion was mutual, as it had been Anne who had spared Millie from the noose some years earlier.

Millie had been purchased from Barbados in the West Indies. At the time, English colonists who had been given land grants in order to produce massive sugar plantations heavily settled the island. The American colonists would transport Indian slaves to Barbados—the women to be used as house servants and the men as hunters—in exchange for their excess of Negro slaves to be utilized as field workers back in the American colonies.

Before arriving to South Carolina, Millie, just eighteen years old, had been purchased from an English plantation owner who no longer took value and had sold her to a merchant. Millie had held out against the treacherous journey up through the Caribbean Sea and across the Atlantic and, upon arriving in Charles Town, had been welcomed as a woman possessed by the spirit of black magic. As if by destiny, Anne had arrived at just the right moment and asked the magistrate if he would release the Negro from the gallows into Anne's care; and to Anne's great surprise, he did.

Millie held tight to Rebecca as the young girl held her peace, making sure not to stain her gown with Rebecca's bloody knuckles. Her nostrils were flared, and her eyes were afire as she watched Thomas stagger in the direction that he ought. Millie guarded Rebecca through the front door with a watchful eye as to not be seen by her mother and swiftly ascended the staircase holding tightly to Rebecca's wrist. In the second-story bedchamber, her grandmother was waiting.

The bedroom belonged to Anne, and it was there that she spent most of her time because it reminded her of her mother, Mary Cormac. The room still appeared the way it had been left when Mary had died in 1716, decorated tastefully in soft blues and whites from the finest of French fabrics, delicately adorned with lace. An oriental vase remained on the oak chest in which Anne refreshed a bouquet from the garden daily, as her mother had been a woman with an earnest affection for flowers.

Anne, sitting in the spindled chair by the window, expressed no emotion at the sight of Rebecca, which caused the young girl's heart to race as she wondered what her punishment might be for such ill behavior.

Anne whispered to Millie. "Cleanse her wounds, and try not to bring attention to her mother."

Rebecca released her breath. Although it was concerning that her grandmother did not address the thirteen-year-old directly, Rebecca knew it was a good sign that her grandmother was attempting to hide the incident from her mother.

Rebecca was the youngest of the seven children, born to her parents long after they thought they could no longer conceive. She bore a striking resemblance to her grandmother, and secretly, Anne had always considered her the favorite. Rebecca even had the same strawberry curls that Anne once prized. She possessed intelligence, beauty, and, apparently, strength, as she had taken Thomas for an awful jaunt, leaving him a gap through which to tell his depraved tales.

Upright in her chair, Anne was the picture of a Southern colonial matriarch seated on a throne, but from such, she couldn't have been at a greater distance. She held herself with dignity and grace, and her physical beauty was still recognizable. The special oils she would apply had almost erased the sun damage that she had allowed to her skin in her youth, with the exception of two small faded spots, which Anne wore with pride.

She had an astute intuition honed by a lifespan of experiences that no other colonial woman had ever owned. She was treated outwardly with respect from the people of Charles Town, but inwardly, she sensed their true thoughts concerning her. Mainly, she was accepted for being Chancellor Cormac's daughter. He had passed some thirty years prior, but her beloved father was still esteemed as having been a pillar of the elite society in the formative years of this thriving seaport community. If it weren't for his grand reputation, Anne believed she would have been ostracized altogether.

Anne watched as Millie squeezed a hand towel over the congealed blood on Rebecca's fingers, letting the water trickle into the porcelain basin, turning the reservoir pink.

Thankfully, Johanna was not privy to Rebecca's misbehavior, or she would have presented immediately to display her wrath upon the poor child. For if there was one trait that Johanna had inherited from Anne, it was a temper.

Johanna was Anne's firstborn living child and was delivered in the mansion by a midwife on Anne's twenty-first birthday. Two and a half years prior, Anne's first pregnancy had resulted in a stillbirth. She had named him Jonathan. Anne proceeded to have seven more children after Johanna, all of which had turned out to make their mother very proud, as they were all good-hearted individuals.

Johanna had always been different from her siblings in appearance. She had a slight olive complexion, brown eyes, and dark mahogany hair, while the rest of Anne's children were all fair skinned, blue eyes, with hair of various shades of strawberry blondes and reds. Anne had pointed out to Johanna that she was merely a picture of her great-grandmother and that appeased her, explaining a reason for her unmistakable differences. With exception, her great-grandmother had peered through pale blue eyes.

Pertaining to her character, Johanna was much more bold and adventurous than her more conservative siblings. But what truly set them apart was her laugh. It came from somewhere deep within, and Johanna saw the humor in things that others couldn't quite comprehend, except for Anne. Anne admired Johanna's differences, and the two women shared a closeness that few others have ever experienced.

Anne addressed Rebecca nonchalantly. "Rebecca, would you like to tell me why you felt the need to strike Thomas Johnson in the mouth?"

Rebecca began to sob, and that gave Anne a moment to contemplate, as she knew the answer already. Anne was set to tell the truth to Johanna. She knew that it was only a matter of time before someone would publicly divulge the mystery. And she thought it strange that no one had confronted her father in his lifetime, being that his name was clearly published in the book. They had probably kept the matter to whispers, not wanting to be the one who outwardly disrespected the honored chancellor. As far as Anne's name was concerned, she had never been addressed in Charles Town by anything other than Anne Cormac or by Joseph's last name. That is one benefit of being a woman; her identity can be concealed behind the surname of her husband.

The book was published in 1724, over fifty years earlier, and the author was Captain Charles Johnson. The title was *A General History of the Robberies & Murders of the Most Notorious Pyrates*. The book had been so wildly popular that three further editions were printed in the two years after its release.

Due to the sheer number of people who devoured its pages, it was actually puzzling to have not had to address the subject prior. The only excuse Anne could imagine was that the church had banned the book from Charles Town, claiming it to be the devil's seed, and for that, Anne was grateful. She was relieved that the subject did not surface during the years that she was raising her children or when her Joseph was alive. He was a good man, and she would have never wanted to see him suffer public reproach on her behalf.

But now at this season of her life, she was ready to free herself by making the truth known—the truth that swelled inside her so much at times that she felt as though she would burst. How she found herself among the pages of that book was a bittersweet journey of what seemed like another lifetime.

Rebecca spoke in between sniffles from the tears draining through her nose. "Thomas said . . . that you were once called . . . the mistress of the sea." Rebecca's lips trembled.

Anne was unaffected and remained silent, as she rather relished the term.

"He called you a pirate!" Rebecca began to sob again.

Anne allowed her time to purge.

"Rebecca, dry your eyes and try not to let what other people say affect you so badly."

Anne held her granddaughter against her chest.

"Rebecca, does it *really* matter about what these people think?"

Anne's tender arms and her words were like soothing balm flowing over the young girl's soul.

Anne had always planned on telling Rebecca's mother the truth. The opportunity had just never presented, but now was definitely the appointed time, being that Beaufford's tongue was wagging. Anne was bewildered, as she wouldn't figure that Beaufford was even capable of achieving such intelligence as to read. One thing she did know, however, is that she did not want Johanna to hear it first from another source. And she was thankful that she had not passed before this moment, taking her secret to the grave. There would be so many questions from Johanna, and Anne wanted to answer them all with the uncut truth.

It wasn't that she was ashamed of being called a pirate; she was incensed that the legend had gotten so vilified, and that no one had ever uttered a word to Anne about it that she may vindicate herself. They simply whispered behind her back and believed what their bitter hearts wanted them to believe—that their lies were of truth about the one for whom they gossiped, only to make themselves feel more righteous. And poor Thomas, being the only one who had the courage to speak out openly, suffered an awful fury by the hand of a young girl who fervently loved her grandmother. And now Anne was ready to be forthright with Johanna, as she believed her daughter had the right to know the truth about who her mother really was and had been.

CHAPTER 2

I T HAD BEEN fifty-five years prior in the year 1720 when England had finally removed the rights of the lords proprietors and had appointed a royal governor to South Carolina, being initiated by a petition signed by the colony's majority. Albeit a temporary mend to their bewailing, for the people of Charles Town were no more satisfied with their leadership than they had been with the lords proprietors. The looming dialogue concerning England's revolutionary invasions against the northern colonies only cast a further grimness upon their inconsolable tendencies. But as the end of June neared in 1775, the mood was elevated, as it was time to reap the wealth from their lush fields. The tilled outgrowth had matured, and the citizens of Charles Town stood rejoicing on the threshold of the harvest. The Cormac plantation was numbered among those who anticipated great yield.

It was Johanna's husband, Charles, who was now executor of the estate; and he held his position as the plantation manager with all diligence, almost as well as Anne's father had years prior.

Charles was a good man. Although he avoided deeper conversations, making it difficult to ascertain his intimate thoughts, he kept many other valuable qualities, mainly that he dealt honestly and entreated Johanna as if royalty. Unbeknown to Johanna, Anne had never considered Charles to be a handsome man whatsoever, but Johanna desired her husband, and for that, Anne was thankful and was completely resolved to dismiss such vanity.

Anne attended all matters concerning her differences with Charles with instant resolution and a humble submission, as Charles opinions were somewhat potent, and Anne didn't care to engage in a verbal sparring with anyone, as she had long ago discovered the futility of such. Besides, it was apparent by his actions that Charles loved Anne dearly, displaying a great amount of respect for her. She always kept a careful guard on her tongue, protecting against casting even the slightest bit of contention between Johanna and her husband, and that was probably her main reason for not confessing to Johanna much earlier.

Anne anguished with the idea. She had been so confident a moment ago, but her courage had waned as Millie completed the rinsing of Rebecca's wounds.

"Millie, she needs further cleansing. Take her and wash her wounds with lye."

Rebecca's face was gripped with fear.

"But it will sting!"

"I know, my love, but the human mouth can cause extreme illness, so it must be scoured."

Anne once knew of a man who had become blind after being bitten on the hand by a crazed child. The doctors reckoned that something in the spittle had traveled upward into his brain and had robbed his sight. The man never beheld the light of day thereafter, and Anne was determined that the same fate would not fall upon her granddaughter.

Millie coddled Rebecca from the room, being careful to conceal her from her mother, while Anne was left isolated with her thoughts. She figured she should get up from that chair and accomplish something of value that day, as she'd not even refreshed the flowers in the vase that rested on her mother's oak chest.

Thankfully for Rebecca, Johanna was unaware of her conduct, since her mother was out of earshot, being summoned to the stable to assist in the birth of a calf that had presented compounded and in the breech. Johanna had always been midwife to the animals and had been miraculous at salvaging many a calf, but in this particular birth, she had not been able, and Anne arrived to find her holding the demised newborn in her arms as if a dear child.

The scene distantly reminded Anne of her experience with Jonathan, and Anne marveled at how a simple implication as such could resurrect the agony of something that had occurred so long ago, leading her to wonder if the pains of the heart really ever vanished. She looked on until Johanna broke the silence.

"Mother, life is sprinkled with pain, is it not?"

"I'm sorry, Johanna."

"As am I, I just couldn't intervene quickly enough."

George, Johanna's fifth son, who entered the barn being sent by his father, interrupted their thoughts.

"Good morning to the both of you lovely ladies."

George suddenly realized that his mother held a dead calf.

"Oh, I'm ever so sorry, but look at the positive, if every calf lived, the whole world would be overrun with calves."

"George!"

"Well, it's of truth," he jested with his mother, his brilliant smile and quick wit brightened their sallow moods.

George was in his twentieth year, and he was attached to the right hand side of his father, as he was apprentice to the management of the plantation. He had shown an earnest interest from early in his youth, and it was George who would eventually ascend to the throne of the Cormac manor. He favored his mother with his auburn hair, and Anne was secretly thankful that George had not acquired his father's awkward color of red. When George smiled as often he did, he could illuminate an entire area, and Anne believed that his smile was the finest in which South Carolina had ever encountered.

"Mother, directly after I fetch father's horse, I shall bury the calf." George received the dead animal with all gentleness, and the women left the stable.

They strolled back toward the mansion in silence, Anne being pleased that Millie surely would have completed Rebecca's cleansing by that time, and her mother would be unaware.

They meandered past fields of breast height tobacco. The plant known as nicotiana was named in 1559 to honor the French Ambassador to Portugal who sent the herb as medicine to the court of Catherine de Medici. In addition to believed medicinal properties, the plant was known to repel insects. And for that feature, the slaves were well pleased as they worked among the fields.

Johanna noted that the broad deep-green leaves had turned to a golden hue on their edges, which signaled that harvest time was near—which meant for her that she would soon be overwhelmed with drudgery, as fall represented the most laborious time of the year on the plantation. While the women walked toward the mansion, they could see the Negro slaves busying themselves with the preparation and placement of the tobacco sticks, which would be used to string the harvested tobacco leaves.

During the harvest, the Negro men would reap the plants using a sickle, and the women would accomplish the stringing. The stringing involved securing the tobacco leaves to a stick by skewering them one at a time through the stem and aligning them in neat rows. It was important not to compress the plants to tightly together, as they needed room to breathe. Afterward, the tobacco-laden poles would be hauled by oxen to the tobacco barn to be hung leaf-side down in order to cure properly before export to Europe. The barn had been reinforced, as the Cormacs expected an impressive crop that season.

"Johanna?"

"Yes, Mother."

"Would it be possible that I have some of your uninterrupted time in the near future? I really need a space to talk."

"But of course. Would you like to talk now?"

"No, I need an entire day."

"An entire day? What could possibly be so pressing that we should need to converse an entire day? Mother the harvest is coming, and my tasks are overwhelming!"

"Johanna, can you not just give me one day? Out of your entire life, I'm just requesting a single day."

Johanna pondered on her words.

"But of course. I'll free the entirety of my day tomorrow if you wish."

Johanna wondered what her mother could possibly have to say as they broke paths, and Johanna continued in the direction of the mansion. Anne went to the garden as usual.

The mansion had borne its own accounts over the past five decades as it had sprung forth with life. When the chancellor was laid to rest in 1738, Charles and Johanna were courting at the time; and if not for Charles, Anne would have been in a difficult position, because her beloved Joseph was then in a feeble state, and sadly, he passed soon after the chancellor. Even though he was still quite youthful, Charles boldly assumed the position of master of the plantation as soon as he and Johanna were married.

The mansion was filled with wonderful commotion, as Johanna's seven younger siblings still resided at home. As her brothers and sisters matured and moved away, Johanna filled their beds with seven children of her own, all of which had been born within the shelter of the Cormac manor.

The Cormac estate was fully equipped to handle the volume of its residence. A central corridor was the entrance into the grand home with its six bedchambers, a great room, a parlor, a study, a small dining room, and the grand dining room where a long oak table expanded its length. There was a seat for each member of the family, and they had spent many a good time dining together and affixing themselves closely to one another.

Outside, there was a large kitchen made of stone for which the slaves would prepare their meals. The kitchen was not attached to the main dwelling, as the threat of fire was far too great a risk. Then there was the smokehouse and the root cellar and, of course, the outhouses, but they were quite a distance for obvious reasons.

Anne thoroughly enjoyed being a part of their family, as the home was abundant with eclectic vitality, which was a stark difference to her upbringing as an only child. She had a special closeness with each of her grandchildren, even more so than her very own children, with the exception of Johanna.

Her eldest grandson, Charles Whitney Wood II, was now in his thirty-sixth year. He had married a woman of the elite persuasion, Abigail Spencer, and the couple had been unable to bear children as of yet, so they busied themselves with finer things such as grand balls and galas, feeling quite comfortable with the aristocrats. Anne suspected, by the company they kept, that Charles was a loyalist, but he never spoke openly about the subject, for loyalists were of the minority in South Carolina, and his parents were certainly not of that persuasion. Anne was determined not to judge her grandson, as her father too had been instrumental in securing the royal governor, being wholly devoted to the mother country. Charles's poetry was simply divine; and Anne would lose herself in his writings, which laid bare a true reflection of his heart, revealing that he was, in fact, not an aristocrat at all.

John was born two years and a day after his older brother. He had never married, because his passion drew him away, as he was a merchant mariner, and his whole existence was devoted to the sea. Anne waited patiently for John to return for their family gatherings, only to hear his tales of unabated adventure.

John's twin brother, Jeremiah, had felt the call of the ministry until he had taken his first journey with John to the West Indies, and thereafter, he was called to the sea. His wife, Victoria, had given him a son, Mathew, and a daughter, Genevieve. Jeremiah's wife spent much of her time on the plantation assisting her mother-in-law, Johanna, while Jeremiah was away. Anne believed him to be the kindest soul for which she had ever encountered.

Luke came along four years after the twins, and when he was twenty, he married a French girl named Antoinette. They settled close to the frontier in a quaint home, where they were currently expecting their fourth child. Luke was an excellent hunter and kept his grandmother well supplied with venison, and Anne considered Antoinette's peach jam to be the finest in which she'd ever tasted.

Eight years later, George was born, and then there was Sarah, Johanna's first daughter. She was now in her eighteenth year and was betrothed to a young artist named David. When Sarah was christened, Anne had been adamant against the name, but after seeing that Johanna would not concede, Anne was determined not to allow the name to sour her against the precious child, and thankfully, she didn't believe it had. However, as darling as Sarah was, she never had the ability to hold such a place in Anne's heart as Rebecca did, and for that, Anne harbored quite a bit of guilt.

The summer perennials were still holding out, so Anne selected a bouquet of yellow foxgloves, sun drops, and coreopsis to revive the vase. She would add them to the purple-crested iris, pink astilbe, and white shasta daisies that Anne had arranged the day before, as they still appeared fresh. She adored spending time in the garden, as it had been her mother's. William Cormac had created the meditation garden for Mary, and it was filled with perennials that had returned every year since. The iron bench where her mother once sat remained in its same location. It was from that bench that Anne's life had taken a turn in a certain direction—a pilgrimage of which she planned to recount to Johanna the next day.

Rebecca was smug as she had believed that she had gotten away with her misconduct, and just as Anne had arranged the last flower in her mother's vase, Millie appeared in the doorway with utmost concern.

"Miss Anne, come queeck. Eets Mr. Johnson!"

Anne figured it was not a good omen that a man was rapping at the front door using his cane, and she never could have imagined such, but coming from Beaufford, she would expect it.

Anne had known Beaufford Johnson in his youth as they both were of the same age. He had always been a queer young man, being provoked by the other children of Charles Town, and his peculiar nature was even more pronounced in his old age. And now he stood on the verge of the corridor hunched to such a degree that when he peered forward, he confronted the doorstep. His face appeared bitter as if he'd sucked an entire lime in one sitting. Thomas, the grandson, stood at his side, being completely absent of his two front teeth.

"Mr. Johnson, how may I assist you?"

Millie stood behind Anne, her eyes jutting with trepidation.

Anne wondered how long it would take Johanna to hear the commotion and to respond. Rebecca peeked around a corner. Her smugness had completely departed, giving way to a tremble.

D.A. NASH

"I'm here to chastise the wicked child who's done this to my grandson," he said while shaking his cane.

"Mr. Johnson, I believe I should step outside with you to discuss this matter."

Anne was somehow able to reason with Mr. Johnson after the odd fellow greedily snatched up the sizable endowment that she offered as if he feared she might change her mind. Anne would have never resorted to bribery except for under these circumstances, and just when she thought Rebecca's name had been set right, Johanna stood at the threshold.

"Mr. Johnson, why are you standing outside? Do come in."

Anne repented that she had taught Johanna to be so polite in her youth, as Beaufford Johnson proceeded to sit upon the parlor divan and expose the entire event to Rebecca's mother, except for the part for which he had instigated the event by his unruly tongue.

Johanna held her composure until she had seen Mr. Beaufford and Thomas to the door and they had disappeared down the path leading away from the mansion with his pockets stuffed full of Anne's lost attempts to silence the outrageous old man. And to Anne and Rebecca's great surprise, Johanna excused Rebecca from the room and snickered about the incident saying, "Well, maybe that will teach old Mr. Johnson a lesson about the way he spreads his convoluted accounts of others." For she knew about his reputation as a devoted snoop, and his grandson being exposed to such a negative influence was in danger of following in his pathway.

That night, Anne wrestled with her thoughts about the conversation that was to take place the next morning. At one point, she resolved to write the story in a diary, making sure it would be easily found after her death. But then she relinquished the idea as she wanted to share her thoughts from the heart with the woman for whom Anne had considered to be her most precious friend throughout the span of her entire life, and so she found her courage again. She planned to let Johanna read the book, the one known as the devil's seed, and then she would explain everything.

It was fair to say that Anne in her youth had been void of all wisdom and that her father had horribly spoiled her. It was also true that she possessed a temper, although it was far from the monstrous accounts reported. Surprisingly, Anne didn't care the least that she was considered a ruthless killer, because she knew that Johanna would consider that to be embellished, but what really disturbed Anne was to be noted as a promiscuous woman.

Why couldn't a woman fall in love more than once in a lifetime without being called a harlot? And why was it that legends of men focused on their bravery and death defying feats, while the same stories about women only wanted to answer the question as to whether they were lewd or not? That eager placement of the scarlet letter from society in general greatly disturbed Anne, and so she firmly resolved in her heart that she would share every detail with her daughter. She ardently did not want to go to the grave, and after being laid silent, have her daughter be poisoned by those who would cast a doubt as to whether her mother had truly been an unchaste and lascivious woman.

That next morning, Johanna was thankful for Anne having requested her company, as spending time with her mother was what Johanna cherished most. Millie was ever so gracious to absorb Johanna's responsibilities and free her for a day of rest, and Rebecca was eager to help.

From the meditation garden, the women sat on the iron bench and enjoyed its ambiance as Johanna read from Captain Johnson's book on page 94, the chapter entitled "The Life of Anne Bonny." That day, Johanna was enlightened for it was truly her mother who rested within its pages, being inscribed as a pirate of long ago.

CHAPTER 3

A DENSE FOG descended upon the Charles Town seaport and crept inland toward the plantation long before dusk. Anne filled her nostrils with the aroma of raw soil as she knelt, her tears moistening the earth that consumed her beloved mother. The cemetery was located on the property and in close proximity to the mansion. Mary Cormac was the first to be laid to rest within its gates. She had died after being taken by a high fever.

"I'm so sorry," whispered Anne. Unbearable anguish swelled within the young woman, now in her sixteenth year.

"I've such regret. I would that I'd not been so precocious."

Enveloped in her grief, Anne reflected.

"You are all I aspire to be a virtuous woman, and I'm ever so ashamed of the way I entreated you."

Her mother's unending love surely had covered a multitude of sin, as Anne had been far from a submissive child, presenting a challenge in her raising. As her tears flowed over her mother's grave, Anne remorsefully thought about how upset her mother had gotten the time that Anne had threatened the English servant with a case knife. But then Anne quickly resolved in her heart and uttered, "No, the cheeky maid well deserved it, and she's lucky I didn't stab her." Nevertheless, Anne was truly heart-stricken about so many other times that she had misbehaved.

From the graveyard, one could see the sun's luster penetrating the fog and casting its illumination on the waters of the Atlantic Ocean, while it slowly descended toward the horizon in the west. The year was 1716, a vigorous era in the golden age of piracy.

Commanding the open water, a merchant galleon brimming with African slaves was within a short distance of its destination, the port of Charles Town. The ship named the *Golden Hind* carried its coveted cargo purchased from British Jamaica. The merchandise was set to be delivered into the hands of a wealthy planter, Chancellor William Cormac.

Practicing law was the chancellor's primary occupation. However, he had found a far more lucrative ambition in that of the slave trade, which was essential for the mass production of tobacco on his plantation. He had recently become supremely interested in Jamaican slaves, as they yielded a higher price due to their knowledge of cultivating rice, a new rage in Charles Town.

The shoreline was barely visible by telescope from the crow's nest as Captain Hawthorne guided the ship due west. In the hold of the vessel, Negro men and women, packed tightly, endured their chained, sweltering journey with stoic heroism. The stench of urine, feces, and vomit overwhelmed their breathing space. Hawthorne was proud and knew that the chancellor would be pleased to discover that few slaves had died while crossing the Atlantic. He reveled in his victory from the helm as the breeze wafted against his ruddy cheeks.

Suddenly, dreadful shouts emanated from the crow's nest. Although not one of the captives spoke the English language, below deck they studied the ceiling of their tomb wide eyed. Fear swept over each face as if they understood the universal word being uttered.

"Pirates! Pirates!"

From the crow's nest, Nathaniel cursed as he peered through his telescope. Surfacing from below the horizon was a sloop. A black flag with the feared skull and crossbones was being hoisted to the mainmast. It was a sure sign that they were being pursued, seeing that there was no other ship in the vicinity. He swung over the side of the masthead and repelled toward the deck.

The small crew of only five men, not counting the captain and his first mate, scurried to prepare for attack, each man knowing his task. With pupils dilated and muscles performing at maximum capacity, adrenaline pumped through the arteries of each man.

Captain Hawthorne remained calm and introspective, assured of himself and his men. Nathaniel arrived at the helm, dividing his words by deep gulps of breath.

"Cap'n . . . pirates . . . port side aft!"

"How far out?"

The captain reached for Nathaniel's telescope and verified the report.

"About two leagues, sir . . . Shall I display the white flag?"

"No, we may be able to outrun them. The harbor's almost in sight."

James Bonny corrected his commander as he approached the helm. The crewmen ceased working momentarily, so they could hear every word that the charismatic first mate had to say.

"Captain Hawthorne, it's a sloop. It will surely overtake us due to the weight of our cargo. Shall we dump some of the slaves into the sea to lighten the load?"

James was a ruggedly handsome young man of only twenty-three years old. His blue eyes were nicely contrasted against his tanned face. His hair was ashen but easily lightened by the sun and fell in tresses just grazing his shoulders.

Captain Hawthorne weighed his options.

"No."

Discouragement washed over each man as they returned to their work. They knew that James Bonny was right, and the pirates would soon overtake them. As any nautical man knew that a sloop was far more efficient with speed than an overfilled galleon. Why Captain Hawthorne didn't heed to James Bonny was perplexing and puzzling at best.

Captain Hawthorne was originally from England. He was a tall man with a solid build and a stubborn streak. The chancellor had named him as captain of the *Golden Hind* because of their Irish bonds, as Hawthorne's mother had been Irish. The captain had also been valued for his amazing skill to navigate in difficult situations, for which the chancellor had been witness on several journeys. But the feature that made Captain Hawthorne of utmost worth was that the Royal African Company had previously employed the captain, providing him with much experience in which to ship slaves.

The Royal African Company, established in England by the royal family, held a monopoly on the Atlantic slave trade with West Africa in the late seventeenth and early eighteenth centuries. The ruling class of West Africa had an agreement with the English company to trade its people for firearms and textiles, as these items were highly coveted by the African leaders. The guns were used to maintain their power, and the textiles were displayed in their grand homes as sign of their wealth and prestige. Men employed by the rulers of West Africa generally hunted the slaves from rival tribes, delivering them back to their employers who sold them to the English company.

It had been such a lucrative business that at the time, the slaves were more valued than the gold that was readily available in West Africa. The captured men, women, and children were shipped to their destinations in the Caribbean, South America, and the American Colonies, where they were greedily snatched up and used for labor. During the time that Captain Hawthorne was employed with the company, he transported a healthy percentage of the one hundred thousand slaves that were taken from West Africa from that short period alone, so the captain had a vast amount of experience in the trade.

Captain Hawthorne's character was that of a strict authoritarian, and James often strove with him, as James was averse to being dominated. The first mate covertly felt that he possessed more wisdom than the captain did, and in this particular occasion, he had. For as feared, the sloop closed in on the galleon and ensnared the vessel's rigging with its grappling hooks.

A host of pirates swarmed aboard. These men were not depraved savages, but well-dressed men of confidence, working as an experienced team, each man keeping his rank. Their marvelous attire had been plucked from previous plunders or purchased with stolen gold.

Hawthorne's crew humbled, almost paying homage, knowing that the pirates possessed the finest ability with sword and musket and that they were no contest. Captain Hawthorne adversely clenched his jaw and drew his cutlass. His eyes turned to bloodshot, and his face reddened by at least four shades.

John Rackam observed the scene while standing on the bulwark with one leg propped in a casual manner. His attire was somewhat unusual, as he wore white cotton breeches as opposed to the darker treated silk and velvet preferences of the day. This had afforded him the nickname of Calico Jack, as he preferred the cotton calico due to its ability to provide comfort.

Seeing Hawthorne in such a defensive state entertained John immensely, and he offered a hearty laugh.

"Have you lost your senses?"

He truly enjoyed this humorous affair.

"We mean you no harm. We only want your ship and your cargo."

John's men parted as he jumped down and approached Hawthorne, who remained ready to strike.

John was a devastatingly handsome and debonair individual. He had gained an abundance of confidence in his thirty-five years, and one could gaze upon his face without wearying. His smooth sun-kissed skin sported a healthy glow; his bronze eyes were soft with dark lashes, and he possessed the most beautiful smile to ever cross the Atlantic.

John arrived at Hawthorne's helm and stood dangerously close.

"Now put down your cutlass and—"

—Swoosh. Captain Hawthorne swung his sword slicing the air, as John glided out of the blade's path with ease. Hawthorne gritted his teeth.

"Okay, one more chance for us to sit down and have a cup of punch together. I *don't* want to hurt you."

Hawthorne, with all the guttural tones he could muster, rushed John, who once again easily avoided contact. John walked away shaking his head and motioned with his right hand, which signaled his first mate to proceed in subduing the crazed captain.

The blades of their cutlasses collided, but Hawthorne, being no match for the swordsman's ability, fell to the deck after being skewered. John turned to see the blood gurgling onto the deck and felt deeply regretful that Hawthorne had chosen that fate for himself. John addressed his men.

"Let that be an example of how pride truly does go before a fall." John lowered his head for a second. "Now help these men prepare the boat, so they may be safely on their way."

The rhythmical slapping of the water with the ores was the only sound that could be heard as James Bonny and his five men rowed toward the shoreline of Carolina. Thankfully, a half-moon rescued them from being completely enveloped in darkness as they distanced themselves from the *Golden Hind.*

John Rackam was not yet the captain of the sloop and crew who had overtaken the chancellor's galleon. He was quartermaster to a certain Charles Vane, who was absent on this particular voyaging due to more weighty matters. John was merely sailing in his steed. It would be approximately two years from then that his men would cast lots, selecting him as captain and procuring Vane's title. Pirates practiced a form of fair entitlement, allowing them to elect their captains by popular vote.

The stench of excrement antagonized their nostrils as John and a few men descended the stairs leading to the lower deck. He forlornly scanned the pitiful sight of men and women bound together in such putrid conditions.

"It's absurd for men to think that they can own another soul," John seethed. "The aristocrats are dregs, the lot of them."

John addressed his men, "Release their shackles and give them nourishment."

#

The silence was particularly heavy the next morning as Anne sat for breakfast in the mansion's smaller dining room. Her father, seated directly across, studied his daughter as she moved her fork in zigzag patterns through her food, having no intention of taking a single bite.

Ahyoka, a middle-aged Yamasee Indian woman, filled their teacups then placed the redware teapot on the table. Her name, derived from the Cherokee, meant, "she brought happiness." The frontiersmen, during a counterraid against her tribe, had captured her. Ahyoka was offered as a gift to the chancellor to be utilized as a house servant, and their motive was most likely to encourage the Charles Town leadership to provide security against the Indians on the frontier. Although she had learned some of the English language during her stay in the mansion, mostly she remained silent. She was not opposed to learning the language because it was to her benefit, but inwardly, she rejected the Christianity that was forced upon her. Her gentle eyes seemed to behold everything, and she would share bits of spiritual truth with Anne as she worked in the home.

Anne's thoughts were far away as she stared at her plate. Her beauty was of a rare nature. Although she had an Irish influence about her nose, her magnificent blue eyes, porcelain skin, and delicate lips were a perfect balance. Her strawberry curls were trimmed by a draping black headscarf, which was tucked into the collar of her black satin gown, donned over a fine black wool calamanco petticoat.

Chancellor Cormac, with his powdered hair and fine apparel, had wearied from seeing his daughter pout and was losing patience over her apathy.

"Anne, it's been over a month. I would that you please replace your mourning attire with a calico gown."

"I would that she had never died."

"I know, love, I too miss her more than life, but we must move forward."

Anne returned to gaze at her plate.

"In your mother's absence, it's of utmost importance that you assume the role of the mistress of the plantation."

The chancellor paused to let Anne process.

"Today, I would that you please rid the estate of all remembrance of your mother—"

"But, Father!" Anne gasped.

"Consequently, we are not constantly reminded of our sorrow."

The chancellor's physical features were predominantly Irish. However, his character was finely sculpted by Protestant English mannerisms, which were acquired in his youth as the British crown reigned over Ireland. Presently, he appeared somewhat impassive, but just below the surface, his heart was bursting from the unbearable pangs of Mary's passing. He spoke just above a whisper.

"Please place her portrait in a secure place."

"What about the advanced schooling you promised me?"

"Under the circumstances, it won't be feasible for you to tour Europe. I'm sorry."

She knew that his regret was sincere, but Anne resolved not to comment due to the overwhelming disappointment. In that era, only men were given the opportunity of a European tour, which provided for higher education and further refinement. The chancellor was proud to have planned such a trip for Anne, as he had offered her every benefit of a son during her upbringing. It was his design to shape Anne into a powerful woman.

Anne had truly been embellished by her father, and she had been elevated as if a jewel in his crown. He must have missed the passage in the Holy Bible that read if you spare the rod, you'll spoil the child. For Anne had never been struck in her entire life, and although she was entreated as if a royal son, she was guarded as if she were made of delicate porcelain.

A stern knock at the front door leading into the central passage suddenly brought them away from their dismal conversation.

James Bonny fidgeted while he removed his tricorne hat. His hair was now pulled back to make himself more presentable. The door opened to reveal Samuel, a Negro servant wearing a powdered wig, a waistcoat, and breeches.

"I'm here to see the chancellor."

William Cormac surfaced from the dining room and was truly puzzled to see the ship's first mate standing before his door. James bowed in a show of respect.

"It is with all regret that I must be the bearer of bad news."

"Do come in."

Master Cormac turned to excuse Anne as James entered the central passage, and from behind the chancellor's back, James caught a glance of Anne in the adjacent dining room.

He thought, "Oh my, she is far more beautiful than what I had heard."

Their eyes locked, and James tipped his head still holding his hat over his heart. Their encounter was brief yet potent and left Anne tingling in her private parts. She had a slight blush as her father excused her from the table.

James, soiled from laboriously rowing ashore all night, faced the chancellor in the eye, appearing as though he had not even noticed Anne as she exited the dining room. Her eloquently erect disposition emitted monarchy as she gracefully ascended the staircase. She glimpsed over her right shoulder to gaze at him once more, and although he so desired,

James resisted the urge to take a second glance. The chancellor studied the exhausted seaman's face with anticipation, waiting for Anne to be out of earshot.

"Deliver your news."

"Pirates have seized your ship returning from Jamaica."

"Vermin, the lot of them." The chancellor's blood pressure dangerously surged due to his adamant hatred of those sea-roving thieves.

From the second level hallway, Anne had stopped to eavesdrop.

"Were any souls lost?"

"Hawthorne tried to resist." James cast his eyes downward. "The rest were allowed to escape to the shoreline of Charles Town. Chancellor, I regret having cowered, but the sheer number of pirates—"

"Halt, it's pure foolishness to have risked your life to no avail. You are no match for those barbarians."

The chancellor turned away, perplexed by his thoughts.

"Did they sink the *Golden Hind*?"

"No, they seized it along with your slaves. I overheard one of them say that they were headed for Providence."

Upstairs, Ahyoka confronted Anne in the hallway, and before words could be exchanged, Anne grabbed the servant by the arm and pulled her tiptoeing into her mother's room, closing the door behind them.

"If you say one word of this to my father, I will thrash you myself. Do you understand?"

Ahyoka was silent.

"Don't play me for a fool. I know you can speak."

Anne slapped the woman who remained motionless.

"Now stop playing dumb!"

Ann, incensed, went to the window and peered from the second story in time to watch James briskly walking down the long narrow path leading away from the mansion. Entranced, she espied until he had disappeared from the Cormac estate toward the harbor. She mumbled under her breath.

"It must be fascinating to sail the open sea."

On the plantation below, the overseer drew a slow drag from his pipe as he carefully guarded the Negro slaves who worked unfailingly to prepare the tremendous amounts of tobacco for export. His men had been sent to watch over the Indian slaves who hunted game for which to fill the smokehouse for the coming winter. But the typical proceedings of the plantation were the farthest affects from Anne's mind as she daydreamed.

When she had finished, she spun around in a show of impatience toward Ahyoka.

"Now help me accomplish this daunting task of disposing of my mother's precious belongings!"

Anne's angry tirade resolved to tears, which touched Ahyoka's heart.

"You mother was good woman."

Because of her kind words, Anne almost felt sorry for the way she had struck Ahyoka as she opened the bureau. Anne lifted out a jewel chest and caressed the precious gems that had been crafted into the finest jewelry that gold could afford. The chancellor had truly lavished his beloved wife in her short lifetime.

Ahyoka folded an embroidered silk gown and was stopped by her thoughts. She knelt down, reaching under the bed. This annoyed Anne.

"What are you doing?"

The Indian woman's withered hand felt the floorboard until she could find the interrupted pattern in the hardwood slats. She pried open a small trap door and reached into the cavern to retrieve a small book.

"You mother write in it."

Anne was aghast.

"It's a diary!"

Ahyoka delivered it to Anne, who opened the book and stroked the soft pages with her dainty hand. A gentle smile crossed the old woman's face, while she watched Anne marvel at such an unexpected find. Anne promised herself that she would never again mistreat Ahyoka, and then she said with a whisper,

"It's as if I have a piece of my mother again."

CHAPTER 4

THE PORT OF Charles Town was taken with merchant ships. Men eagerly disburdened the vessels of their payload of sugar and slaves, while others were being packed with exports of tobacco, rice, and deer hide bound for England. In the harbor were countless other ships anchored and awaiting such opportunity to turn their wealth.

James combed the dock searching for his men who were found camped out of the way from the main traffic. He nudged Peter firmly with his boot.

"Wake up! Get up, you lazy dogs!"

Peter squints at the light as the others began to stir.

"Bring in the *Carolina* at once, Chancellor Cormac has ordered that we make some revisions to his ship."

The rest of the men were conscious but looking fairly hung over. Nathaniel replied,

"But, James, we've been up toiling all night."

"Don't you think you ought to go the extra mile seeing that the chancellor is going to furnish his galleon with cannon and extra men for our next journey?"

Jacob, the eldest of the group, was now fully awake. "Did you say cannon and extra men?"

James could not contain a grin.

"Looks like he plans to fight the pirates at their own game."

The men processed in awestruck wonder, as they envisioned themselves being victors over the pirates. Henry had a sudden idea.

"But hey, maybe you'll be the lucky man who the chancellor will appoint cap'n of the *Carolina*!"

Charles chimed in, "Yea, you're well suited being that you served as a British privateer!"

Nathaniel agreed, "I cast me lot for you as cap'n."

Peter stood with sword lifted. "All in favor say aye!"

The men chorused together, "Aye!"

James, pleased with the possibilities, marveled at his potential prospects. It makes sense that he should be the captain. He was the first mate and with Hawthorne removed, it would only be logical for James to move up into his rank. He would truly be honored by such a notion, but there was one thing that he would prize even more greatly. He crouched down speaking to his audience as if he were a dramatic actor on a platform.

"Although . . . what would truly make me a lucky man . . . would be to marry the chancellor's daughter . . . She is a fair maiden of truth . . . and her dowry alone would be more than an honest man could make in one hundred lifetimes."

The men were drunken by his performance and bewildered at James's vision and brazen courage. He was regarded as a very tall man in all their eyes as James said,

"Now, let's get to work."

The men responded with hardy enthusiasm.

After that, James completely dismissed Anne from his thoughts, but back in the mansion, Anne thought incessantly about the handsome young man, only to be contested by the discovery of her mother's journal.

"You have to promise not to mention a word about the diary to my father."

Anne searched Ahyoka's face for understanding and felt assured when the servant answered with a simple nod.

"Now go on out."

Anne closed the door behind her and placed the diary under her mattress but was unsettled with her decision. So she retrieved the small book and placed it in a hatbox in the upper part of her wardrobe. She then selected a floral calico gown and delicate lace cap, so she could resign her mourning attire as her father had requested. A final inspection in the looking glass left her feeling alive again.

Anne raced down the stairs just in time to see Samuel assisting her father with his overcoat. The chancellor admired his daughter, reminding him of the way she had been before Mary's death.

"Much better now, darling"

"Have a blessed day, Father."

Her father kissed her tenderly on the forehead and relished the sweet sight of her cheerful demeanor.

"As well as you, my love."

"Father?" Anne hoped he would not sense her hesitation. "What is the name of the gentleman who came calling this morning?"

"I hardly call him a gentleman. He's nothing more than a sailor. Why do you inquire?"

"I figure since I'm to be the mistress of the plantation, I should be privy to all the affairs that affect our livelihood."

The chancellor was reluctant.

"His name is James Bonny, and you need not concern yourself. I shall deal with him."

Anne was a crafty one for sure, but one thing was certain. She truly had a fond love for her father and thought the entire world of him, as he did of her.

The chancellor departed the mansion to begin what he considered his sacred duty, delivering justice in Charles Town, for he sat on the judgment seat. Horse and carriage drew him to the downtown district, the vigorous hub of South Carolina, where he arrived at the Court of Guard.

The inner city of Charles Town was a brick-fortified municipality laden with Protestant houses of worship. The crafted brick buildings housed the English church, the Anabaptist, the Presbyterian, as well as the French church. Religious tolerance was a trademark of the southern colony as long as Protestant doctrine was adhered. The Quakers were allowed a house of worship, but it was without the fortress, as they held the unpalatable doctrine that each member was a priest of sorts, and the Catholic Church was simply not welcomed anywhere in the region whatsoever.

In addition to the churches, there were two substantial buildings within the fortress. They were the Powder Magazine and the Court of Guard. The Powder Magazine housed the artillery necessary to defend the colony and the Court of Guard was the place of justice. In the Court of Guard, the upper level was utilized as the courtroom, and the lower level contained the dungeon, where unlawful citizens and pirates were jailed and tortured. Both the Powder Magazine and the Court of Guard resided on the harbor's edge situated on the Cooper River, which provided ready access to the Atlantic.

On this particular day, the chancellor was prepared to try the details of an alleged adulterous affair. Inside the courtroom, seated at a wooden table in front of the judgment seat, was Herbert Ford, a slender and fairly decent-looking man in his forties. Sweat soaked his pits as he waited for his lord to come forth. A sweet young maid wearing a simple gown and mop cap was seated away and to his left. She stoically endured what may become of her.

Finally, the judge appeared from behind the rostrum, and all in the small courtroom rose. A long white wig and majestic black robe exhibited his authority. He stood in his place at the bench, the highest position in the center of the platform.

Two barristers, one of which was Chancellor Cormac and the other Nicolas Trott wearing shorter wigs and less elaborate robes, entered and stood on either side of the judge at a lower elevation to His Majesty. Mr. Trott was positioned to his left and Mr. Cormac to his right.

In unison, the men were seated behind the tiered podium. The small group of courtroom observers was then seated and tarried with all reverence. A magistrate stood to the side of the room with utmost solemnness. All were awaiting the judge's oration, which finally came forth.

"It is my honor to deliver justice according to English common law on this day in 1716. Shall we proceed?"

The audience resonated softly in unison,

"Aye, my lord."

The judge inspected Herbert and the maid with all diligence and for some time.

"Who shall bring forth allegations of adultery against this man and woman?"

A woman, quite unsavory to the eye and about ten years Herbert's senior, rose from the audience. Her two chins were a sure sign of over nourishment, and her nose turned upward to such a degree that she appeared porcine.

"I do, my lord."

"Please come forward and take your rightful place next to your husband."

She marched down the courtroom aisle and pressed into the chair on Herbert's right-hand side. She leaned over and shot a dagger glance at the sweet maid.

The judge remained emotionless.

"You may speak."

Herbert's wife drew a kerchief to dab a tear.

"Verily, I was returning from a journey to assist a relative in childbirth. Now mind you, I returned a day earlier than planned, and upon entering my bedchamber, I found my husband in the arms of this woman, the maid. They were lasciviously thrashing about on our holy bed of matrimony."

Her chins giggled as she sobbed. A holy hush swept the courtroom. Every woman was feeling such sorrow for the dear wife. Every man, after taking one look at the wife, was thinking, "Poor bloke."

The judge turned to his right.

"Chancellor Cormac?"

The chancellor contemplated.

"Were your husband or your maid disrobed in any fashion?"

Herbert's dear wife clutched her chest, the pain almost unbearable to recall such a tale, and then to talk openly about it was simply shameful, yet she choked out the words.

"Her dress had been pulled down over her shoulder, and her cap had been removed."

Herbert comforted her as she decompensated. The judge addressed left. "Chancellor Trott?"

Mr. Trott was quick.

"Can you produce another witness?"

She gave a blow of her nose into the kerchief. "Yes, my mother."

Chancellor Trott scanned the small courtroom, and his eyes fixed on a woman who had risen. He resisted not widening his eyes as he thought, "Oh, my Lord in heaven, she is even more homely than her daughter and twice the girth. What in God's name was Mr. Ford thinking to have married an offspring of such?"

Herbert appeared to be the dotting husband and son-in-law, sitting next to his dear wife and mother-in-law at one end of the long table, while the maid was seated alone at the far other end. They all waited before the judgment seat.

Nicolas Trott cross-examined the mother-in-law.

"In your humble opinion, would you say that your son-in-law and the maid were in the throes of passion?"

"Beyond a shadow of a doubt, my lord."

"Mr. Ford," said Chancellor Cormac, "what do you have to say for yourself?"

"I was attempting to remove a spec from the maid's eye, and I lost me footing and toppled upon her. I was struggling to arise when me wife and dear mother-in-law came upon us."

The chancellor retorted. "Don't you think that there would be a more appropriate locality to conduct such matters rather than the bedchamber?"

Herbert's tongue had been bound for loss of words as Chancellor Trott deliberated.

"Mr. Ford, the Holy Bible says out of the mouth of two or three witnesses, let every word be established. We have two witnesses who speak against you."

The judge pondered as complete silence loomed over the courtroom and then handed the final decision. "I find them both guilty of adultery."

The maid burst into tears. "But he forced himself upon me."

The judge disregarded her plea and addressed her sternly. "You will be whipped and sent to the pillory for your transgressions."

She collapsed into a sobbing heap as the magistrate assisted her from of the courtroom. The pillory was the choice for her punishment rather than the dungeon, because the pillory was intended to publicly display her sin in order to induce shame, rather than conceal her iniquity in the dark caverns of the dungeon.

"Mr. Ford, you will be fined two shillings for your lot in the matter."

"But, my lord, that's a whole week's wage."

"If you dare to complain, you will be whipped as well."

Mr. Herbert Ford held his peace from henceforth, knowing that colonial righteous judgment had been delivered that day in Charles Town.

That evening, from the music parlor, the chancellor reflected on the day while playing an original arrangement on the harpsichord. Anne listened to the exquisite melody while working her needlepoint. Ahyoka tended the fireplace, savoring every sweet note. Only the elite men of that era were educated in music, and William Cormac had studied extensively. He was a fine musician.

"That was lovely, Father. May I please be excused? I would like to read my Holy Bible before retiring."

Later, an oil lamp illuminated her bedchamber from the nightstand, while Anne retrieved the diary from the hatbox and tucked it within the pages of her Holy Bible. She settled in as Ahyoka tucked her bedding. Anne had waited all day to read her mother's most personal thoughts, and she was finally given the opportunity, and so she read.

It was a story beginning in County Cork, Ireland in the year 1698. Carriages were being drawn through the English-style town just on the verge of the eighteenth century. Men and women went about their affairs visiting the various shops and businesses in the downtown area. That is where the law office of William Cormac resided. He was only thirty years old at the time.

It was in that year when Mary Brennen discovered her one and only true love, William Cormac. However, there was one difficulty. He had a wife, and she was merely the maid.

It all began when Mrs. Cormac's breathing was not at ease, and she had taken ill. So she decided to travel to her mother-in-law's for a long span of time, hoping that the air quality would be better and that her condition would recover. Mary was left to attend the home and the family in Mrs. Cormac's absence, and she held her position with all diligence.

Night upon night, when William returned from his occupation, she would listen, as he needed a soft ear to ease his worries. The more they talked, the more fond they grew of each other's companionship.

Soon, she found herself safe within his arms. She tried to resist her heart, knowing right from wrong, but the passion that burned within lured them further and further. His tender kiss was divine, and his touch was ever so gentle.

Finally, she allowed him to lay with her, and Mary discovered that against his bare bosom was where she felt complete and utter tranquility. Leaving her to wonder, how could their love possibly be evil? Mary had never experienced such euphoria in her entire existence.

Well, it turned out that Mrs. Cormac was set to arrive home in three days, and William had to leave for business for only two. He had planned to return and spend one more day together with Mary before his wife's return.

As fate would have it, Mrs. Cormac arrived home a day earlier than planned, and she brought with her the mother-in-law.

Now it was only proper that Mary should deliver up her bed to Mr. Cormac's wife in order to accommodate Mr. Cormac's mother, who was to sleep in the master's bedchambers. However, when William arrived home late that night, he was unaware that his wife had arrived home a day early and was lying in Mary's bed, as he assumed it should be Mary.

"Mary, are you asleep?" he whispered in the dark as he kissed her cheek and down her neck.

His wife froze in disbelief and remained silent. Mr. Cormac slid between the sheets and embraced his wife from behind. For the darkness of the room, he proceeded to make passionate love to his wife, calling her Mary all the while, and Mrs. Cormac took her treatment like a good Christian woman ought. His wife arose early in the morning before William had a chance to discover his error.

After that, their adultery had been revealed. However, Mrs. Cormac desired to keep the matter private, not wanting to publicly disgrace her husband, and Mary was made to leave immediately. Even in Mary's absence, Mrs. Cormac chose to reside with her mother-in-law rather than William, who was left alone.

Mary went to the country and took refuge with a certain relative, but her love for William never waned, as he would meet her in secret for walks, enjoying the privacy of the countryside.

Several months later, when they would steal moments together and dream about their lives as one, Mary informed William that she was with child. William was simply elated.

"When the child is born, we will name him Adam, after my grandfather."

"But, William, what if the child is born a girl?"

"Oh . . . well then, Anne, of course, after the queen."

Anne Cormac was born on March 8 in the year 1700. Soon after, Mrs. Cormac must have reneged upon her promise to keep the matter a secret, because whispers were heard throughout County Cork that William Cormac had sired an illegitimate daughter. William, being privy to such gossip, thought a brilliant plan. In order to spend time with his daughter, he would dress Anne as a boy, telling the townspeople that a relative had left the small lad in his care.

Mary eventually returned to the Cormac home, being that Mrs. Cormac's departure was permanent. William diligently educated Mary in the craft of reading and writing, as it was uncommon for a maid of that era to do such. He knew that Mary would need literary skills for their future endeavors. It appeared as though it would be necessary to relocate the family to the New World, being that the neighbors of County Cork were beginning to place extreme pressure upon the adulterous couple. Mary would be presented in Charles Town as a noble, educated woman, perfected with worldly culture. And so it happened in 1705 that Chancellor Cormac brought his wife, Mary, and his daughter, Anne, to the seaport town of South Carolina, creating an unstained beginning for his young family.

The diary snapped shut, and Anne could not believe what she'd just read. The shock was staggering as she uttered under her breath.

"I'm a bastard child!"

CHAPTER 5

ANNE'S THOUGHTS WERE consumed by the divulgence of the diary. As she pondered, she was able to easily rationalize much of it away. She knew that her father was a good man, and that there was not a kinder, gentler soul to have graced the planet than her mother. She figured that Mrs. Cormac had probably been a horrible nag and had deserved her circumstances. Anne found a scripture in her Holy Bible to support her views, as the book of Proverbs clearly stated that it was better to live in the corner of an attic than to dwell with a contentious woman. Nevertheless, Anne's love for her parents was unfaltering.

As far as being a bastard child, it didn't change a thing. Anne knew that with the exception of a pirate, there was no lesser a person to be loathed than a bastard in Charles Town, but she never believed that to be true. As in her younger days, she had befriended a girl named Catherine, unbeknown to her father, who was labeled as a bastard child. Anne rather found her friend to be quite delightful, and it grieved her heart to observe the townspeople entreating Catherine in such a cruel manner, which eventually forced her parents to move to the frontier, where Anne would never see her friend again. But pertaining to Anne, the people of Charles Town didn't know about her predicament, so she herself wouldn't suffer their reproach. She was completely resigned to keep it that way, as it would be her little secret. Although Anne didn't believe anything had changed by the knowledge she had acquired from the diary, everything had indeed changed, because from that day forward, she began to conduct herself with much less caution than she had prior.

Among the pages of the diary, there was one particular theme that caught her utmost attention. She was ever so curious about the notion of true love. She had certainly witnessed the romance played out by her parents and knew that there was some special enchantment between them, but she wondered if she would ever find the equivalent for herself.

Another matter consuming her thoughts was that of James Bonny. Maybe what she had experienced at the table yesterday morning, when their eyes met, was true love. She couldn't be sure, but she was determined to find out. Nonetheless, she would not utter a single word of any of this to her father.

It was a couple days later that Anne had developed a scheme. She recited the plan over and over in her mind as she arose early to prepare herself for the day. She donned a fresh gown, she had a delightful breakfast with her father, and she graciously sent him on his way to be about his daily standard. Then Anne addressed the servants.

"Ahyoka, you know what to do, just conduct your business as always. Samuel, you will come with me."

She motioned to the Negro servant, as Samuel had not yet learned the English language. Anne knew he possessed some aptitude because he was a fair butler, but he had presented a little thick when it came to linguistics other than his native tongue.

The chancellor had purchased Samuel at the selling block about a year prior. His previous owner had great prospects for the slave, as Samuel had been brought from Jamaica and he was believed to possess the wisdom to grow rice. After a short while with his master, the plantation owner grew impatient, believing that Samuel was dull in the head and had probably been touched since birth. He sold Samuel—bringing attention as to how marvelously the Negro could keep a rhythm upon any solid piece of matter, whether wood, iron, or stretched cloth, never mentioning his concerns about Samuel's mental capacity. The chancellor eagerly purchased Samuel with the thought in mind that he may be valuable to help the chancellor perfect his musical tempo. And Samuel was a cherished part of the Cormac manor thereafter.

Although the Cormacs entreated their slaves far better than most in Charles Town, they didn't shun slavery in the least, as it had been a well-accepted part of their culture and easily justified, since the Holy Bible made reference as to the normalcy of possessing slaves.

Anne continued to detail her contrivance in her mind as she treaded to the stables with Samuel in tow, and she addressed the overseer.

"Prepare the chaise. I need to be about my business."

The chaise was a sporty mode of transportation developed in the France in the early 1700s. It was a single horse-drawn pleasure carriage used for light traveling. Anne's chaise held two passengers and had been given to her as a gift for her sixteenth birthday. It was black with a folding calash top.

Samuel drove while Anne talked incessantly as they followed the path away from the plantation toward the Charles Town harbor. She told him practically everything.

"He teaches her all proper manners, and then they come to Carolina presenting themselves to polite society as man and wife! *With* their precious daughter, *me*, who's not even legitimate! It's a very twisted tale. Can you believe such things?"

Anne knew that Samuel lacked the ability to respond, as he hadn't understood a single word, but she just felt the need to ventilate her thoughts aloud. Samuel's expression was such that a crazy woman had taken him captive.

"Oh, I know you can't understand me and probably all the better. If word of this got around, we would be reduced to ruins!"

The chaise pulled up to the dock, and Samuel lifted Anne from the carriage. She approached a mate loading a ship, interrupting his work.

"Can you tell me how I may find James Bonny?"

After searching a short while, Anne and Samuel stood before the *Carolina*, a massive galleon, being outfitted with seven cannons that would protrude through portholes being hewn. The ship was being prepared for battle against the sea-roving dogs that had stolen the *Golden Hind* from her father. A salted deer hung from the rigging to be placed in the hull for sustenance.

"I'd like to speak with James Bonny."

The crewmen came to a dead standstill as James appeared from the lower deck.

"Mistress Cormac. It's my pleasure."

He removed his tricorne and bowed.

"How may I assist you?"

"I'd like to come on board."

The crew was watching in disbelief.

"This is certainly no place for—"

"A lady?" she interrupted and boarded the ship void of invitation. Then she commanded a crewmate adorned for his pirate-fighting adventure.

"Hand me your rapier."

Every jaw was gaped, and every mind was thinking, "For the love of God, what is she doing?"

Anne proceeded to slice the salted deer with precision and pierced it through with a final blow. Her fencing skills were supreme for a man, let alone a woman and certainly of that era. James stepped forward.

"Where'd you learn that?"

"I am my father's son. He gave me fencing lessons when I was younger. He figured I may need it for defense against unsavory fellows."

She looked down at a crewmate who quickly backed away.

"Up until recently, I would practice daily in the smokehouse," she gloated as she tossed the sword back to its owner. She still had audience, as no soul could speak for bewilderment.

"Why, it came in handy only last year, as an overseer tried to take advantage of my feminine youth. I thrashed him so badly. He took to bed for two weeks in order to recover. He's lucky I didn't kill him."

The men processed the story imagining such a sight.

"Now, James Bonny, do you still believe that a ship is no place for a lady?" she flirted and then moved in close for a whisper into his ear,

"Meet in my garden tonight at nine."

James was punch-drunk as he watched her gracefully float away.

In Anne's youth, her father had been concerned as she was somewhat of a tomboy, and although the chancellor was shaping her to be a potent woman, a hoyden was not what he had intended. And so he decided to afford her fencing lessons, thinking it would be an estimable means of channeling her masculine energies. In addition, he wanted to complete a way in which she could defend herself. The instruction came by means of a man named Chidley Bayard.

Mr. Bayard resided in England and had befriended the chancellor during one of his many visits to Charles Town as he captained his own ship and frequented the colony. After their fond meeting, the chancellor invited the gentleman to reside at the Cormac mansion annually when Mr. Bayard would arrive to receive his goods, being the deer hide that he purchased from the frontiersmen. He had become quite wealthy by transporting the hide back to England and selling it at a good rate. During that time interval, approximately fifty thousand hides were being exported annually from the South Carolina seaport, as the commodity was coveted in England.

Mr. Bayard had been schooled in France in the art of fencing, and his ability was said to be exquisite. The chancellor asked Mr. Bayard to pass the skill of dueling on to Anne, and he did so even though he thought it was a most unusual request, being that Anne was a girl. So every autumn when Mr. Bayard arrived in Charles Town, he provided Anne the lessons, and they would practice a good spell, as he would remain with the Cormacs until the threat of hurricane subsided in December. Anne was considered by Mr. Bayard to have been his most successful student, and he marveled at just how well she took to it.

Anne hadn't planned on displaying her fine dueling abilities that day; she was simply hoping to mesmerize James in some way or another, and luckily by serendipity, Anne had left the young man completely spellbound.

After pulling away from the dock in Charles Town, the chaise was drawn through the middle of the brick-fortified town of churches, and as Samuel navigated the shay, he had a look of pride about him as he escorted Mistress Anne after witnessing her grand show of talents. Anne was much more subdued than earlier as she savored the sweet thoughts of her infatuation with James Bonny.

Being that the Court of Guard was located on the wharf, it was convenient for the chancellor to frequent the site and inspect the progress of the *Carolina*. He came as usual, but no one dared to mention a word that his daughter had just left the vicinity and that it was Anne who had practically destroyed the hanging venison.

Samuel and Anne passed by the Town Square where the young maid stood shackled in the pillory. Anne thought of her mother as she read the sign displaying her crime. She read aloud,

"Caught in the act of adultery."

Anne motioned to Samuel. "Stop."

He pulled the carriage to the side of the road, and Anne approached the young woman, her heart feeling exceptionally heavy as she saw the red whelps upon the maid's arms due to the whipping. Anne spoke tenderly.

"Why are you here?"

The maid's eyes had been robbed of their life, as tears gently flowed from their corners. "I've been accused."

Anne had instant compassion for the dear woman and simply would not tolerate this deplorable decree, so she approached the magistrate with all confidence.

"Mistress Cormac—"

"My father has ordered this woman to be released at once as she has served sufficient time."

She leaned in and softened her tone,

"And you best not mention a word to him, or he shall perceive that you are questioning his judgment."

The magistrate readily heeded Anne's admonishment, and Anne was pleased to have helped the maid and to have brought her form of justice to Charles Town on that very day.

That afternoon, Anne delicately removed her mother's portrait from the wall. She longingly gazed at the heavenly figure. Mary was an elegant, petite woman arrayed in the finest clothing that high society could produce. In her bedchamber, Anne gently placed the portrait under her bed, having wrapped it carefully in a fine quilt. Finally and against her wishes, all traces of her mother had been removed from the mansion as her father had requested, with the exception of her mother's bedchamber. It was to remain intact, and the bedroom door was to remain closed.

That evening in the parlor, Chancellor Cormac entertained the elite members of the council who addressed the agenda one concern at a time. Pertaining to the Indian attacks, and after much discussion, all were in agreement to let the frontiersmen deal with those issues, because there were much weightier matters.

Chancellor Cormac allowed the men plenty of time to hash over smaller concerns, as he did not want to minimize their worries. However, they were now ready to discuss the true reason for which the chancellor had called the meeting. His audience was engrossed as William Cormac captured the center of their attention.

"Heed my words, gentlemen . . . there is a peril that threatens our prosperous reign in Carolina more so than any other aforementioned adversary . . . It's piracy. They are nothing more than filthy rabble and must be eliminated completely before they destroy us."

One of the councilmen consorted, "Of truth, Governor Craven has put much energy and supplies toward the fighting of the Indians. However, he has neglected to secure our ports."

Nicolas Trott chimed in, "And the lords proprietors seem to have gone on a long holiday. I do hope their enjoying their stay."

The men relished a hearty laugh. Then one of the other councilmen added, "Perhaps when the new governor, Robert Daniell, takes office, he will consider a petition to help remedy the predicament."

Chancellor Cormac was not convinced.

"I believe our only hope is to petition England to dismiss the lords proprietors and make Carolina a royal colony . . . That would guarantee the presence of British naval forces in our harbor. Gentlemen, there's no other way."

The men contemplated the serious consequences of such a decision, as they had all previously resided under the tight control of English rule.

While the council meeting preoccupied her father, Anne took full opportunity to sneak from the mansion, her destination—the meditation garden.

The garden was a short distance behind the mansion toward the river, and it currently bloomed with fall perennials of aster, mums, eupatorium and helenium, and sunflowers precisely placed in graduating layers of color.

Thankfully, the moon was on the verge of becoming full, and it illuminated Anne's path as she stepped lightly toward the garden. She used care not to snap a single twig as it might alert the overseer's dog. Slave's quarters could be seen in the distance with the warm glows of dim light seeping from their small paned windows. Although it was a cool night, it was temperate enough for crickets and frogs to sound their final choruses before surrendering completely to the cooler weather. The smell of smoke lingered in the air where the fields had been burned after the harvest to allow the earth to rest.

Wearing a cape over her gown for warmth and modesty, Anne reached her destination to find James waiting. He was dressed in a clean white calico shirt with dark breeches. He had cleaned up quite nicely, although his rugged appeal was still very apparent. The sight of him stole her breath, and she looked down, hoping that he would not notice her blush.

"You're shy," James flirted.

"I've never been alone with a young man. I don't quite know how to behave."

"You didn't bring your rapier?"

"No, silly." Anne felt more at ease.

"Why did you want to meet with me?"

Ann sat down on the garden bench, while James stood. "I can't quite remember . . . oh, I know! I'd like to hear about your sea travels!"

"We would be here for days." James was puzzled by the strange inquiry.

"All right, how about what is your favorite place in the whole world to which you've sailed?"

"Oh, that one's easy."

James sat down on the bench, but a healthy distance away from Anne.

"That would be Providence."

Anne jumped up aghast. "Isn't that where the pirates took my father's ship?"

"Yes, and there are pirates there for sure, but everyone gets along. It's a paradise of sorts. There are no rules."

"No rules?" Anne was amused.

"They've no governor."

"*No* governor?"

"Yes, pure freedom."

Anne could barely picture of such a place in her mind's eye and then returned to her place on the bench.

"So is that why you really wanted to meet with me tonight, to hear about my seafaring adventures?"

"Well yes, but . . ." Her courage was not easy to muster. ". . . I wanted to know if you would like to court me."

"Of course I would, but shouldn't I have asked your father first?"

"Oh, you probably shouldn't do that. He says you're nothing but a sailor. He probably has me betrothed to some . . ." Anne suddenly realized that she had hurt James's feelings. ". . . But don't worry, because I believe that if I introduce the idea slowly, my father will eventually give his blessing. Until then, we can just meet in the garden!"

James pondered the consequences of being caught with the chancellor's daughter alone at night and certainly without permission but conceded.

"Well then . . . since we're courting, would you mind if I kiss you?"

"James Bonny, you should be ashamed of yourself!"

She stood up and leaned in a bit in a teasing manner.

"I plan to save my first kiss for the altar."

"Well then, you best get in before you're not alive to go to the altar."

He arose from the bench, took her hand, and gave a gentleman's bow.

"Until tomorrow evening?"

"Yes, tomorrow," said Anne dreamily.

With one last look at the lovely lady, he turned to leave.

"James?" Anne hesitated. "Do you believe in true love?"

He pondered for a second as he turned back to her.

"Well, I believe in truth, and I believe in love, so I must believe in true love."

Anne, satisfied with his response, watched as he disappeared into the shadows. She was tingling again, and James resigned quit swollen.

Anne slipped past the closed door of the parlor just in time to hear her father concluding his council meeting and went directly to her bedchamber.

As was customary, Ahyoka tucked Anne's bedding as Anne watched the servant wistfully.

"Ahyoka?"

The aged Indian woman stopped to listen.

"How do you know when you're in love?"

Ahyoka knelt beside her bed searching her mind for the words, and then she caressed over her heart. "Here."

Anne was pretty sure that she had felt James Bonny in her heart and was appeased.

"Ahyoka?" Anne spoke just above a whisper. "I'm really sorry for striking you the other day. Can you find it in your heart to forgive me?"

Ahyoka had long since forgotten the insult and would have never held a grudge against the young woman whom she had grown to care for so deeply. Ahyoka saw nothing but goodness in Anne's spirit. She stroked Anne's hair as Anne drifted off to sleep, dreaming of her true love, James Bonny.

D.A. NASH

CHAPTER 6

IN PROVIDENCE, THE *Golden Hind* had been docked and was being prepared for its next voyage. The pirates rejoiced over their plunder of such a massive ship in which to outfit many men. The Jamaican slaves had been freed, and some had chosen to flee into the wild, knowing that they would be able to live off the land as freemen. Others joined efforts with the pirates, being regarded as kinsmen. This would account for the many African pirates who sailed during that golden era, where rum, distilled from West Indies molasses, flowed freely.

John Rackam boldly declared as he lifted a bottle of that very rum,

"I dedicate this vessel to our dear Captain Vane, and I propose to name it the *Revenge*."

He then smashed the bottle on the bulwark as the men cheered wildly.

Back in Charles Town from the small dining room, the chancellor's impatience was building as he waited for Anne. Ahyoka added the teapot to the table and tarried in silence.

"Where is she?" the chancellor snorted.

Finally, Anne appeared at the doorway with a bouquet of flowers and handed them to Ahyoka as she hastily made her way to her seat.

"What's become of you? You know not to be late for our morning spread."

"I apologize father. I was gathering flowers from the garden to dress the table, and the time escaped me."

"Well, you almost missed out on your surprise."

"Surprise?" Anne was elated.

"Today, I would that you have Samuel carry you to the dress shop. You'll find a new ball gown that's just arrived from England."

Anne's joy leapt and left her unable to speak.

"We are hosting a ball to welcome the new governor."

"Will it be a masquerade?" Anne was hopeful, as she loved such an occasion.

"We've decided not. We don't want to encourage unsavory fellows from infiltrating our company in disguise."

"Nevertheless, a ball!" Anne responded dreamily as she tried to picture the brilliant gown that she would discover later that morning.

And brilliant it was. Anne was aghast as she stood before the most magnificent garment on the planet. The gown was ivory satin with delicate embroidery. The hoop in the skirt was one of the most accentuated that had ever graced the colonies. The woman at the dress shop assisted Anne.

"It's a brand new design and all the rage in England."

"I can't find my breath."

"You're father thought you might like it," the woman added with delight.

"I don't just like it, I adore it!"

The bell on the front door resounded, and two well-dressed women holding their heads quite erectly entered the dress shop. Anne could overhear parts of their conversation as they murmured in low voices between themselves.

"They're a congregation of dissenters. Why they even allow bastards to worship in their midst."

"Noooo," resounded the heavier of the two women.

Anne's countenance fell, hearing the term bastard being smeared in public, but fortunately was not noticed, as the woman attending the dress shop turned to greet her new customers.

"Mrs. Perry, how nice to see you."

As Samuel guided the chaise in the direction of the plantation, he listened to Anne's rant.

"It's funny how things work. One minute, you're a gift to the queen, and the next, you're nothing but a slag in society. Well, I guess I'm not really a slag because nobody knows."

Anne sighed deeply.

"You know what, Samuel? It doesn't really matter, because I've decided that I don't like aristocrats anyway." Anne was smug in her decision.

"Oh, Samuel, I do wish you would hurry and learn the English language because I'd like to hear your thoughts on these matters."

After that, Anne relinquished to the silence of her brooding, and the only sound to be heard was the horse's hooves pounding the worn path leading back to the mansion. Anne spent the rest of the day preparing for the grand ball.

That evening, from the illustrious parlor in the inner district of Charles Town, the orchestra resonated the most majestic of baroque music to grace one's ears. The ball was simply divine. The men were stunning in their pure white powdered wigs, satin waistcoats with colorful embroidery, and breeches with shining buckles below the knees. The ladies appeared angelic in the finest ball gowns that England could supply, but no one was as picturesque as Anne in her satin ivory gown, soft curls cascading from under a feathered headdress.

She was positioned at her father's side as he introduced her to the new governor, Robert Daniell.

"May I introduce to you my daughter, Anne Cormac."

The governor was well pleased.

"Named in honor of the queen I presume and quite fitting."

Anne curtsied ever so gracefully, while small groupings of women coyly observed from the periphery, pretending to admire the sight but inwardly writhing with envy. They skillfully concealed their wretched jealousies behind their lace handheld folding fans.

Later, Anne and her father had center stage as they performed the most enchanting minuet together. Anne, as well as her father, was experienced in the art of dance, and to observe such was simply dreamlike.

Directly after their performance, the chancellor whispered in her ear,

"I have another surprise." He paused, anticipating her thrill. "Tonight you will meet the gentleman to whom you will be allowed to court."

Anne instantly disguised her emotions with a sweet smile, and the chancellor, being preoccupied by the thoughts of his daughter betrothed to such an ambitious young man, never perceived her ill surprise.

He led her by her satin-gloved hand into the presence of an exceedingly gracious fellow, yet Anne could not help but instantly notice his imperfection as he wasn't James Bonny. She blushed, but this time, it was caused by attempting to constrain her true feelings.

"Anne, I'd like to present you to Joseph Burleigh." The chancellor beamed. "Joseph just returned home from his grand tour of Europe."

The chancellor delivered her hand into Joseph's and then departed to mingle with other prominent guests at the ball.

Anne was completely dumbfounded, which made for an awkward silence. Joseph, being a gentleman and sensitive to a lady's feelings, suggested that they step out onto the balcony for some fresh air.

On the balcony, Anne stood in complete silence, gazing out over the moonlit ocean, as the moon was now full. Her eyes glistened in its light, yet she was able to constrain a full-fledged tear.

"Are you shy?"

"No, I just don't quite know how to handle such an occasion."

"Would you like for me to give you some distance?"

"No, that's not necessary," Anne replied as she worked up a good bit of courage.

"Joseph, I discern that you are truly a virtuous man." Anne's tears were now apparent. "But my heart belongs to another." She whispered, "I'm ever so sorry."

He was touched by her sweet address, which left his heart reminiscing of such pain.

"I understand." Joseph looked down. "Before I left for Europe, I met a most extraordinary young lady I'd ever envisioned."

Anne, having turned to face Joseph, hung on his every word.

"My parents forbade me to see her. She was a French Huguenot."

Joseph met her eyes and gently reached for her hand.

"You can't alter your heart now, can you?" He smiled sweetly. "I know from experience."

If one were to view the couple out on the balcony, one would perceive that the love they were feeling was for each other and that the chancellor's grand design had been a success.

"For you, I will petition your father to give his blessing, and maybe your circumstances will end in your favor, unlike mine."

At that moment, a bond formed between the two youth caught in a world where outward appearance, religion, and social status reigned supremely.

Anne chose to remain in her solitude as she peered out over the balcony. She wondered if James was waiting in the garden when her father suddenly appeared. It was evident that he was hiding anger, as his cheeks were red as rubies, yet he portrayed a forced smile as he did not want to draw attention.

"Your heart belongs to another, does it? And just when have you had the opportunity to fall in love?"

The chancellor's sarcasm was magnified by his smile. He glanced to make sure that no one was eavesdropping. His jaw was clenched when he turned back to Anne.

"Now you get in there and put on your best manners—"

"You mean, put on a façade?"

It took all of the chancellor's restraint to not strike her at that very moment. But then he thought how silly he would appear, spanking his daughter in her ball gown in front of everyone that was anyone, and the very thought of it helped to diffuse his temper.

"I've not been strict enough with you." He paraded his control. "You will be escorted home immediately, and I will confront with you when *I* am ready, which may be a very, very long time. So you may sit and wait for your judgment."

Anne's displeasure was just what she needed at that moment to squelch her tears and confidently surface from the balcony. With utmost grace, she glided straight in the direction of the governor.

"Governor, it was certainly an honor to be in your presence this evening."

"The pleasure is all mine, Mistress Cormac."

The carriage ride home was solemn and reminded Anne of the procession that led to her mother's funeral. Her father had chosen to remain at the ball, as to not cut the evening short and provoke gossip, but he had given Anne strict orders to restrain herself to her bedchamber and not to surface.

Instead of obeying, Anne waited until the coachman was out of sight and then rushed toward the garden to find James seated on the bench, picking the petals from a sunflower, which had wilted in the night.

"You're late, and you've been crying."

Anne could not speak as she was choked by grief.

"Did your father react unfavorably to the suggestion of our courtship?"

That made Anne stifle even worse.

"I have a bit of bad news myself. I'm leaving for Providence."

"*No,*" Anne forced a reply.

"Seems like, just as I have completed the task of preparing your father's ship for its grand voyage, I've been replaced as captain by a man named Virgil Jackson."

James, not sensitive in the least to Anne's raw emotion, seethed with bitterness.

"He doesn't even compare, and I refuse to be subordinate."

Anne finally found her voice and retorted,

"Marry me, and I will leave with you."

James displaced his resentment momentarily to carefully ponder the risk.

"Your father would have me hung."

"He can't hang you if he can't find us. Besides, I have such love for you that he would have to hang me first . . . Please, James, I don't want to be here any longer."

Anne's heartfelt pleas took a favorable toll on James as he took her hand, admiring her beauty.

"Well then, leave with me tonight. I have kinfolk on the frontier, and they can provide a safe haven. We can be married, and then depart for Providence together. We can make a fresh start."

Anne knew that she had but a short while before her father would return from the ball, so she made haste in gathering her belongings. She packed only a few essentials in a soft leather bag and suddenly remembered the most important items, her mother's diary and her Holy Bible. She tucked the books into her bag with care. Her gown was left crumpled on the floor in the middle of the room as she exited the still mansion. She wished so badly that she could say goodbye to Ahyoka and Samuel but certainly did not want to draw attention to her departure, and so she didn't.

Under the full moon, the castaways, with stealth-like ease, removed two horses from their stables without being suspected by the overseer. James cursed the light of the moon under his breath, fearing discovery, but was appeased once they disappeared into the shadows of the tree line on the periphery of the plantation. As they made their way toward the frontier, Anne had not one ounce of regret for her decision, but James, however, thought long and hard about the possibilities of acquiring Anne's dowry under such circumstances and hoped that they would not encounter Indians along their journey. That night, they headed away from Charles Town, their destination—the home of James Bonny's father situated in a remote region in western South Carolina.

The Bonny family had migrated to South Carolina from England in the late 1600s, and although their ancestors had resided in England for centuries, the mother country was not the source of their seed, for they were the descendants of the Vikings or Norsemen, meaning "men from the north."

The Vikings were Scandinavian pirates who terrorized the coasts of Europe in the eighth through the tenth centuries, and they were said to have been unusually aggressive. When the Norsemen invaded France in the middle of the ninth century, the northern territory claimed was called Normandy. In 1066, the ancient Normans conquered England, and it was then that the surname *Bonny* surfaced.

The name *Bonny* was given to a handsome person or large and well-built individual. It was derived from the Old French word *bon*, meaning good or fine. The Bonny ancestry lived in England for over six hundred years before James's father would relocate his family to South Carolina.

They currently resided on the frontier, and James's father made his way by hunting deer and selling the hide to merchants to be shipped to England for the making of fine leather products. James had been an avid hunter with his father in his youth but was called to the sea as he matured.

It took James and Anne a few good days journey to reach their destination, and they never met with any of the Yamasee Indians as feared. They arrived at the Bonny home to the smell of fresh-baked bread. The aroma wafted the exhausted couple in the face as they entered the family residence. The essence reminded Anne of home, but after inspecting the rustic cabin with the large hearth clad in caste iron, she thought, "This is nothing like home. It's worse than for which we provide the slaves to cook." After that, she quickly repented of her thoughts, as she did not want to judge her new family too harshly. Besides, all she could really think about was how sore she had become from sleeping upon the ground like an animal for the past week.

In the days following, Anne got along well with James's family, which eased her initial concerns. She actually found them quite entertaining. His mother was a large-boned and broad-minded woman with a jovial spirit. His father was soft spoken and introspective, but a strong silent leader of the family. James was the oldest of one brother and three sisters, all whom favored James in appearance. But more important to Anne than finding camaraderie with his family, she was relieved to find that she would be married in a Protestant church. If James's family had been of the Catholic faith, her father would have disowned her more so than for her elopement.

The day of the wedding, Anne looked sweet and simple in her wedding gown. The dress reminded her of an undergarment, but it was pretty, nonetheless, with its fine lace edgings. James was handsome as always and drew her breath, although even Samuel's attire was superior to what James had worn on the day of their matrimony.

The wedding night came as quite a shock to Anne. She was baffled at the way a man's private parts changed so drastically. It was painful and somewhat bloody, and she was sure that she did not want to do that again anytime in the near future. However, she was resolved to be a good wife and fulfill her duties, but only if she could not think up a believable excuse.

After the wedding, they remained on the frontier during the winter, and then just after Anne's seventeenth birthday, the couple returned to Charles Town. That is when Anne had her first encounter with her father since she had vanished some six months prior.

The chancellor was in his study penning a script from his writing desk. He appeared gaunt and plain haggard due to the emotional toll of his daughter's charades. Multiple attempts to complete his publication had failed, as his thoughts were elsewhere; his concentration weakened for lack of sleep. The majority of most days and nights were spent mulling over ways that he could make James Bonny suffer. And just as his mind had drifted back to how much he missed Anne, she appeared in the doorway.

He so wanted to wildly embrace her and celebrate her homecoming, but he resisted and succumbed to sarcasm instead.

"Oh, I see you've chosen to return, Mistress Cormac." He pretended to return to his writing.

"My name is now Anne Bonny, and I'm here to collect my dowry."

The chancellor broke into forced laughter.

"Oh, you are being waggish."

"I'm being sincere."

His countenance abruptly changed.

"And I'm being sincere when I say there's no way in *hell*!"

Anne gasped, and the chancellor's anger had caused him to stiffen.

"You ought to be whipped and placed in the pillory."

"I've done nothing wrong. We were married in the church, and I waited until my wedding night to consummate. I've found my true love."

"Oh god."

The chancellor's stomach churned, and its contents were threatening to soil his writings at the very thought of his daughter consummating with James Bonny.

"And where is that bastard, your so-called true love?"

"He's preparing for our departure."

"Oh, and where do you think you're going?"

"Providence," Anne said with confidence.

"That filthy rogue is taking you to the den of iniquity?"

Anne was a little puzzled as she hadn't heard the term before but remained strong.

"No, he's taking me to Providence."

The chancellor gritted his teeth, slamming his fist hard against the desk.

"I want you to know if I find James Bonny, he will be hung."

"Maybe that judgment should be bestowed upon you."

Her father was in shock for the audacity.

"I beg your pardon?"

"Passing off your maid as your wife and presenting me as some kind of a royal princess when I'm nothing more than a bastard child."

The chancellor appeared as though he had been dealt a fatal blow.

"Where did you hear that?"

"Father, don't you know that your sins shall find you out?"

Anne was feeling remorseful for the way her father had become so pale, and she would never forgive herself if he did not survive.

"Now if I please may. I'd like to take one ship, of my choosing, for my dowry, and I will never ask you for another thing, I promise."

CHAPTER 7

THE *CAROLINA* BLAZED across the azure sea as the wind set perfectly in its sails that day, pushing the ship toward Providence. James Bonny stood proud at the helm, as he was now the captain of his ship, having with him his five faithful crewmen and his wife Anne Bonny. They all anticipated the adventures in store for them on the island known as "a pirate's paradise."

Providence is situated in the middle of the chain of the Bahaman islands, beginning fifty miles off the coast of Florida and stretching hundreds of miles to the coast of Cuba and Haiti. Columbus first discovered Providence in 1492, making Spain its rightful owner, but the Spanish quickly lost interest due to its lack of gold and riches and thus neglected their claim. In 1648, English settlers migrated to Providence and began development of the colony that was named Charles Town. In 1684, the Spanish returned with a vengeance and completely demolished the settlement with fire, but the determined colonists rebuilt the town in 1695 and renamed it Nassau to honor the Dutch Stadhouder and also the king of England, William III, from the Dutch House of Orange-Nassau.

In the early eighteenth century, Spanish and French allies briefly occupied Nassau, and upon their departure, pirates began to claim the land to such a degree that no honest citizen desired to dwell in such a vile place. Consequently, the remaining settlers abandoned the well-constructed colony, which had been erected of brick and wooden buildings just off the northern coast of Providence and had left the hopeless locality to the pirates. The new inhabitants considered Nassau to be far from hopeless, as they took a stronghold of the tropical island, being most pleased with the lack of empyreal regulation.

Anne daydreamed of Providence as she leaned against the bulwark of the *Carolina*, port side, while the midmorning sun warmed her face. She had never felt so liberated. Everything was new. Everything was fresh. She delighted in the feel of the breeze washing over her skin and the way the sunlight dispersed into glimmers dancing across the vast ocean. She was sure that she wanted to live like this forever.

At times, she truly missed her father and was remorseful for having broken his heart so badly. But she resolved in her mind that all children must grow up and find their way in the world and that the pain that ensued was inevitable for all parents. Besides, she knew that her father would finally come around when he had found her to be so happy and getting along so well in Providence. She planned to write to him on a regular basis and update him on her progress.

James found relief for the helm and joined Anne as the two basked in the sun's warmth together. He gently removed her delicate lace cap and then tossed it overboard. Anne was delightfully amused and attempted to snatch his tricorne hat, but James was much too swift. They laughed as they watched the cap drift upon the gentle waves and finally disappear.

Continuing to flirt, he removed her hairpin, allowing Anne's hair to fall into long relaxed strawberry curls, which flowed in the breeze. He placed his hat on her head and enjoyed the view as she posed. Anne rested against James chest, and the couple kissed. Anne was sure that she had found her true love, and it was wonderful to be able to express her affection openly for James without fear of recourse from the people of Charles Town. And pertaining to laying with James, although he was not gentle whatsoever, Anne tolerated the whole ordeal now, only using an occasional excuse as to why she couldn't.

Anne was learning about a whole new world. She had her first sip of rum, which made the men laugh by seeing her nose crinkle. However, she was determined to show her bravery and went for a second gulp. She laughed at the comforting warmth that rushed over her body and the way it made her head feel like it was floating. James taught her all about the mainmast, rigging, and various parts of the ship. He even let her take the helm as he carefully guarded over her shoulder. She was at the pinnacle of euphoria, and it was there that she desired to remain.

Later that evening, the coupled nestled on the open deck, lying on a quilt. They gazed heavenward at the billions of celestial bodies sparkling in stark contrast to the blackened, moonless night.

"James?" Ann propped up on one elbow. "How can we be sure that we will not fall prey to pirates?"

"I have a little secret that I will show you later."

"What is it?"

"You will have to wait my love."

Anne reveled in the playful attention from James and breathed a deep sigh of contentment, turning her attention toward the star-filled heavens.

"This reminds me of when I was a child."

"What, gawking into the sky?"

"No, sailing at night . . . When my parents and I departed from Ireland to Carolina, I was only five years old. At night, my father would take me up on deck, and I remember those very stars right there. Oh, the feeling, I can still remember . . . Maybe that's why I've had such a fascination with the sea."

"I'm going to the cabin," he said, his attitude now soured, which completely caught Anne off guard.

"Did I say something amiss?"

"You've made reference to your father, more than a dozen times in the course of the day. Anne, you no longer belong to your father. You belong to me."

James walked away, and Anne's heart was catapulted to the ground as she sat alone in her silence with so many conflicting emotions. She loved, she hated, she was angry; but after a bit of a cry, she decided that she'd better try and remedy her husband's ill feelings.

When Anne entered the captain's bedchamber, she found James bare chested, sitting upright in bed, resting against the headboard with the sheet draped just below his navel. His body was tanned and lean from years of toning labor. She wanted so badly for James to hold her, but he resolved to ignore her as she undressed for bed.

"I'm really sorry. I didn't realize."

Anne offered affection, but James turned away.

"I still cannot believe that he replaced me as captain."

"But you are the captain now."

"It's not the same," James huffed.

He continued to pout, so Anne quickly changed the subject, attempting to draw him out of his foul mood.

"Wait a minute, where is the secret you were going to show me?"

Her plan worked, as James reached under the bed and pulled out a chest. From inside he fetched a black piece of cloth, which he gently unrolled to reveal a skull and cross-boned flag.

"Oh, that's dreadful. What is it?"

"That, my darling, is a pirate's flag. It is my secret weapon. You see, pirates won't attack other pirates. There's a silent code among them. So if we are approached, we simply hoist the flag, and they will pass us by."

"That's brilliant, but you're not truly a pirate, are you?"

He pulled her onto his chest and caressed her face.

"Anne, with this small piece of tapestry, I will make you more wealthy than your father ever could . . . I will take away the riches from those who think they are more powerful and righteous than everyone else, and you, my darling, shall reap the blessings of their lost treasures."

"But you would never rob from my father's ship, would you?"

"Of course, I wouldn't. I'd simply pass over him and wait for a Spanish or French vessel laden with gold."

Anne took comfort in his words, as she could easily justify in her mind the robbing from the French and Spanish as they had been long-standing enemies of Charles Town. Besides, she was smitten with James Bonny, and at that point in her young mind, she didn't even fully comprehend the significance of the black flag. From that time forward, she resolved to never mention her father to James again.

"I don't care about any of it as long as I'm with you. Please promise me that you'll always keep me by your side."

He ran a finger over her lips.

"You will never leave my side . . . ever." He embraced her more tenderly than he ever had, and they made love in the hold of the vessel that night. It was the first time that Anne had actually somewhat enjoyed the experience.

Up on the deck, Charles responsibly guided the ship from its helm, while Nathaniel stood guard in the crow's nest. The *Carolina* cut through the blackened sea heading south under a moonless sky.

Back in Charles Town, her father lay awake in his darkened room; having exhausted his anger, he was now swallowed in anguish. His love for his daughter was endless, and he'd been cut far more deeply than the day his Mary had died. He whispered a blessing for Anne as he drifted off to sleep.

After some days of sailing, Anne awoke alone in her captain's bed. As she became fully aware, she realized that the ship was no longer in motion. She hurried to dress and ascended to the upper deck to find James staring out over the bow. The sight set before her was unlike anything she'd ever witnessed. She gasped.

"I never could have imagined such an enchanted place!"

The water glistened of transparent and crystal blue. The sand on the seashore was white with a backdrop of diverse soft leaf palms and broad leaf foliage, each having distinctly different forms, but all tinted in deep emerald hues. The sky above competed for the water's color and was dotted with snow-white clouds. Anne had never beheld such a palette of vibrant blues and greens. It was vastly different in appearance from the Charles Town seaside, with its gray overcast skies hovering above the wild grass herbage dotting the tanned beaches being lapped by verdant waters. She wondered if what she was witnessing was the way in which heaven would appear.

By late afternoon, the *Carolina* was securely anchored in the harbor, and the men lowered the boat so they could row ashore.

Although the abandoned colony was well appreciated, the true reason the pirates had taken to Providence was for the harbor of Nassau. The harbor was one of the finest naturally occurring of its kind. It was a large channel along the northern coast, which was shielded by Hog Island. The most valued aspect of the harbor was that an infinite number of pirate vessels could moor within its safe confines, but the sand bars and reefs were too pronounced to accommodate men-of-war ships. There was an exit on the east side of the harbor and one on the west.

Providence was also ideal for piracy as there were multiple cays and islets surrounding the island in which to lie and wait for Spanish merchant ships laden with precious tender. The Spanish used the Bahamian islands as a route from the West Indies returning to Europe, and the pirates had plundered countless ships of their kind. One scheme that the pirates used to draw ships toward the island was to wave lanterns at night from the reefs and sandbars. The ships were coerced into the area believing that the lanterns belonged to other ships safely anchored in its deep harbor, only to discover that they were easy prey, having been grounded by the shallow waters.

James directed his men as they rowed ashore. He was certain of his destination, since he'd been there before.

It was early evening when they arrived at the tavern situated in the center of Nassau. The town was assembled of buildings aligned along the avenue that would much later be called George Street as Nassau evolved. The tavern was the remains of a puritan church that had been erected by the colonists in 1695 and had been enhanced with the remnants of pillaged vessels. Fine oak and cedar planks paneled the saloon's walls, which were tastefully decorated with plundered artifacts. A second story had been added to provide rooms for passing voyagers.

It was currently active with the raucous conduct of pirate pastime. An arousing tune resonated from the harpsichord in the corner of the room. The fine instrument had been snatched from a ship crossing the Atlantic coming from England and was practiced by its musician until he had perfected his invigorating melodies.

Shelves behind the bar housed a healthy assortment of mead, gin, rum, wine, and beer, which flowed freely to its patrons. Attending the bar was Pierre, an ornate and gloriously celebrated homosexual, a sturdily built Frenchman who had a manly appearance, but his mannerisms were accented with femininity. Pierre's hair was meticulously groomed and was as black as coal. His eyelids were lightly lined, accentuating his piercingly dark but gentle eyes. His smile was angelic, brightened by pure white teeth that were aligned to perfection. The stunning Frenchman held immense respect among the most infamous pirates in Providence, and he was famed by all as being the "madam" of his popular ladies establishment in Nassau.

Toward the back of the room, a cluster of men surrounded a table and shot craps, the game was called hazard during that era. The shooter rolled a seven, and wild cheers erupted. The sore loser tossed the dice on the table with a stomp and headed for the bar to sulk. The lucky fader greedily scooped up his winnings of golden Spanish coins and mocked his opponent.

At nearby tables, a few pirates had befriended women with flowing hair and bountiful cleavage, a far stretch from the conservative colonial women of Carolina. For a cost, men could pair with them and take their fill of love for the evening.

At a table isolated from the crowd was Edward Teach, who would later acquire the nickname of Blackbeard. He was frightening in his appearance, as one could not discern where his bushy black hair ended and his mangy black beard began. His harshly bloodshot eyes, hollow of all emotion, and his crooked nose, barely protruding through the overgrowth, were his only distinguishable facial features. He was given ample space, as everyone was aware of his antisocial mannerisms. He faded as the gin began to take hold and didn't seem to notice when John Rackam entered the brothel with a few of his men.

Pierre was most giddy.

"Well, if it isn't John Rackam. You've been away far too long, my friend."

"Pierre, I've missed you as well," John retorted with a grand smile.

The crowd offered a hearty cheer, confirming that John was well esteemed in these parts. Two ladies approached him immediately and vied for his attention as he announced,

"I propose to entreat everyone to some very fine rum."

His men held up several bottles as the crowd cheered more fiercely.

"Pierre, serve up a round of bumbo for all."

John removed a generous helping of gold and silver coins from his coin bag and slid them in Pierre's direction.

"As you wish, sir."

Avoiding distraction from his lady friends, John searched the room and found his subject, Edward Teach. He arrived to find Edward's eyes at half-mast. "Edward, I hear congratulations are in order."

John held out his glass for a toast, but Edward ignored the gesture, taking a hearty gulp of his gin.

"Rumor has it that Captain Hornigold has named you as captain of his latest prize."

John moved closer to obtain better eye contact and with a smile placed a hand on the Edward's shoulder.

"May you have many prosperous journeys, my black-bearded friend."

Edward finally responded, showing a bit of pride. "I've named her the *Queen Ann's Revenge*."

John offered a hearty laugh.

"Ah, a most clever name for a pirate's ship, very well, Captain, very well."

Edward gave a slight nod and accepted a handshake from John who then turned and addressed the two women by his side.

"Ladies, be a love and show Edward a good time tonight, won't you?"

The women pierced John with their eyes and then reluctantly took seats next to Edward, having no way out without offense. John chuckled inside at his roguish prank, knowing that Edward is the last man they would have chosen to lay with that evening.

"Edward, best wishes to you and do have a good evening."

With a wry smile, he tipped his hat at the trio as he left for the bar, where he found the glasses of bumbo lined up ready for the taking. Pierre announced to all.

"Come and get your bumbo!"

Alone at the bar, John was enjoying his punch as James, Anne, and the five crewmates made their entrance into the tavern. Pierre looked up.

"What in bloody hell, if it isn't James Bonny. And who may I ask is this very lovely lady?"

"This is my wife, Anne Bonny," said James with pride.

Pierre pranced from behind the counter.

"Let me have a better look . . . Oh my, you are lovely, simply lovely. What in God's name are you doing in a place like this and with—?"

"Pierre," James sternly cut him off just in time to avoid insult, as he knew Pierre was capable of doing.

Pierre admired the innocent creature with her golden curls falling gently over her lean breasts accentuated by the fit of her bodice. Her waistline was cinched, and her figure resolved to a full-length calico gown. She was a stark comparison to the ladies of the evening that served Pierre's establishment, and he delighted in the goddess set before him.

The five crewmates dispersed into the crowd, allowing for a better look by John who sat unnoticed from the sidelines, sipping his drink while evaluating the couple. John remembered James as the first mate of the ship they had once plundered, and as for Anne, he had never seen such a gorgeous creature before—ever. His breath fogged the inside of his glass as he coveted James's wife.

"Pierre, we need to rent a room for a short while, until I can provide a more suitable residence for my new bride."

"But of course,"

"And I need you to look after her while I go—"

"While you go? I don't need anyone to look after me. I thought I was not to leave your side ever?"

James jaw stiffened with ire at the embarrassment of Anne's incensed public challenge to his authority.

"We will discuss this in private."

John looked down, pretending he had not witnessed a thing, resisting laughing out loud, being thoroughly amused by this spirited young woman's brazen character. Instantly, he was magnetized to Anne.

Suddenly, the party was interrupted by urgent pleas resonating outside the tavern, and a young man burst through the front door out of breath.

"Spanish ships are circling the island!"

James grabbed a key from Pierre and hastened up the stairs, holding tightly to Anne's hand. The skeleton key turned the lock of a solid wooden door to reveal a room that was dimly lit by an oil lamp. The space was quaintly decorated, with just enough area for a double bed, a wardrobe, and a chest. The sound of resuming nightlife could be heard downstairs. James felt rushed, being preoccupied by the lad's announcement. Anne was still stewing as she looked around dubiously at the tiny room that would be her new home.

"You stay here while I—"

"You lied to me. You're a liar!"

James grabbed Anne by the shoulders and pushed her to the bed.

"Don't you ever challenge me again like you did in front of the audience down there!"

He leaned over her threateningly, but Anne would not back down.

"You said I was not to leave your side—ever!"

"I need to go to the other side of the island to recruit men and—. I don't need to explain myself to you."

"And why not?"

"You are a spoiled child."

He grabbed her by one arm, lifting her to confront his enraged face.

"You will do what I say. Do you understand me?"

Anne shook free, and he slapped her violently and then grabbed her hair, drawing her close. She attempted to release herself once again, but he had such a hold of her hair that she was painfully restrained.

"I want to go home."

"This is your home, Anne Bonny, and you are my wife. Now stop your defiance, so I can go help the men fight."

James forcefully shoved her back to the bed and walked out with a slam of the heavy door. Anne wept bitterly. She had never been struck or entreated like such in her life. She caressed her reddened cheek, which felt as if a flame had scorched it. She was sure a swatch of hair must be have been removed by his aggression, and she thought about how James viewed his wife as more of a possession needing to be dominated similar to that of an unruly slave. This was not the example she had been shown in her upbringing, as her father allowed his wife to reign as an equal partner, being cherished and adored by his side, and that is what she had envisioned her life would be like with James Bonny.

She spent the better part of the night striving with her thoughts and searching her Holy Bible. "Surely there's a passage in here that relinquishes a wife's entitlement to her husband when she is struck. What kind of a God would allow such?" she thought. She exhausted herself trying to find the scripture and was fast asleep when James returned later to unload some belongings and dirty laundry.

When she awoke in the morning, she was still tarnished by the incident, but as she lay there in bed, she resolved to attempt at being a better wife, and maybe that would affect a positive temperament from James. And so she decided that she was going to attempt the washing of the laundry that day. However, she had absolutely no knowledge for which to achieve her plan.

CHAPTER 8

ENGLAND HAD RECENTLY decreased the number of privateers as peace treaties were actively being negotiated with the Spanish and French. The privateers were common sea captains operating under the letter of marque, which was a document issued by England to make them equivalent to British naval forces. It was a means of bolstering the volume of British naval artillery in the Atlantic, and the marque granted permission for the captains and their crews to attack the Spanish and French ships who were opposed to England. When the privateers were successful, the booty obtained from their victories was divided equally among the English crown, the captain, and the crew. The decline in the number of marques left many privateers unemployed, and many of them became outlaws known as pirates. In the current year of 1717, approximately five hundred such villains resided on the island of Providence.

Although the Spanish were dealing more civilly with England, they still held deep resentment for the island. For one, Providence had been discovered by one of their own, so they felt entitled. And secondly, the inhabitants of the island were the souls of who had caused the Spanish much grief from loss of lives and goods from the frequent ambushes off its coasts. And so the Spanish took every opportunity to cross Nassau and harass the pirates.

James and the other men stayed vigilant all night, but the violence never mounted, as only a few cannon shots were fired in the harbor. Then the Spanish sailed away, taunting the men of Providence with their lofty display.

Some of them had returned to the tavern that morning, but James was not to be found. He and his five men had gone to the other side of the island to recruit men in order to expand their crew so James could attempt at pirating once again. He had left Pierre strict instructions for the care of Anne, and Pierre intended to take his assignment seriously, so he knocked at Anne's door.

"Are you hungry? Are you well?"

Anne opened the door to Pierre dressed lavishly. She admired the choice of color and texture coordination of his clothing. Anne had an immediate affection for this strange fellow. She had certainly enjoyed the attention he had bestowed upon her the night before, and if James felt it necessary to leave her in anyone's care, Pierre would most definitely have been Anne's first choice. As far as James was concerned, he knew that his wife would be safe with Pierre, knowing that the tavern keeper's sexual preference was unmistakably not for a woman.

"I'm fine, thank you. Can you assist me in doing the laundry today?" Anne replied.

"Oh, but of course. I am a laundry expert. Just look."

He posed with one foot forward as if a dancer of ballet.

"Oh that's wonderful, I know nothing about it, as the slaves always performed those menial tasks back home, but I'm a wife now, and I am willing to learn."

Anne's countenance radiated a childlike zeal.

"Oh, I see." Pierre was quite amused by her naivete.

Pierre was eleven years older than Anne and had been born into the urban commercial class of Paris in 1689. It was the urban class from France that comprised the bourgeoisie that defined aristocracy. It was they who enlightened the entire world as to the ability to procure happiness through the acquisition of possessions and servants, thus leading to a more fulfilling life. In addition, the notions of romantic love and paternal affection began to surface from among them. So Pierre was raised in a family like Anne, with a doting father and with a thirst for the more excellent things in life.

During his upbringing, King Louis XIV reigned with royal absolutism over France, and the country was undeniably the major power of Europe. King Louis XIV referred to himself as the Sun King, and it was he who persecuted the Protestant Huguenots who opposed the Catholic faith, as the king himself maintained a strong tie to the pope. Pierre's family had always been devoted Catholics, but as Pierre matured, he dabbled in the Protestant faith. It caused extreme contention between him and his father, but religious persecution was certainly not his reason for departing from France.

Although Pierre's father pampered his other children, he entreated Pierre quite differently, as Pierre was effeminate from his youth. His father believed that if he thrashed the young boy long and hard enough, Pierre would resolve into a manly individual. After receiving the beating that almost claimed his life, the young Pierre set out on a trade ship headed for the West Indies, and as fate would have it, they shipwrecked off the coast of Providence in 1709. Pierre found solace among the pirates and had been on the island ever since, leaving the harsh memories of his father far behind.

As Anne felt for Pierre, he too had an instant devotion to this special lady. He felt as if a goddess had been plucked from the universe and delivered into his care. He knew that she was far too innocent to be left on her own accord, and so he purposed to keep her close at all times, a task that he would discover he thoroughly relished.

Later that morning, after Pierre had served breakfast to his new-sprung companion, they carried down piles of James and his men's soiled clothing, keeping their heads turned to avoid the stench of dampened decay. Out behind the tavern, a fire was lit under a large cast-iron pot just on the verge of boiling, and Pierre instructed Anne on the art of doing laundry his way.

"While we're waiting for the pot, take this and work it into the visible stains."

He handed Anne the lye soap. Repulsed, she took it and daintily agitated it into a spot on the dungarees.

"No, like this."

Pierre scrubbed heartily. "You have to put some knuckles into it."

Anne returned a good demonstration.

"Very well."

Shortly after, the pot was at a rolling boil, and Anne had worked up a sweat, her hair somewhat disheveled.

"Now we will place the garments into the pot and wait a spell, but first, I need to add a special ingredient, guaranteed to vanish any stain."

Anne was intrigued as Pierre added a generous portion of yellow fluid from a jug.

"What's that?"

"It's piddle."

"Piddle?"

"You know, urine."

"Urine!" Anne was completely disgusted and withdrew her hands. Pierre laughed.

"Be patient"—he chuckled—"The ammonia from the urine will give you the brightest garments that you've ever witnessed. It's simply amazing. Just look!"

He referenced his attire again.

"Here's your example."

After boiling the laundry, Pierre and Anne were hanging the clothing to dry.

"I really can't believe that I left a sprawling mansion full of servants to come and do this . . . And for a man for whom I struggle to find affection anymore."

"Hmm, I was wondering how you ended up with James Bonny. Look, give it a quick snap to get the wrinkles out before you hang it."

"What do you mean about ending up with James Bonny?"

"Well, I didn't want to cause a stir."

Pierre looked down.

"No, tell me. I want to know the unbridled truth about your thoughts concerning James."

Pierre calculated about how much he should tell Anne, as he knew she could not be told everything. He repented in his heart that he had mentioned the first word.

James had been to Providence many times in his younger years when he privateered for the British. In fact, one night, when James had been unusually drunken, and seeing that there were no ladies readily available, the young lad propositioned Pierre. Being the weak man that Pierre had been and not having known more about the character of James, Pierre consented to lay with James for the night. After that, Pierre was regretful for his decision and was pleased when James acted as if not a thing had occurred. Pierre was relieved when the British voided James's letter of marque, being that James was unable to produce any revenue for the crown and that his cancellation had forced him to leave the island in search of employment. James headed to South Carolina after that, and Pierre had hoped that he would never see him again, but here he was back on the island.

Pierre wagged his head in sympathy toward Anne.

"First of all, I want you to know that I care deeply for you in just a very short time. May I call you Anney by the way?"

"Of course, you can."

"And secondly, you are much too precious for a rogue like James. His luck is putrid. He never prospers at anything in which he sets his hands to accomplish. He's been known to be rough with the ladies and . . ." Pierre suddenly realized that he was ranting and needed to give Anne a chance to rebuttal.

Anne was downcast by that point, and Pierre offered comfort.

"I'm sorry."

D.A. NASH

"No, it's not your fault. I was wrong. I thought he was my true love, and I had such hopes for happiness, but after he struck me last night—"

"He struck you!" Suddenly it was as if Pierre was reliving the horrors of his past. "Oh no, he will never strike you again, and you have my solemn word on that."

Remorse flooded Anne's heart.

"I wish I'd never left Charles Town. My father treated me as a queen, and I took it all for granted."

"Your father sounds like a very good man."

"Oh, and he is a wonderful man."

Anne was grateful to have found someone like Pierre that she could share her heart concerning her father, unlike James who writhed at the very mention of his name.

"As much as I don't want you to go because you've brightened my existence, I think you should return to Charles Town and pretend that this whole thing never occurred."

"I wish I could."

She pondered such a thing and resolved in her mind that it might be quite plausible. She knew that her father would certainly not have told anyone about the marriage. Her father would have just added this to his collection of little secrets. He was probably boasting of her grand European Tour as they now stood there. And quite frankly, it sounded quite pleasant, the idea of returning and living out the rest her days as mistress of the plantation, being known as the chancellor's daughter—the old maid who never chose to marry.

Pierre thought long and hard about a way to get Anney back to Charles Town, but he did not want to harp on the subject and cause her to renege, so he kept the matter to himself. He thought about having a pirate sail her home to Charles Town—"But no, that would never work!" For Pierre knew that not one pirate in Providence would dare set foot on the port of South Carolina, knowing they would be lynched immediately or, worse yet, placed in the dungeon and kept alive, only to be horribly tortured.

After hearing about the abuse in which Anne had suffered at the hand of James, Pierre was completely resolved to hide her in the meantime from her husband, until Pierre could safely see Anne on her way back home to Charles Town. If James returned before then, Pierre would contrive a story that Anne had been horribly abducted by a crazed pirate and send James away on a wild chase. Pierre could even work up a tear at the very thought, making his story all the more believable.

Until then, Pierre decided that since he was responsible for Anne's care and since he didn't know how long she would be on the island that he should teach her everything he knew just as he had with the laundry. He would instruct her on all the valuable skills necessary for survival on the island. So Anne and Pierre spent all of their time together and became closer friends than Anne had ever experienced. It puzzled Anne, because in some strange way, Pierre reminded her of her mother.

After they completed the laundry about noon, the first thing on Pierre's mind was to move Anne out of the room that she and James had shared upon their arrival to Nassau. Pierre did not want James to return in the night and find Anne alone, thus compromising her safety. Anne was agreeable, as Pierre had only confirmed what Anne already knew deep in her heart that she needed to leave James Bonny.

After settling her in to her new room, the two took a walk by the ocean, and Pierre helped Anne to release the guilt of so many things. It freed her heart to hear Pierre say that no matter what Anne did, like by trying to be the good wife, she was not going to change James Bonny's behavior. Also, he encouraged her not to be so hard on herself because she was simply human and all humans make blunders. Marrying James was simply an oversight, and she did not need to live the rest of her life in misery because of one tiny lapse in judgment.

With Pierre's excellent counsel, Anne was able to firmly resolve in her heart that she never cared to see James Bonny again, especially after hearing Pierre's poor report of her husband's character. As far as Anne was concerned, James was a liar who had abandoned her on that dreadful island, and he was certainly a brute who didn't deserve a wife.

"Oh, and one more thing, he hates my father, and I am ashamed of myself for ever allowing him to be so disrespectful without putting up a fight!"

"Well, it's probably better that you hadn't put up a fight or he may have resolved to completely snatch you bald headed."

Anne and Pierre snickered at the thought as they walked along the white sandy beach. The sound of the blue waters lapping the shore was a nice reprieve from the exhausting subject of James Bonny.

Every night, Anne would stay in her room while Pierre tended the bar just in case James should appear. One morning, after making a quick survey and finding James still hadn't returned, Pierre took Anne along with his musket and a large jug into the pine yards to show her where to fetch fresh water.

Anne marveled at the wilderness, as the vegetation was completely different than on the frontier. The Bahamian pineyards are a short and shrubby timberland with the Bahamian pines being the majority of its trees, although not exclusively, for there are also variations of flowering trees as well as palms. The tree height is not nearly as grand as the tall oaks, pines, maples, and birches of South Carolina. Flowering shrubs and climbing bushes are abundant in the forest with all colors of pinks, reds, and purples. The yellow elders competed with the hibiscus of yellows, pinks, reds, whites, and peach, and wild orchids were found in soft blues and lavenders.

On their hike for water, a pygmy boa frightened Anne, but Pierre reassured her that it was not poisonous and the meat was actually quite tasty. She saw types of birds that she'd never seen, such as the yellow throat and the Bahaman woodstar. But the things that intrigued Anne mostly were the dwellings built in the trees. Many of the pirates had built tree houses among the pines to elevate themselves from the dangers of the wild animals on the forest floor, and Anne thought the idea of living in a tree was quite peculiar.

During their walk, Pierre picked wild onions and mushrooms, placing them in his side bag. He also shared information with Anne as they trekked along the well-worn path. He instructed her on the craft of extracting sea salt from the seawater by allowing it to evaporate in the sun. He took her by a natural hot spring and told her that is was a marvelous place in which to take a proper bath. The tropical surroundings mesmerized Anne, and she delighted in all the knowledge that Pierre was so gracious to share that she almost forgot to ask about the dangers.

"Do you think we will come across any Indians?"

"Indians, what are those?"

"You know, savages"—Anne searched Pierre's face for understanding—"they're a breed of beastly humans who attack innocent people who've crossed over onto their land."

"Are you sure there's such a thing and not just a plot by the leaders of Charles Town who desire to scare the people?"

"No, they are real, one of our servants Ahyoka is an Indian."

"So you have a beastly savage serving in your home?"

"No silly—"

"Wait, look over there."

Behind a bush was a wild hog rooting for food. Pierre loaded his musket with powder and shot and took aim. With one blast, the hog fell to the ground with a thud. Anne was shocked at the amount of blood that poured from the dead animal's side.

After Pierre was sure that the pig was dead, he cut a branch off a tree and secured the pig's legs to the pole using strands of bark. Afterward, he and Anne suspended the pig upside down by each holding an end of the pole upon a shoulder. Pierre was surprised as to how strong Anne really was. Anne didn't enjoy the walk as much thereafter, as they were forced to walk in line, with Anne in the rear having to gaze at the ugly, bloody animal.

They finally reached their destination at the spring that gurgled from the ground and flowed into a stream. Pierre filled his pot with the fresh water and let Anne know that if she ever lost her way to follow the stream and she would eventually end at the ocean where she could more readily find help. So with the pig suspended and a jug filled with fresh water, they made their way back to Nassau.

Anne asked Pierre if he would teach her to shoot the musket, and he promised he would, but tomorrow he was going to teach her how to milk the cow, as Pierre had kept a cow in a stable close to his tavern. That evening, they dined on fresh wild pork seasoned with sea salt, wild onions, and mushrooms, and as sides, they had potatoes and zucchini from Pierre's garden. Pierre opened a bottle of fine red wine to enhance the flavors, and Anne resigned completely satisfied as Pierre went to work in his tavern.

He was so thankful for his fellowship with Anne, as she was the true friend for whom he had always dreamed, and he desired to share so much more with her. However, he didn't know if he'd have the time, seeing that he didn't know how long she would be on the island. He wished she could stay there forever, but he knew it wasn't feasible.

Pierre awoke Anne early in the morning to accomplish the milking as he had done every day at that hour. Anne had never milked a cow, but she resolved in her heart that she was going to be brave, so Pierre didn't get discouraged and consider Anne to be a poor student. After a bit of instruction, she actually did quite well, and Pierre was pleased. Anne developed such skill in just a short while that she was able to spray Pierre from across the stable.

Of course she was familiar with all the normal uses for cow's milk, like butter, cheese, and curds, as they had owned cows in Charles Town; but Pierre wanted to show her his little creation, the making of beauty cream.

Pierre would skim the cream off the top of the milk and add the liquid from a coconut, mixing the two together, and then he showed Anne how to apply the blend to her skin to affect a soft and supple texture. It worked wonderfully, and Anne was pleased that Pierre had shared such a secret with her. The ladies in Charles Town would be green with envy if they could see how soft Anne's skin was now. In fact, Anne noticed that Pierre had the softest skin of anyone she had ever seen, let alone for a man.

That night, as Pierre tended the bar, he talked to John, who had just returned from a successful voyage with Captain Vane. John informed Pierre that he had seen James on the other side of the island, and one of his men said that they were set to return shortly, which caused Pierre to cringe. He thought deeply as to what to do with Anney as he scanned the room, looking out over the patrons in the tavern, and suddenly Pierre got a brilliant idea.

CHAPTER 9

PIERRE ALLOWED ANNE to sleep late that morning, and it was directly after milking his cow that Pierre had reached Anne's doorway. As he grabbed her by the hand, he could barely contain his bliss.

"Come with me!"

Pierre giggled like a child as he tugged Anne through the hallway until they reached the threshold of a room tucked away in the corner. Pierre's face was lit with anticipation, and Anne chuckled at his sense of playful antics. With Anne close by his side, Pierre pounded on the door and excitement filled his whispers. "This man sails to Charles Town frequently."

To Anne's great surprise, Chidley Bayard, completely unbuttoned, answered the door, guarding observation into the room. Anne gasped. "Chidley Bayard!!"

Pierre was jilted off guard. "You know each other?"

Mr. Bayard composed a fatherly tone. "Anne Cormac, *what* are you doing here?"

Anne rebutted quickly, "What are *you* doing here?"

"Oh, I know what he's doing here," Pierre smirked as he strained a bit to see beyond the gentleman.

"Pierre, that's enough!" Mr. Bayard said with all firmness.

A lady's voice could be heard from inside the room. "Chidley, who's calling, darling?"

Anne's mouth was agape at Mr. Bayard's awkward position, and Pierre addressed the gentleman boldly.

"We're here to ask a favor."

"I'll be down in a few moments after I compose myself, *Pierre*." And Mr. Bayard snapped the door shut.

Anne rushed back to her room to prepare herself more presentably. She twisted her hair up and donned a fresh lace cap and rushed downstairs to wait for Mr. Bayard, where she waited for a very long time. Mr. Bayard was allowing a lengthy delay out of pure embarrassment over the whole situation.

"Damned Pierre," Mr. Bayard mumbled as he finished getting himself together.

Although Mr. Bayard was truly considered to be a gentleman, he was familiar to all the residence of Providence. The pirates rather liked him, as he would frequent the island to take his fill of the ladies without any censorship from his comrades, the aristocrats of South Carolina. He was so well respected among the pirates that his ship was passed over while encountered out in the Atlantic as he transported his deer hide from the colonies to England.

Anne was bored of waiting so long, so she busied herself by helping Pierre polish glassware behind the bar.

"Pierre, I can't thank you enough. Mr. Bayard is practically family. He used to stay with us in Charles Town every autumn. In fact, he taught me how to fence."

"*You* know how to fence?" Their conversation was interrupted by a voice resonating down the stairwell as he descended. "*That,* I would love to see." John offered a hearty laugh, which did not amuse Anne; and as John came in to view, Anne reproved him sharply.

"Don't you know it's rude to interrupt a conversation?"

"Oh, I do apologize. Where are my manners? I'm John Rackam." He gestured for Anne's hand on which to offer a kiss, but being the decent woman that she was, Anne firmly drew back.

"You are a treasure, my darling, and your husband is certainly a lucky man. Where is he, by the way, that I may congratulate him?"

Anne exhaled, and in her agitation, she had not even noticed how dashingly handsome he was, but Pierre did. "Oh, to be able to have and hold John Rackam," he thought.

"He's left me here."

"Oh, what a foolish man."

"So I've been told. I plan to leave him anyway and return to Charles Town."

"Well, if you're leaving him anyway, why don't you come with me instead?"

"I beg your pardon!" Anne was thoroughly aggravated by his brashness, which amused John, and he laughed the more. "I plan to set sail in the next few days. Come with me."

Mr. Bayard descended the last few steps just in time to intervene. "No, John, she's coming with me."

Pierre was tickled at such a comedy of commotion surrounding him, and he chuckled to himself thinking, "Oh my, this is a very twisted saga."

John bowed in a show of respect, and with that, he conceded his taunting. "Sir Chidley Bayard. It's certainly a pleasure."

John then gestured for Anne's hand, which she reluctantly responded after giving it quite some thought. John commenced to place a tender kiss on Anne's soft skin. He followed it with a sultry gaze.

"Mrs. Bonny, It's been my pleasure."

Anne felt the tingles again as John departed and felt a good amount of guilt being that she was a married woman, but she was determined not to be tricked again into thinking that such a feeling was true love. Besides, he was twice her age. She dismissed the whole situation fairly quickly, as she had more important business to conduct, and she was anxious to discover when Mr. Bayard could take her home.

She told him everything, pertaining to her father and her dealings with James Bonny, and he readily agreed that her leaving the island was for the very best. But before she was to discuss travel plans, she insisted on knowing why Mr. Bayard was visiting Providence in the first place. Thankfully, he was able to create a believable story, which appeased Anne.

Pierre was thrilled as he listened in on the plan that Mr. Bayard unfolded for Anne of getting her away from James. It was simply brilliant, and Pierre was proud that he had come up with such a grand idea.

"So they're hosting a ball in Jamaica to present the candidate for the royal governor, and as chance would have it, your father is scheduled to attend."

Anne inhaled for joy and then suddenly stopped. "Oh, but I have nothing to wear to a ball."

"Not to worry about a thing. There are plenty of dress shops in Jamaica. I will make sure that you are ready to present to the new governor as well as your father. Now go prepare yourself before your husband returns, or it will place us in a very precarious situation."

The next day, Anne said goodbye to Pierre, who could not cease from sobbing violently. He would miss her more than anything he had ever loved, and it made it even worse to know that he would never see his Anney again. She had brought pure joy to his soul, and now it would be completely void. He truly didn't know how he would survive such an ill travesty upon his life.

After they had pulled anchor and set sail, Anne wept bitterly for Pierre, and she vowed to keep him in her heart forever. As far as John Rackam, Anne never gave him a second thought, well maybe one, but she quickly repented and resisted the devil so he should flee from her thoughts. Although she was thrilled to be on her way home, she was even more thrilled to be sailing again. She so enjoyed her trip to Jamaica, as it took much longer to complete than the trip from Carolina to Providence, and for that, she was truly grateful, for it gave her time to reflect.

She thought of James Bonny, and she had not one ounce of regret for leaving him behind. She thought of Pierre again, but the sorrow of their parting was remedied by the tender thoughts of reunion with her father, Ahyoka, and dear Samuel.

James Bonny finally returned to Providence to find that his wife had vanished with Mr. Bayard, and knowing of Mr. Bayard's reputation, James viciously accused the gentleman of seducing and carrying away his wife. And from that time forward, Anne Bonny would possess somewhat of a reputation for being an adulterous woman. But Anne had a clear conscience, and the longer she sailed, the clearer things became—that what she was doing was not only right but was necessary for her well-being. Not only had she cleansed her mind during her journey to Jamaica, but her body as well.

Pierre had sent her away with a healthy supply of his sea salt and beauty cream. Anne spent the entirety of her trip exfoliating with the sea salt, washing her skin, and then applying the cream. She was determined to rid herself of the grime that she had accumulated in Providence. After her scrubbings, she would apply fresh clothing that she herself had laundered but had decided to leave out Pierre's secret little ingredient.

By the time they arrived in Jamaica, Anne was ready to greet her father and be on her way to Charles Town. However, as much as she loved galas, she didn't feel in the spirit to enjoy one at this time. Her mood was so downcast that she hadn't even thought to notice how beautiful the island of Jamaica was, as the recent events of her life had taken such a toll that she was emotionally exhausted.

Jamaica was an enchanting island just below Cuba a certain distance. It was well controlled by the English Crown, and the culture was ever so grand as England itself. The ambiance of the island eventually lifted Anne's spirits, and she marveled at the dress shop. She wondered how it could possibly surpass the dress shop in South Carolina to such a degree but it did. She selected the most perfect ball gown; although it was barely feasible, she thought it might have been even grander than the one her father had purchased for her the night he attempted to betroth her to Joseph Burleigh. Mr. Bayard was nothing less than a gracious host and embellished Anne with many fine possessions while in Jamaica.

Anne's father had been known to frequent the island due to his interest in the slaves, and he was well respected by the leaders of the royal colony, which was tightly controlled by the mother country. He had probably already arrived on the island, but Anne was completely resolved to conceal herself and surprise him at the ball that evening. She had visions of falling into his arms with sincere repentance and of his meek acceptance, desiring to kill the fatted calf on her behalf for the joy of her return. Witnessing their grand reunion, everyone at the ball would simply think that their gayety was the result of the reuniting of a father and daughter after her lengthy absence caused by a grand European tour. No one would ever suspect that Anne had just come from living among the pirates, washing her clothing in urine, and was leaving a man whom she had married on a whim.

The evening finally arrived, and Anne entered the ball on the arm of Chidley Bayard. Her crimson ball gown was a gift to her ivory complexion, and it accentuated her blue eyes. Her strawberry curls cascaded in loose tresses below her feathered headdress. Unfortunately for Anne, she was a sight to behold, and envy swept the crowd of women.

The gala was even grander than the ball hosted in Carolina. This event was orchestrated in order to introduce the new candidate for governor of Jamaica, Sir Nicholas Lawes. He had even more clout than the leadership of Charles Town, since Jamaica was a royal colony. The energy was elevated in the ballroom, and it was abundant with anticipation for the new candidate, who was once knighted in England for his grand accomplishments.

Anne glided gracefully by the side of Chidley Bayard for a good while, but she became restless when her father was nowhere to be seen. Her mind began to wonder about so many things. She took note of the people around her and how differently they behaved than the pirates and Pierre. How was it that she could feel completely comfortable on a ship or enjoy Pierre's company so greatly, but she had not one ounce of interest in conversing with any of these people? She did not want to inquire about the latest novel one had read, only to brag about another that she had read that was more profound. She viewed the whole thing as a charade, and it sickened her stomach. They were all like the aristocrats in Charles Town, even on a worse scale.

"Where is he?" she mumbled under her breath, while she hid behind a smile.

"Don't worry, my darling. Your father must be here somewhere. We'll locate him."

Unbeknown to Anne, Mr. Bayard was leading her in the direction of a certain group of ladies. He figured that since Anne was bored, she might enjoy being left with the elites, so they might entertain one another. The ladies coyly eyed Anne as Mr. Bayard introduced her to Sarah Lawes, the sister-in-law to the candidate for royal governor. Then to Anne's horror, Mr. Bayard left to go join the men. Anne felt completely awkward, as Sarah and her snide group of friends practically turned their backs to Anne and ignored her very existence, leaving her with no one in which to converse and completely ill at ease in this foreign place.

Suddenly, an announcer stepped to the podium and commanded every soul's attention. Anne left the congregation of catty women in search of Mr. Bayard.

"All hear yea. Announcing the candidate for the new governor of Jamaica, Sir Nicolas Lawes."

The audience applauded as a well-built man took the podium. "It is my good pleasure to be announced as a candidate for governor of Jamaica by the king of England." He relished the applause. "I shall promise to serve you well. Tomorrow I shall conduct some business on the island, but for tonight, I shall enjoy this fabulous celebration, thank you."

During the speech, Anne drew some attention as she made her way through the crowd to join Mr. Bayard, as it was a blatant show of disrespect to mill about during the prospective governor's speech. However, Anne didn't care, for she needed to find Mr. Bayard, her pillar of support in such a dreadfully coldhearted, callused room. Anne was beginning to perspire from mental anguish by the time she finally reached Mr. Bayard, and just when the speech had ended, a messenger approached the couple.

"Sir Chidley Bayard? I was told to deliver word to you that Chancellor Cormac will not be able to attend the governor's reception due to a devastating fire on his plantation."

That was the final blow to Anne's feeble state, as she could hardly contain her grief. Thoughts raced through her head. Thoughts of her beloved home in tortuous flames, and then there was the question if anyone had been injured or, worse yet, had died. She felt the blood rush from her face, and she felt as though she may lose her perception. She hid her face in her handheld Victorian fan and wanted so badly to retreat, but where?

Throughout the evening, Anne and Mr. Bayard had been scrutinized by countless women congregating along the periphery of the room, all wondering just what were the terms of their relationship—Mr. Bayard, with his reputation of an eye for the ladies, and the young daughter of Chancellor Cormac of Carolina. One of the more critical in her judgments just happened to be Sarah Lawes, and she whispered in the ear of her close confidant,

"Look, she appears as if she's been upset by Mr. Bayard. Do you think they've had a lover's quarrel?"

"It certainly appears that way," her friend chided.

The women turned their heads to avoid being caught staring, as Anne scanned the room for an exit. Suddenly, Anne viewed a passage leading to the corridor containing the powder room, and she hastily moved in its direction. She feared that she would make a public display due to her building of ill emotions that were ready to gush out.

Inside the powder room, Anne gazed at herself in the looking glass, while tears streamed down her cheeks. Her feelings were overwhelmed, and she could not sort them properly at the time. Perhaps she could have a good cry now and sail tomorrow for Carolina with Mr. Bayard. Then she would be home to help her father sort through the mess of the fire, if he was still alive. That thought caused the tears to flow even more so, and she was sobbing hopelessly as Sarah entered the powder room. Anne attempted to make a quick recovery, pretending to freshen up her face.

"Good evening." Anne was polite

Sarah was quick and to the point. "What was your name again?"

Anne hesitated, sensing the animosity, but then conceded. "Anne Bonny."

"I'm Sarah Lawes, sister-in-law to the royal candidate."

"Very nice to meet you," Anne replied politely.

"So if your name is Anne Bonny, and you are the daughter of Chancellor Cormac of Carolina, you must be married." Sarah looked her up and down. "So why would a married woman be traveling with a gentleman who is not your husband? You know it's causing quite a stir out there, don't you?"

Anne could feel the anger mounting as this elite cow was unrighteously judging her. Besides, Sarah had no idea what pain and tribulation Anne had just endured, but Sarah pushed on.

"Well, don't you even care about what people are saying about you?"

"Actually, I don't give a *damn* about what they're saying about me."

One would think by Sarah's reaction that Anne had just blasphemed the most high, and she spewed.

"You're despicable, and I'd like to put some distance between us."

Anne's temper flared at the insult, and it's as if she had lost her good senses. "I'll put some distance between us," Anne proceeded to release her fury from the end of her fist as she clocked the snide bitch square in the mouth, knocking out her two front teeth and creating a blood bath in the process.

Sarah touched her mouth, and seeing the blood, she fainted straightaway. She hit the wall of the powder room hard and slid down the wall to the floor, which wedged her chin against her neck, allowing the ruby-colored fluid to flow over the upper part of her white gown. The blood reminded Anne of the pig that Pierre had killed, and seeing Sarah Lawes lay there on the porcelain, Anne feared that she might be dead, so she fled the powder room. Anne happened to make it outside the ballroom without being suspected by anyone, and she fled toward the harbor knowing they would come looking for her very soon.

She planned to find a ship for which to stow away and that would give her time to think. Her mind was racing, and her thoughts felt jumbled. She felt as if she had fallen into a pit, and the more she tried to surface, the deeper she sank. She needed time to sort it all out. However, one thing was very clear in her mind; she knew that she was in horrible trouble. Because, if they whipped a woman and placed her in a pillory for the accusation of adultery, her punishment for knocking out the two front teeth of the royal governor's relative would certainly be much more severe.

On the dock, she appeared rather peculiar in her ball gown as she paced back and forth attempting to fetch a ride, but thankfully her luck played into her favor. In this particular occasion it held true—the pirate's belief about bastards having the best of luck.

CHAPTER 10

IT WAS NEAR the end of July in 1717, and Pierre was in a dismal state ever since Anne had left the island to the effect that he was having a difficult time finding delight in anything he had prior. His poor cow had been horribly neglected to the point that her utters were beginning to dry of their milk. He hadn't been to the hot springs in weeks in order to get a proper bath. Even the once-enjoyable trek to fetch the water was only done if he was out completely. But most surprisingly, he took no pleasure in counting his coins that he received from the tavern.

His grim outlook was remedied somewhat as he fantasized about the grand reunion of Anne and her father. Although Pierre had never experienced the love of a father himself, he found serenity in Mr. Cormac's unending love for his daughter, which Anne had tenderly revealed. Such imagery lifted his spirits, and he figured that Anne should be at least halfway to Charles Town by that point. And rewarding as well, he delighted in seeing James Bonny seething in his loss.

James was frantically trying to busy himself in order to attempt to take his mind off his extreme hatred of Anne and for all she had done to him. He indeed had been industrious by supplying the *Carolina* with men, and since it was already equipped with cannon, one would speculate that he should return a wealthy man as others had when they had been so well endowed. But not for James, he had returned empty handed once, twice, and thrice again, each time having excuses of how the merchant ships had already unloaded their gold and silver prior to his arrival and he found nothing to pillage, or the stories of grand dueling battles won by him and his men—but no booty to show for it. Pierre thought it was all rubbish.

Besides, Pierre was getting impatient, for James had not paid him a cent for the rental of his room that his wife had occupied. Pierre would have gladly let Anne remain with him at no charge, but it was the principal of the matter that bothered Pierre. Thankfully, for Pierre's sake, James had taken to sleeping on his ship when he was moored in the harbor of Nassau after Anne had left. Pierre wondered how long he would have to endure the ill-fated pirate this go round. Nevertheless, Pierre terribly grieved the loss of his Anney.

Unfortunately for Anne, she was not having the grand voyage home as Pierre had envisioned. She was frantically pacing on a dock in a red ball gown, while she imagined that half of Jamaica was diligently searching for her only to apply the noose, and she was sure that they would be there at any moment. She had worked up quite a bit of panic in her mind, but it couldn't have been further from the truth because of Sarah.

Sarah had crawled into a dark corner of the powder room to hide herself from being discovered in that deplorable condition. She would have never marched out into the crowded ballroom with blood splattered all over her gown to lisp her dilemma in front of all the royal guests, and so she had remained in the powder room until the last guest had gone home. And then she surfaced to plot her revenge.

Initially, Anne's luck was failing on the dock, as she had approached two crewmembers of different ships and had been refused by both. The first ship had just unloaded slaves from West Africa, and it was set to return to its destination, and the second ship mate Anne couldn't understand a word because he only spoke Dutch. It was the third ship that she approached that would turn her luck in her favor.

The galleon was preparing for its departure, and a young man was busy loading sugar. He was a small-framed lad who looked rather unclean, as his face was stained with soot; but he was as able-bodied as anyone of a larger size, for he was working very diligently.

"Excuse me, sir. To where are you headed?"

"Providence."

"Oh, that's perfect! May I come aboard?"

He inspected the young aristocrat, standing there as if decked for the queen, then replied. "Don't you know it's bad luck for a lady to be on board a ship?"

"Oh, that's foolishness. I've sailed many times. Now please, I need your help."

Anne looked back from where she'd come.

"If they catch me, they'll surely hang me."

It must have struck a chord with the lad, because he immediately consented.

"All right, but you must disrobe yourself."

Anne left the ball gown swaying in the surf just below the pier. The young man covered Anne with a woolen blanket from head to toe and assisted her on board, guiding her every step. They passed by one of the lad's crewmates, and he made a quick excuse.

"Poor bloke fell in, too much rum."

He managed to get Anne into his cabin without notice and quickly closed the door.

"You can stay here with me, but you must don men's clothing."

The cabin smelled of sweet pine diffusing from it paneling into the cool, moist air. It was compact with only room in which to store minimal supplies and allow its two bunks.

"But wait! Is there not a private cabin for which can accommodate me?"

"Are you concerned about bunking with a man?"

"Of course, I am. I know that I am at your mercy for your kindness, but I'm sorry, I don't even know your name."

"My name is Mark, and I regret to tell you, but you must stay here with me as the ship's full."

Anne's discouragement was evident, so Mark offered reassurance.

"But don't worry. I intend to allow you your privacy. Here put these on."

Anne put Mark's honesty to the test.

"Wait a minute, if the ship's full, then how come you have an empty bunk in your cabin?"

"Because of fever—"

"You have a fever?"

"No, I had a fever."

There was no greater fear at the time than a fever, as it was often a death sentence. With the increase in rice fields in the tropics, the mosquitoes carried deadly malaria and yellow fever in which there was no cure. Although Mark was healthy now, it was certainly a sure method of obtaining a private room, and he would use it often, as he truly was susceptible to fever.

Mark handed her a shirt, a pair of dungarees, and a hat and then left the cabin. Anne was quite surprised as to how comfortable she felt in the clothing. The pants were way more forgiving than her bloomers, and the blouse was not nearly as constrictive as the dresses she had worn. It was rather quite liberating. Besides, she could change into her clothing when she got to Providence, but no.

"Oh no, the diary!"

She had left all of her earthly possessions on Mr. Bayard's ship with no chance of retrieval, and although she grieved the loss of the diary the most, she was thankful that she had gotten to read the entire contents within its pages. She was determined to keep those precious words of her mother written upon her heart. Pertaining to her Holy Bible, she would certainly miss it, but she had read it so many times that she figured that she would be just fine with her memory alone. Everything else was insignificant, and she resolved that she would be fine in men's clothing, since it was the only means of covering her nakedness, with exception to the undergarments she had been wearing.

Anne remained concealed in the cabin the majority of the time during her journey to Providence, and although Anne was much more convincing as a man when she smeared soot upon her face, she was not as realistic a man as Mark was.

Unbeknown to Anne, Mark was actually another woman named Mary Reed. She was employed as a crewmate on the Dutch merchant ship, and they were scheduled to deliver sugar to Providence. The pirates had a favorable trade agreement with the Dutch, being that England and Holland were allies beginning with the Nine Years War. The pirates coveted the Jamaican sugar to create fermented beverages and paid for it in golden Spanish coins, and the Dutch crewmen coveted the ladies on Providence and paid for them with more sugar.

Mary Reed had worked on the Dutch ship as it was the only way she knew how to provide a living for herself, and so she dressed as a man and did an honest man's job, placing the soot upon her face to hide her femininity. Not one person aboard suspected Mark for a woman, as she was very believable.

Mary never revealed her gender on the journey back to Providence, as she never wanted to compromise her employment, but she and Anne became great friends. In the daytime, Mary would work her position as an able-bodied sailor. She would visit the cabin from time to time to sneak Anne food and water, and at night, the two spent hours talking about everything. Once or twice, they stayed up practically all night long enthralled in riveting conversation.

The journey back to Providence helped Anne to clear her mind and sort her thoughts. She knew that she could not return to Charles Town, or she would be discovered and returned back to Jamaica and probably hung. She did not want to return to her lawful husband, as Pierre, with his excellent wisdom, had enlightened Anne as to James's true nature. She did, however, love sailing the open seas, so she decided to attempt to stay on with Mark and obtain a position as a crewmember on the Dutch merchant vessel. Mark wasn't so taken with the idea and discouraged Anne, being that he perceived her as much too frail. He encouraged her rather to return to

Providence to live on the island and allow a trustworthy Pierre to continue to conceal her from her husband, James.

The idea settled with Anne, and thereafter, she sailed with joyful anticipation of rejoining her best friend, Pierre, once again. As far as Mark was concerned, he too was counted as a dear friend to Anne, and as close as they became, one would think that there was a romantic inclination between the two. However, that couldn't have been further from the truth, for Anne only loved Mark's heart and his soul.

During one of their many conversations, Mark confided that he too was a bastard, as Mark had never known his father. He told Anne of all his military excursions. He marched and rode horse with the English army; he enlisted with Holland, and after he resigned Holland's army, pirates captured him while en route to the West Indies. The pirates chose him out of the entire lot, because he was the only Englishman aboard. He remained with them until his opportunity arose for his current position on the Dutch ship.

Anne was enthralled at Mark's exciting life. To talk with him was as if she were reading an adventure novel. Although the stories were ever so true that Mary had told Anne, Mary had accomplished all of those things dressed as a man, unbeknown to her comrades. Mary was glad for her friendship with Anne, but what she really craved was to be able to tell Anne the whole story as a woman heart to heart. As she drifted off to sleep that night, Mary reminisced about her conflicted past.

Before Mary was conceived, her mother lived in England and married a man who sailed the seas. Shortly after they were betrothed, her husband took to the sea, never to return again. He left Mary's mother alone and being with child in which she delivered a son. Directly after, Mary's mother, being young and foolish, found that she was with child again; but this time, in the absence of her husband.

As her belly grew, she didn't want to be discovered as she had built a good reputation for herself, so she moved away from her husband's relations and took refuge in the country with others who were friends. She never did reveal to anyone who sired the child, so it should remain a mystery. Sadly before Mary was born, her brother died, not even reaching his first birthday, but Mary was born shortly thereafter in 1690 to fill her mother's empty arms.

Her mother remained a few years in the country until she was financially exhausted to the point that she could not feed her daughter, Mary. Mary's mother knew that her husband's relations would surely secure their future, but she had the dilemma of returning with a daughter instead of the son whom they assisted in childbirth.

Her mother devised a plan to return to her husband's mothers with Mary dressed as a boy to decoy as her deceased brother. When her mother-in-law offered to take the lad and raise him as her own, Mary's mother told her that she could not stand the painful thought of parting with her son. So her husband's mother took pity and agreed to give a portion of money every week for the child's keep, and he could remain with his mother.

As Mary grew older, her mother revealed the story to her daughter in order to encourage her to continue living the life of a boy as it was to both of their benefits. When the grandmother died, the weekly allowance was cut off, and Mary's mother placed her daughter for hire as a footboy to a French woman to continue their revenue.

Mary's employment for the French lady was short-lived, and because she was older and wiser, Mary began to seek out opportunities as a young man in which she could excel.

That is when she boarded herself upon a man-of-war ship, and the adventures that she told Anne were derived from her experiences thereafter. However, it was during that time in her life that something magical happened, and she so wanted to share that component of her life with Anne, coming from her heart woman to woman. Mary wanted to tell Anne that she had fallen in love.

It was during the time that Mary, using the alias of Mark, was assigned to an English regimen on horse. She had performed so well that she had received a considerable amount of recognition from her superiors. Well, it just so happened that one of her comrades was a young man named Peter from Flanders, and he was exceedingly handsome. Mary fell deeply in love and began to neglect her military duties and quickly fell out of favor with the officers, and soon she was discharged.

During her jaunt with the regimen, she and Peter had become the best of friends, and he didn't think it strange in the least that Mark would visit him on the field. He readily let his friend share his tent as any good friend would. Peter's fellow soldiers, however, thought Mark was crazed for putting himself in harm's way without an assignment. As their friendship grew, Mary allowed Peter to enter the tent while she dressed, and he discovered that Mark was truly a woman.

The discovery thrilled Peter because he now would have a mistress in his tent all to himself, while his comrades were lonely for a woman. However,

Mary was not unchaste and resisted Peter's attempts to get closer to his friend. After meeting much resistance, Peter asked Mary to be his wife.

The couple took what money they could muster between the two and bought a lovely dress for Mary and a looking glass so she could behold her beauty. Mary would spend hours gazing and admiring what she beheld in the mirror, as she had never owned a dress a day in her entire life. Peter so loved Mary, and he took her hand in marriage soon after.

Word got around to the regimen that two of their soldiers had gotten married, and they were drawn by the peculiar nature of such an event. Finding the rumor to be true and being gleeful for the couple, they arranged a celebration and imparted gifts necessary to set up housekeeping. With all the favorable talk about true love and circumstances, Peter found favor with his officers and was able to secure an honorable discharge from his post.

The happy couple straightway founded an eating establishment near the Castle of Breda called Three Horse Shoes, and it was filled daily to capacity with many military officials. And only when Mary felt she couldn't be any happier, she experienced more grief than she could ever imagine, as her loving husband had died suddenly.

She attempted to keep the restaurant in business in her husband's absence, but with the troops moving from the area, her patrons dwindled, and Mary was forced to don men's clothing once again and seek a means to provide for her victuals.

Mary had borne so much pain during her life, but at that moment, she was peacefully unaware as she lay sleeping in her cabin on that Dutch ship. For Mary, slumber was her only reprieve from her harsh past.

She was truly a gentle, romantic creature that longed for the arms of a husband to hold her, and when she awoke, she knew that she could not tell Anne anything else about her past, as it was too risky to reveal her gender and forfeit her livelihood.

As the Dutch merchant vessel pulled into the harbor, Anne's mind was at ease, for during her journey from Jamaica to Providence, she had resolved in her heart that she could be quite satisfied living in Nassau forever. Although she would continue to miss her father, she was far away from the aristocrats, and for that, she was happy. She looked forward to introducing Mark to Pierre, for she believed that they too would become great friends. She was determined to hide her presence from James Bonny, as she didn't care to ever see him again. And as far as John Rackam was concerned, she was fully determined to shun him as well and not allow that sly dog to coerce her in any way, and Anne was steadfast about that.

Mark never did reveal his gender and was unsuspected when they arrived in Providence. Anne's reunion with Pierre was more special than she had ever imagined, as he wept violently at her return, and then he laughed more violently than he had cried when Anne told him the story about her crude dealings with the governor's sister-in-law. He said that she definitely deserved her royal treatment.

Anne's plan of avoiding James was working brilliantly, as he was absent from Nassau a good amount of time. Her plan of ignoring John Rackam, however, was not as successful as she had hoped, for she had placed herself in an unusual situation. Well, actually it was Pierre who prompted the occasion. Then again it was probably Anne, for she had bragged to Pierre in the first place about her ability to fence.

CHAPTER 11

BACK IN SOUTH Carolina, Anne's father had extinguished the fire on his plantation without any harm to the mansion, and no souls had been lost. Chidley Bayard eventually informed Chancellor Cormac of the entire matter concerning Anne's marriage to James, Providence, and then Jamaica, and once again her father's heart was badly bruised. However, he was pleased to know that Anne loathed the very thought of James now.

Her father figured that Anne would return to Providence for fear of punishment for her misbehavior in Jamaica, but he was not concerned in the least about Jamaican penalty toward Anne, as he had very strong ties with all the leadership of Jamaica. His concern was getting Anne home safely. He thought of sailing to Providence himself, but he knew that he would not last a day among those lowbrows. He knew that Chidley Bayard was not a means to her escape, as the chancellor was sure that Chidley would not be returning to Providence anytime soon out of shear embarrassment over the whole situation, so Mr. Cormac devised another approach.

The chancellor and other South Carolina residents were exhausted by the attacks against their harbor, and if England was not going to provide military defense on their behalf, perhaps the king would consent to a plan to eradicate the source by providing regulation in Providence. The chancellor figured that if they worded a petition to reflect a benefit to England, the colony may obtain more suitable results, so the petition to the king requested the placement of a royal governor in Providence in order to dissolve piracy and restore unrestricted trade with England. Once Providence was restrained, the chancellor planned to remove his daughter from the island known as a pirate's paradise.

But in the meanwhile, the legend of Anne Bonny was building. It was mouthed that Anne had started that fire on the plantation as vengeance toward her father for disowning her because of her marriage to James Bonny. That was added to her already unsavory reputation, making Anne Bonny now an unchaste, vindictive young woman, when the only thing she was really guilty of at that time was the force of her temper unleashed on Sarah Lawes's mouth.

Sarah Lawes stopped smiling ever since the night of the ball. By practicing in her looking glass, she had figured a way to speak that still looked natural but never revealed her unsightly gap, but every time she looked in the mirror, she loathed Anne Bonny even worse. Her husband lovingly reassured her that he would make sure that an ivory prosthetic was created that would return her beautiful smile, which he couldn't wait to see.

Chidley Bayard was taken in and forced to tell about his relationship with Anne, as he had been clearly viewed with her all night. He let them know about her circumstances with James and Providence, hoping to extract a little bit of sympathy for his best friend's daughter, the chancellor of South Carolina, and he swore that he had no idea to where she had fled.

After their investigation and finding Anne's ball gown floating in the bay, they figured that Anne Bonny had been taken to one of three places, either West Africa, the northern colonies of America, or Providence with the export of the sugar.

Sarah Lawes believed that Anne had retreated to Providence where she belonged among the whoremongers and thieves, and she was determined to find her and bring her to justice.

Anne, unaware of her father's determination to get her back and her rising fame in Jamaica as an outlaw, was living carefree with her best friend, Pierre, on a tropical island where there were no rules. Anne had been able to keep her word to herself about all the decisions she firmly made on her journey, except for one—John Rackam.

It happened when Anne arrived in Providence dressed as a man in Mark's clothing. She wasn't concerned about her attire, because she had everything she needed right there to craft herself some women's clothing. Pierre had all types of beautiful fabric from calico to velvets to satin. He also had sheers that had been plundered and plenty of needles and twine, which had probably been snatched right from the hand of a frightened Puritan woman as she was crossing the Atlantic. But the fact that Anne was dressed as a man was most likely the impetus that reminded Pierre of what she had told him before she left for Jamaica. *That* was what put her directly in the path of John Rackam once again.

It occurred a few days after they had arrived home, and Anne and Mark had already exchanged their tearful goodbyes. Well, Pierre, having a vigorous memory inquired about her ability to fence as she had mentioned in her leaving. Being proud of her skill, Anne had to brag, and she expressed to Pierre that she would love to engage in a match.

At that time, the pirates would practice their sword-fighting abilities by casting lots on an opponent and placing a set amount of coins in a pot. After the duel, the champion would take a large portion of the coins, and all the rest would be divided among the men who had correctly chosen the winner. The only solid rule of the game was that there was to be no killing; otherwise, there would only be one pirate left on Providence. Not one man suspected that Anne was anything but a man when she arrived with a cutlass secured to her left hip. Pierre became nervous as he whispered to her,

"Are you sure you can do this?"

Anne offered a wry smile.

Pierre worried. "I will never forgive myself if anything happens to you." Pierre repented in his heart for his foolish decision to mention fencing as he squinted through his fingers.

Anne's opponent was equally matched with her size as she was not of a short stature. Although her frame was lean, she possessed amazing strength. As the match began, Anne was definitely able to hold her own; and as a result, a fierce sword fight ensued with a pirate who was greedy for the win. He appeared as if his temper had skewed his judgment away from the universal rule of no bloodshed while dueling a comrade.

After a bit of a battle, the pirate intended to throw a fatal blow. The crowd went wild as Anne avoided the insult and took the upper hand. Their eyes locked, and she could discern his true intent.

With a final swift move, she disarmed her opponent, and he fell to the ground. He winced at the discomfort of her blade at his throat and her foot upon his chest. And that is when Anne pulled off her hat, revealing her gender as her curls fell below her shoulders. She replied coyly,

"That is certainly no way to treat a worthy opponent."

Pierre could not have been any prouder of his Anney than he had been at that moment. He was even more proud of her than Samuel had been that day that Anne had revealed her talents to James Bonny. Pierre reveled in Anne's force as a major contender and at her impeccable grace and pure magnificence. Another onlooker was taken as well.

It so happened that John had watched the whole match from a distance, and now he was intrigued more than ever with Anne Bonny. Her intelligence, her strength, and her beauty enraptured him.

Since James was absent from the island, Anne could celebrate that night openly and without constraint. In fact, she was the vigor of the party. There was singing and dancing and an overabundance of rum. Anne had never

D.A. NASH

had such a jolly grand time in all her life. It was a stark difference from the stuffy galas to which she was accustomed. It was apparent by the look on every pirate's face that she was revered as a female divinity of sorts.

Even though Pierre had witnessed her ability, he still felt the need to watch over her, and he did try to intervene.

"No, Anney, no," he said, but to no avail.

Anne took a healthy portion of the stout rum with not even a hint of a grimace. The crowd cheered wildly. Pierre winced, knowing that she was way over the limit, as he had counted seven by that time.

John had decided not to attend the celebration for reasons unknown, but later, as Anne's head was hung over the wash basin, retching violently, John appeared at the doorway of her room.

"Is she going to be all right?"

"I fear she's had a deadly amount." Pierre repented in his heart that he didn't insist on refusing Anne her last portions. "Someone will have to stay up and keep watch of her all night, lest she die in her sleep."

Pierre assisted her with her clothing, allowing her to slumber in her undergarments. John Rackam turned his head until Pierre had gotten her into bed and covered.

"Pierre, please allow me."

Anne had passed out with the covers pulled up just far enough to reveal her young cleavage, accented by the lace of her camisole, rising gently with each breath.

John, being completely trusted by Pierre due to their lengthy history, was allowed to stand guard over Anne all night. Pierre could sense that John had truly grown to admire the young woman, and if Pierre was going to trust any man with Anne's care, it would surely have been John.

After Pierre left the room, John gently covered Anne to protect her privacy. He placed a cold cloth on her brow and tenderly lifted her head to offer her sips of water when she would moan during the night, until finally the darkness had faded to morning radiance.

Anne awoke from her stupor, feeling as if she would prefer death to this sickness. She suddenly realized her half-nakedness and pulled the covers to her chin. She was ever so frightened at the sight of John hovering at her bedside.

"What are you doing here—?"

"Not to worry. You're completely safe here with me. I would never harm you."

Anne, unable to contest, just grabbed her head and moaned.

"That's from too much rum. Here."

John lifted her head gently and fed her a sip of water. Then he rung out a cloth and replaced the stale one on her brow.

"You rest as long as you like. You're over the danger now."

"Danger?"

"Of dying in your vomit. I must go, but I'll inquire about you later."

Anne sunk back into the bed and tried to ignore her misery. She then knew why the Holy Bible referenced to only give strong drink to those who perish. She made a firm decision to never partake of rum again. However, she was not always steadfast in keeping her promises that she had made to herself, and she reneged upon the firm decision she'd made concerning John. Because over the next few months, Anne saw a good bit of John in between his voyages with Captain Vane, as she had truly been touched by his kindness bestowed upon her the night she almost perished in her vomit.

John Rackam was born on Dec 21, 1682, to parents who had moved from Bristol to Jamaica. At the time, England was offering land grants in Jamaica in order to encourage sugar production, and English citizens were thronging to the royal territory to take good advantage of a wealthy opportunity.

John's upbringing was typical for any English Protestant family. His mother was a devout Christian woman, and his father ruled the home with strict discipline and emotional detachment. His father taught his five sons how to read and write by using the Holy Bible as a learning guide, and although John learned some, he was deficient, as he preferred to be active rather than be placed in front of a book. And so it caused much tension between him and his father.

As he matured, his attention was drawn to the sea, and he began to spend a considerable amount of time at the port of Jamaica talking with the men arriving and departing on their ships. His fascination grew for the prospects of wide-open adventure, and the contemplation of such brought him great pleasure, and he also discovered another delight—rum. John had his first taste at a young age and had craved it ever since.

As John grew, so did the contention between him and his father, so at the age of thirteen, John boarded a ship and took a position as a cabin boy. The ship was part of the fleet used by the Royal African Company. It was there that John developed an intense hatred for the harvesting of the African people against their will and also for men who have a preference for young boys.

John knew that he could not return home, as he feared his father's wrath for his running away, so he stayed with the company for three years and then joined a crew on a Dutch merchant ship, which transported flour from the American colonies. The Dutch at the time had the largest merchant fleet of any nation and the highest gross national product per capita in the world. John had obtained the position while unloading slaves on the dock in Virginia. In his new position, John would load the flour and then sail to the West Indies or England, depending upon the Corn Act.

Parliament enacted the Corn Act of 1689, disallowing the import of grain from the colonies if prices on the English market fell below a certain level. So when the prices were low in England, the ship would unload its merchandise in the West Indies where trade was less restricted.

John's employment as an able-bodied sailor on the Dutch ship would prove to be a blessing in his life, although he didn't see it at the time, as he had developed a hatred toward God for his prior circumstances. On the ship, John got along well with his fellow crewmates, which were an eclectic bunch of fellows who acted more like brothers than his own.

The captain was a good man and fathered his crew, allowing them much liberty as long as the work was completed. Rum was allowed if not taken in excess, and it was on that ship in which John learned to fence and become an excellent marksman with musket and pistol. He and his crewmates spent hours honing their skills once they had completed their tasks. The employment on the Dutch ship was a cherished part of John's memory and a healing balm to his soul, as he had been able to release his anger and was sincerely able to thank the Lord on their behalf.

When John was nineteen, he felt the need to reconcile with his father and left the Dutch ship when they ported in Jamaica. He was sorely disappointed that his reappearance was met with such impassivity, and he soon left, his conscience now clear for having tried, and he never felt the need to return home again.

He returned to the port of Jamaica in search of his next opportunity; it was 1701. A British privateering ship was attempting to bolster its crew to set out against the Spanish and French in response to the Spanish Succession. The Spanish Succession was an attempt to unify Spain and France under the Bourbon monarch that, if it should occur, would create a superpower in Europe with which no other country could compete. So the British desired to increase their naval forces to intimidate the enemies. The thought of manning a warship intrigued John, and he joined the crew.

It was on the British privateer ship where John developed his leadership skills, as he was recognized for his solid character and fair handling of his crew, and he quickly moved up the ranks, achieving quartermaster. The ship continued to sail under the marque during part of the Queen Anne's War but lost its decree in 1710. That is when John and some of his fellow crewmates were set in Providence, and they continued with their trade of pirating, except now it wasn't done with the blessings of the marque of England. After six years of small-time pirating, John joined Captain Charles Vane to be quartermaster of Vane's ship, the *Ranger*.

It was now September of 1717, and in between his voyages with Captain Vane, Anne allowed John to court her. It was never her plan to fall in love, but she did, as Anne had a wistful heart.

As Anne learned more about John, she appreciated so many wonderful qualities. He was mature, as he was twelve years older than James was, and she was certain that he would never strike a lady in which he never did. He was well respected by all the pirates in Providence. But greatest of all, her relationship with John reminded her of her parents' miraculous love affair that she had witnessed in her childhood. Being that Anne so craved the ecstasy of romance and that the passion between the two was exceedingly potent to such a degree that it couldn't be resisted, it wasn't long before she lay with John. She felt as if she were living out the pages of her mother's diary.

As she lay there bare-breasted against his bosom, she was transported to a paradise that she never could've imagined. His touch was ever so gentle on her private areas, which caused a pleasant swelling and wetness. His kiss was sensually divine. As he entered her, she felt nothing but pleasures. During the crescendo of their love, they heaved together with rhythmic perfection until both had obtained their fill. Anne knew in her heart that this experience could never be considered as evil, although she wondered how because Anne was the wife of another man.

When John would return from each voyage, he would present her with the most precious poetry that she could imagine. His writings were crude, but Anne could extract the beautiful meaning of each inscription, and they lifted her to another place.

It was John who taught Anne how to handle a musket and pistol on their many adventures out in the pineyard of Providence, as John was an excellent marksman. It was in the wilderness of Providence where John kept a dwelling in a tree. To Anne's great surprise, it was a well-constructed, roomy, and comfortable abode lifted above the earth with stairs leading to its door. It was there that they slept together without fear of discovery from James when John would arrive home from his journeys. And Pierre could not have been happier for the couple, as he relished their matchless romance.

At night, they would take a lantern and visit the hot springs and bathe together, making love to the evening sounds of the jungle. Often, they would steal away to a neighboring island called Cat Island and relax for a day, dining on crabmeat seasoned with sea salt and butter, fresh bread and vegetables, and wine—all sent by Pierre. Anne had never been so happy in her entire life. The bliss she was experiencing in Providence completely erased all of her longings to return to Charles Town.

Anne, in just the short time she had been with John, saw herself evolving from a spoiled child into a woman, and it was at the beginning of the new year that Anne discovered that she was with child.

John, being concerned with the possibility of James encountering Anne as her belly grew, thought of a plan. He would take her to Cuba, so she could safely give birth without the looming threat of her husband.

CHAPTER 12

THE PROSPECTS OF beginning a family caused John to reconsider his life. He desired so deeply to provide for and nourish his family, but the only occupation in which he had ever been successful was that of pirating. He knew no other trade, and his heart belonged to the sea. While they sailed to Cuba, John and his men plundered several small vessels, but Anne was not to be considered a pirate at that time. Piracy was the furthest thing from her mind, as she carefully guarded her unborn child that grew in her womb.

When they arrived in Cuba, Anne had just turned eighteen. John placed Anne in the care of a dear friend named Elias and then returned to Providence where he intended to take many prizes during the time of her expectation, fully planning to return prior to the birth of the baby.

John and Elias had met when they were British privateers. Elias, like John, was English, except he was born to a Puritan family in Jamestown shortly after they arrived to the New World. Elias and John considered each other to be as close as any brother. They had secured a friendship through many adventurous voyages as pirates together before John joined Captain Vane. After that, Elias settled in Cuba with a young woman named Avala.

Elias had met Avala at the port of Havana when he and John stopped with their men to clean and dress the ship. Elias could not cease thinking about the Spanish beauty when he had returned to Providence, so he left to Cuba in order to find her after John accepted Captain Vane's offer. Elias never pirated again thereafter, for he and Avala were allowed to marry once Elias had converted to the Catholic faith. He then was taught the trade of a coffee planter by Avala's family.

Avala and her parents were criollos, which was the term originating from Spain to classify a caste of people who were of Spanish ancestry yet were born out of Spain in the Spanish Americas. The term was used to differentiate between them from the peninsulars, who were originally born in Spain but then relocated to the Spanish Americas. The peninsulars had a higher place in the caste system than the criollos, but it only had a mild effect on Avala's family as they managed their coffee plantation in Cuba, exporting their product from the harbor in Havana. It was from that harbor that Avala had met Elias.

Avala was the most beautiful woman whom Anne had ever witnessed. Her smooth olive skin practically glowed, and her large brown eyes were framed with black lashes, but what Anne really loved the most was her nose. It was smaller than Anne's and was formed in the most magnificent shape. Anne was not accustomed to seeing Spanish women, as there were none in Charles Town.

Elias was a tall man with broad shoulders, and although his skin had an olive hue, he rather stood out with his blonde hair and blue eyes. He was as gentle as John had been with Anne in his dealings with Avala, and their home was full of peacefulness and tranquility.

Their house had been constructed of wood and was situated on the corner of the plantation. It had been added on a few times to make a fairly spacious living environment and was large enough for Anne to have her own bedroom. Their home was certainly gigantic compared to John's house in the tree. Avala's parents lived in a much grander home on the other side of the estate.

Elias and Avala had a son named Raphael, who was five years old, and a daughter named Cordula who was two. Avala was expecting their third child, but her girth was much more pronounced than Anne, which was a delight, because Anne figured Avala could show her how to care for a child, and Anne planned to practice until hers was born.

Anne spent the next few months assisting in the home and took a good bit of the responsibility when Michael was born, as Avala needed time to rest. The labor process and especially the delivery were quite frightening, as Anne was present at the birth. The Negro midwife with skilled hands safely delivered the child and placed him at his mother's breast. It was as if Anne was witnessing a miracle. Except afterward, Anne purposed in her heart that she would not scream during her parturition even if she felt the extreme urge, as it had also frightened Raphael and Cordula. The midwife had performed a flawless delivery, and Anne was ever so thankful to have witnessed Ester's gift.

It was refreshing to have slaves once again, as Anne needed much assistance and coaching with her matronly tasks as she helped Avala. Anne had never kept house or children before, and she wanted to learn everything. The Negro slaves, Ester and Miriam, even taught Anne how to cook. The food in Cuba was such to Anne that she figured her palate had been destroyed forever, as she craved the herbs and spices of the black beans and rice, which was a wonderful reprieve from the dull corn mush of Charles Town. Ester and Miriam were a godsend, and Anne was truly grateful on their behalf, as it was also they who showed Anne how to care for Avala's baby, as Anne was a nursemaid to his mother.

While Avala rested, Anne would rock baby Michael for hours. His face was that of a cherub, and Anne would marvel at the child while he gazed up at her, his eyes carefully studying the shapes of her face as he took in his new world. Anne inspected his little fingers and fine lips and dreamed about the day that her baby would be born and the day she would see John again.

It was the end of July in 1718, and Anne had just completed her seventh month of expectation when Elias returned home from the harbor to announce that he'd heard that a new royal governor had arrived in Providence. That was all the information that Elias had received, with the exception that all pirates who did not willingly surrender were to be hanged. Anne's duress was immediate.

"Hanged, oh dear Lord!"

Anne didn't know where John was or how he would react, and the worry was overwhelming. She so desperately wanted him there safely by her side, but it's as if he had vanished. Anne wept in hopeless despair.

Apparently, the king of England had paid respect to the petition from the chancellor and the citizens of South Carolina, and he had positioned Woodes Rogers in Providence to exterminate piracy from the island forever.

The governor's grand entrance came as a surprise attack on Providence the eve of July 22, 1718. John had been talking to Pierre at the tavern when the frantic announcement came.

"Two British men-of-war ships are securing the harbor!"

The tavern turned to instant chaos, as the men scrambled for their weapons and supplies and sprinted toward the water's edge. John immediately ran upstairs to inform Captain Vane who was courting one of Pierre's ladies of the evening, and then John followed the other men. The pirates of Providence sneered at the Spanish, mocked the French, but shuddered at the sight of British troops—but not Vane. As the other pirates watched the British troops lower their boats to come ashore, they were already waving the white flag, but Captain Vane had conjoined with John and his other men and was not even considering surrendering but rather he conspired a quick plan.

Governor Rogers had been wise in his strategy, as he had placed a man-of-war ship at each exit of the harbor, so no ship could escape. But that wouldn't stop Vane.

Captain Vane had a few of his men mount a ship that was anchored adjacent to his brigantine called the *Ranger*. The vessel was a French sloop that they had taken as a prize. The two ships slipped cable and set sail. Once the French ship was headed east toward its target, its helm was stabilized, and the men dumped powder upon its deck. Simultaneously, Vane moved close enough for the men to throw a grappling hook over to Vane's bow and be secured. Once it was fastened, the men moved along the rope one at a time until all men were safe on board Vane's ship. A lantern was then thrown onto the sloop, igniting the powder as the grappling hook was cut from its rope, and the fireship, being of lighter weight than Vane's brigantine, sailed forward. The inferno headed toward the man-of-war ship, which caused the great vessel to retreat enough of the passage that Captain Vane in his six-gun brigantine could slip by the east narrow end and head out to sea.

Captain Vane brazenly fired his cannon at the man-of-war as he passed by, raising his pirate's flag to the mainmast. After he was out at sea, he evaded several other British naval ships and sailed north.

It was rather surprising that John continued to remain as quartermaster to Vane as the two men were very different in character. Maybe it was the constant dosing of rum that kept John numbed and allowed him to tolerate Vane's sinister ways, or maybe that was just an excuse.

Captain Vane was an English pirate who started his maritime life as a privateer on a British ship like so many others. His notoriety as a pirate came mainly from the wealth he received while plundering the silver coins from the Spanish ships as they were recovering the treasure from the shipwrecks off the coast of Florida. He was also renowned as a pirate who was cruel to his victims.

Captain Vane would torture the crews of captured ships, cheat his men out of their fair share of the prize, and kill surrendering sailors after he had promised them forgiveness. Although Captain Vane had immense respect for John Rackam and the captain curtailed his behavior somewhat at John's request, Captain Vane persisted to accomplish evil, and John was tiring of dealing with his harsh unchanging ways. And there was no way that Captain Vane was going to repent and surrender, but John was seriously considering accepting the deal of clemency offered by Woodes Rogers.

Governor Rogers was sent to Providence by England, extending clemency without penalty for all pirates who would surrender by the end of July. With the exception of Charles Vane, John Rackam, and Edward Teach, all the citizens of Providence had readily surrendered the day the governor arrived. The willing submission was most certainly due to the fact that Woodes Rogers held a place of respect in their midst, as the governor was the captain of a ship that had sailed completely around the world.

The pirates knew that Woodes Rogers had accomplished his journey and returned home to England a national hero, and they knew that he wrote about his adventures in a book called *A Cruising Voyage Round the World*, which was wildly popular and afforded him the title of a famous author. Woodes Rogers was a celebrity of sorts in Providence, and because of all of those valued characteristics, he was the perfect man to subdue piracy in Providence.

Although he was considered a deity of sorts, his personal life, his financial dealings, and his character judgment were all far from pristine. He had been divorced, he had been bankrupt, he had been sued multiple times, and he had chosen business partners with histories of miserable past failures caused from their sheer neglect of the basics. But these things didn't seem to matter to the pirates, as they accepted their deal of clemency with Governor Rogers, so with the governor's prior record, it was no great surprise he would see the potential in James Bonny and appoint him as an informant and pirate hunter.

"What on God's green earth was he thinking?" Pierre thought as he hoped that the look of horror wouldn't be gleaned from his face from James Bonny as he bragged about his new position with the governor.

"He must have lost his senses. This man is supposed to be some world-famous hero full of all wisdom, and he has chosen James Bonny as his second in command? Oh my god!" Pierre gushed in his mind, as his true intent seemed to be unnoticed by James.

"Well, congratulations to you," Pierre managed to mouth a somewhat convincing lie.

After his escape from the harbor, Vane redirected his ship toward the Caribbean Sea. Along the way to the Windward Islands, the captain, John, and his men seized a sloop from Barbados and another with eight passengers on board. They commanded the two captured vessels, one with a fellow crewman named Yeats, and the three ships headed for a small island in which they could divide the gains and clean and dress their ships.

After scouring the Windward Islands, they cut between St. Christopher's and Anguilla and took a Spanish sloop, which had departed from Puerto Rico en route to Havana. Vane's crew allowed the Spaniards to row ashore to a neighboring island as they burned the vessel. Typically, they would have returned to Providence at that time, but that was no longer an option, and they were running out of supplies.

Luck would have it that soon Vane and his crew found the prize in which they were in need. It was a brigantine and a sloop with all the necessities to survive on their journey north, and the three vessels of Vane's company sailed on to the North Americas, where they ended off the coastline of South Carolina around the middle of August.

Anne was then in her eighth month, and after wearying herself from anguish, she resolved to let her mind rest. She delighted in the movements of the baby in her womb, and she chose to trust that John would return to Cuba in September for the birth of their child as he had promised.

Vane had indeed promised to have John in Cuba by September, but he had no intention of doing such, as he would risk the loss of his trustworthy quartermaster. And only for the miniscule reason of a supposed wife and a baby, which Vane loathed the very thought. Instead, he pillaged vessels along the coast of the North Americas torridly against John's will. The tension had mounted between John Rackam and Captain Vane to such a fierce degree that it was apparent to the entire crew, who was left wondering as to what their fate would hold. Despite John's objections, Vane continued in his madness, and after taking a brigantine with ninety Negros on board, Vane devised a plan in which to abandon Yeats from his company.

After plundering the brigantine, Vane placed the Negroes on Yeat's ship without sufficient supplies in which to care for so many souls. And Yeats, seeing that he had been lowballed by the Captain Vane, headed to shore just south of Charles Town and surrendered to the king's pardon. Yeats was considered a hero, as he turned the Negros back to their rightful owner, and afterward, Vane combed the coasts of South Carolina obsessed with his thoughts of bestowing a painful revenge upon Yeats for his disloyalty.

September had passed, and Anne was still not delivered of her child. Her girth was such that she could barely breathe, but her time had not come, and she wondered if the baby was holding out for the return of John. Ester supplied Anne with the tea to encourage her labor, but Anne refused, as she wanted to have John with her for the birth, but he hadn't returned by the middle of October, when Anne awoke at four in the morning to pains in the lower parts of her belly.

Anne was able to doze in between the nagging cramps that came regularly, but still fairly spaced, and she rested in bed until later that morning. When Anne arose, Avala, Ester, and Miriam could tell by the waves of mounting agony that Anne's time of travail had come, and Anne paced the better part of the day. Elias was more than happy to care for the children away from the house and would only alert Avala if Michael was in need of her breast. When Anne would tire, she would sit and rock in the chair and partially doze until another god-awful pain would come. Her mind wondered in a dreamlike state, and her head floated as if it were affected by rum. She thought about John and remembered the serenity of the house in the tree and the way he would touch her, and then her thoughts would vanish, being interrupted by another harrowing pain.

The pain would snap her back into consciousness, and it was then that she reneged on her promise to remain silent during her birth, and she moaned in guttural tones with each contraction. The three women remained silently vigilant at her side, gently swaying with the rhythm of Anne's chair as she drifted in and out. Her groans had resolved to deep breathing followed by harrowing screams of anguish that were steadily increasing and coming in rapid succession, which resolved with an uncontrollable urge to bear down during the peak of each pain.

Esther knew that Anne was nearing the end and was thankful, because Anne had now been in travail some twenty hours, with a large portion of it being hard pains, and Ester knew of the possible consequences for the mother and the baby. She stood by ever so gently with her gifted dark hands resting softly on Anne's shoulders, imparting her strength, awaiting the birth . . . Ester was thankful that Anne could not see the look on her face when she saw Anne's water come, as it was dark, thick brownish-green in its color.

Anne was not lucid enough to notice that it was not at all like the clear fluid that had flowed from Avala's body before her birth, but the three women noticed, and they prayed for a miracle despite the ominous sign.

After three hours of trying to expel the baby from her womb by bearing down under the intense pressure, Anne was delivered of a baby boy.

Anne finally awoke from her unconscious state to find that there was no baby on her breast and that the three women surrounding her had reddened puffy eyes from the grief that they shared. When the demised baby was born, he was taken to another room and gently bathed, then they wrapped his lifeless body in a soft blanket that Anne had made for him.

They encouraged her to rest for a while before she saw her son, as she was shivering violently, but Anne firmly insisted on holding her baby, as she needed to see for herself that he didn't have his breath. Maybe there had

D.A. NASH

been some type of mistake in their assessment, and she would be pleasantly surprised, or maybe a miracle had occurred. So Ester brought Jonathan into the room swaddled in the soft blanket and delivered the dead child into Anne's arms.

CHAPTER 13

IT WAS NOVEMBER of 1718, and James Bonny had yet to bring in one single pirate. Pierre smirked from behind the bar as James paraded his new position.

"Oh my god, how much longer must I endure this?" he whispered to Delfina, one his finer women.

Delfina had been named after a French saint when she was born to a peasant family in France. She had come to the island after pirates plundered the ship she was aboard, and it was a fine day for the pirates, as they had happened upon a ship full of French prostitutes being extradited from Jamaica. Although the prostitutes were in high demand among the aristocrats of the royal colony, the authorities in Jamaica had ordered them removed and demanded that they be taken back to their own country where they would be rendered out of sight. The captain of the ship was so embarrassed after he had been plundered that he sailed for a decent amount of time before returning to Jamaica and then he returned with the good report of accomplishing his mission in delivering the prostitutes over to the French officials. However, rather than landing in France, the prostitutes came ashore to Providence and found a haven with Pierre.

After Delfina left with a client, Pierre lovingly thought of Anney and imagined that she and John were probably frolicking around the island of Cuba enjoying their lives as a happy family. He envisioned the baby was a son and probably the spitting image of John. He solidly swore in his heart as he thought of the young family that he would never covet John Rackam again as John belonged to Anney, and Pierre had much higher values than to lust after his best friend's husband. He wondered if Anne would ever return and figured she probably wouldn't, as James was ever so present in Nassau more than he had ever been before.

Pierre had thought to return to his Catholic roots and maybe praying to a saint would assist in removing the bastard from his sight. He also thought about John and hoped that he was right in that John had made it to Cuba safely in time to join Anne for the birth.

Unfortunately, John was being held captive by a tyrant who was slowly losing his mind and the respect of his crew. Instead of heading south toward Cuba, Vane was hovering around the harbor of North Carolina when he came across an old friend Edward Teach, known as Blackbeard. Captain Edward Teach frequented the North Carolina colony and was welcomed by the governor who greedily accepted his briberies and all manners of valuable gifts.

When the *Ranger* sailed by the ship captained by Teach, Vane fired his cannon wide and up into the air, as was common practice among the pirates to offer such a salute. Teach had given up his original ship called the *Queen Anne's Revenge* when he took the king's pardon but had returned to pirating and was now sailing in a ship called the *Adventure*. John was most displeased by the lofty display of respect for Teach, as he had lost all regard for the rogue.

Back in 1717, when the black-bearded pirate had risen to the rank of captaining his own ship, Teach, like Vane, began to develop a reputation of extreme cruelty to his victims as he delighted in terrorizing them before he would mutilate and kill them. He was known for cutting off the finger of a quivering man who could not deliver the coveted ring fast enough to satisfy the impatient demon. The pirates of Providence had also spread stories of his perverse sexual activity, which they claimed that Teach himself boasted.

According to one account, Teach supposedly had married his fourteenth wife while finding a safe haven in North Carolina. She was a planter's daughter of only sixteen years of age. After Teach had lain with her all night, he would have at least five, maybe six, of his men come into the bedchamber where he would lend out his wife to the men while he watched. John, after hearing that accord, refused any more stories and became sickened by the thought of Teach's twisted existence.

It was after Vane's salute to Edward Teach that John firmly decided to abandon his post with Captain Vane, as the captain was now heading further North into New England. John plotted to steal the remaining sloop that they had obtained in the Windward Islands and then he would sail to Cuba to join Anne, but luck turned in his favor, and his plan was never necessary.

Off the coast of New England, they came upon a ship which appeared as if it would easily submit to their hoisting of the black flag, but to their ill astonishment, the ship hoisted a French man-of-war flag, which bravely rippled in the breeze.

Vane at once turned away from the ship and retreated, but the man-of-war ship pursued the frightened captain, and it appeared that the great vessel would readily take the advantage over Vane. John immediately took a stand against the captain and insisted that they fight, for he knew that if they remained docile, they would be captured by the French and rendered powerless or, worse yet, executed, but Vane disregarded John and continued to flee. By chance, Vane's brigantine pulled ahead of the galleon, and Vane's crew narrowly escaped as they headed south. Vane gloated in his decision to steal away from the French, and he made it appear as if he were merely taunting the French ship. However, the majority of his crew sorely disagreed, and a heated argument ensued between John and Captain Vane.

Captain Vane spoke through gritted teeth, "This is mutiny, and I will not tolerate it."

But John stood firm. "No, Captain Vane, it is a pirate's right to vote, and let the men decide their leadership!"

"I don't like your tone, John Rackam."

"And I don't like that you're a coward and man who can't keep his word."

Captain Vane would have attempted to pierce John with his cutlass at that moment, but he knew that the majority of men backed John Rackam and he would be the victim of a mutinous bloodbath. The men voted, and on November 24, 1718, Vane delivered his rank of captain up to John, and Vane and his mere fifteen men of supporters were given the remaining of the plundered sloop with enough provisions to keep them alive, and John headed south to Cuba with his men.

Anne had delivered her child at three in the morning on October 17, 1718, and she held his limp body as she shifted between moods of violent wailing and periods of peaceful awe at the sight of the newborn. She held him all through the night and well into the next day. Although his color was ashen and his lips bright red from the congealed blood below the surface of the skin, Anne saw a living child who was merely sleeping. She marveled at how much he favored John. She pulled back the blanket and inspected his tiny fingers and toes, which resolved into guttural sobs once again. It took a long while before Anne finally realized that Jonathan was never going to wake up.

Ester was ever so patient, but she knew that if she didn't take the child, Anne would become sick from the decay, as she had already shown signs of a fever. Eventually, Anne loosened her hold and released Jonathan to Ester and fell into a deep sleep.

Over a month after the birth, John arrived in Cuba to find Anne sitting by the gravesite of his son. Avala's family had so graciously provided a resting place for the infant in the cemetery where they had laid other dear members of their family. John watched from afar with excruciating agony as Anne grieved the loss of their child. He so desired to run to her side and hold her, but Elias had warned him about Anne's deep hatred for the pirate who had caused her such misery and had abandoned her in Cuba. Watching Anne suffer as she did forced John to his hands and knees, and he wept more severely than he ever had. His broken condition had rendered him powerless, and John wasn't able to approach Anne until his strength eventually returned to his body.

As he had feared, the dynamics between the two had drastically changed, as Anne was hostile toward him. She would not even look in his direction, and she wanted to be left alone. However, John was patient, and he was determined to remain available for as long as it would take her. He prayed for the day when she would begin to talk to him about her ordeals and she could listen to his reasoning for being absent during her harrowing time, which made him feel a good bit of guilt, as it sounded as if he were making sore excuses. He berated himself for not taking a stand against Vane much earlier in his journey, which would have allowed him to arrive on time.

He elected a new captain of Vane's ship who was a man named George Fetherston. John had always chosen George as his quartermaster when he sailed in Vane's steed. In fact, it was George who subdued Captain Hawthorne that day they plundered the chancellor's slave ship en route to South Carolina. George was a man who had shown a great amount of character, and John fully trusted that his men would be successful under George's solid leadership. John sent them away from Havana with his blessings to be free to sail to wherever they decided, but after they sailed from Cuba, they headed for Providence. The men had unanimously voted that they should return to their home and accept the king's clemency, as it wouldn't be the same pirating without John Rackam. Upon their return, they surrendered the brigantine to Governor Woodes Rogers.

John supposed that he and Anne would remain in Cuba and learn the trade of coffee planting, but his heart longed for Providence. Finally, Anne had decided to engage in dialogue, but it was more of a verbal sparring than a conversation.

"I am not going back to Providence, ever!"

"Please, Anne, the governor has extended his pardon on my behalf. I heard it from a sailor at the dock who just arrived from Providence today."

"No, I am not leaving the site of my dead son's grave!" Anne bellowed. "I will live here forever preferably without you!" she spoke through trussed lips. Then she lowered her head as the tears came.

"It's not only about leaving the grave. I don't want to leave my family. Elias and Avala and Miriam and Ester." Anne wept. "They have shown me how to truly love by their example, and they've performed the miracle of cleansing me of the agonizing guilt that I held. They made me realize that what had happened to me wasn't God's punishment for my wickedness . . . But merely a blessed gift that was much too fragile for the harsh circumstances under which he was born. I owe them a lifetime of servitude."

Her words were as millstones, as John wiped his tears with his sleeve to erase the fluid that flowed from his eyes without regard. It's as if the burden of her guilt had been set upon his shoulders, and the weight was such that he was slowly being crushed. It was only made worse by Anne's rejection, as she stood away only allowing John at a certain distance. Nevertheless, John continued.

"Anne, we can return to Providence and visit here anytime you like."

Anne was becoming annoyed. "Why are you so determined to return to Providence?"

"It was there that you and I spent the happiest time in my entire life, and I want us to go back and start over again, but this time doing it the right way."

Anne spewed her cynical disgust. "So we can live in a tree and be pursued by my husband the rest of our lives. That sounds like a bloody paradise!"

"Anne, I have accumulated a lot of wealth in this past six months, and I can buy your marriage decree from James Bonny, so I will be your rightful husband."

Anne seethed at his remarks. "Goddamn you, John Rackam. You presume that I can be bought and sold like a piece of cattle? You're no different than James Bonny, and I loathe the very sight of you!" Anne turned to leave, and John pleaded,

"Anne, please, the governor is going to grant land for the men to build houses upon in Providence."

With her back to John, Anne stopped and waved her hand for him to be silent, but John continued.

"And I want to build you a grand home on a plantation, where we can fill it with children and live the rest our lives as honest citizens with a marriage decree that says we have permission to be together. Anne, I want to accept the governor's offer of clemency, and I plan to give up the sea forever, so I can be at home with you."

Anne turned around and eventually allowed John to hold her, and she clung to him that day. She wept more severely than she ever had, saturating his shirt against his chest with her tears, and John was a pillar of strength guarding the fragile creature in his arms for as long as she needed. When she finally released her grip, Anne had accepted her grief and began to find forgiveness in her heart for John.

It was a slow process, but eventually Anne was able to look John Rackam in the eye again. Then finally, he got his wish as Anne was ready to talk, and bless John for he never wearied as Anne talked and talked and talked some more.

The couple stayed with Elias and Avala for a little over a month and said their farewells to Ester and Miriam and the gracious family as they set sail for Providence on a merchant ship after the New Year in 1719. The trip home was filled with heartfelt reminiscing of the time Anne had spent in Cuba, and John could envision the beauty of his son, which was eloquently described by Anne.

When they arrived, Pierre was ecstatic but wept horribly at her story of baby Jonathan. After a good cry, he suggested that it would be a good idea for Anney to don men's clothing, as James was ever so present in Nassau those days. Pierre feared that Anne would be discovered, but it would only be until John could buy her marriage decree from James, as Pierre loved to see Anney in a dress. To Anne's great surprise, Mark now resided in Providence. In fact, he was staying in John's house in the tree.

Pierre had taken a rare liking to Mark and set him up in the tree, as he figured John Rackam might never return from Cuba. He had given Mark ample supply of sea salt and beauty cream, and Pierre figured it was a good sign when Mark was so delighted, as it showed Pierre that the handsome fellow also had a feminine side. At night, Mary would retreat to the hot springs and cleanse and moisturize her skin and slip into a satin shirt in which she slept. Pierre's products made her feel soft and supple, like a lady ought, but she had no inclination whatsoever to take Pierre as a partner.

Pierre, however, envisioned him and Mark frolicking gleefully in the surf together and taking their fill of romantic bliss. Then he pondered them relaxing to some very fine wine while they enjoyed the moment, listening to the ocean waves beat against the shore as their toned bodies warmed in the tropical sun, but only until Pierre had to go to work at the tavern.

Since the governor arrived, Pierre's tavern was livelier than ever. No one enjoyed women and strong drink more than British troops, who felt that their assignment to secure Providence was a fairly decent shake. One could barely tell the soldiers from the pirates as they enjoyed their pastime together.

Governor Rogers was doing a fine job, and he readily granted John Rackam his clemency, honoring John with the Woodes Rogers seal of courage. The governor hoped that Charles Vane would also respond favorably to his extension. However, John wasn't agreeable, for he knew that Vane would rather die at the end of a noose than to submit to an English royal governor.

With his clemency granted, the only obstacle John faced then was to approach James Bonny and offer to buy his marriage rights, but he wondered how he should approach the subject. Should he simply buy him a round of bumbo and drop a hint? "How would you feel if someone wanted to buy your wife?" And then wait for James's response? "No," John thought. "Hello, James, congratulations on your new position. Can I buy your wife? No, even worse," he thought, "that certainly wouldn't work." It had turned out to be quite the dilemma, but until he figured it out, he could return with Anne and hide in the pineyards in his house in the tree.

Pierre had warned John that he had lent his house out to a friend, which was fine with John, as he was a gracious man. However, when he arrived home with Anne, John was taken back as to how thrilled Mark was to see Anne again, but John composed his politeness because Mark was also delighted to meet John, as Pierre had filled him on the details of their relationship. John was further taken back by Anne's elation to see Mark and couldn't wait to update him on all that had taken place in Anne's life. Anne shared that she was developing her own adventure story, except Anne's was really very sad. Mark showed utmost compassion as he looked forward to hearing all about it. John purposed in his heart to resist his jealousy. Besides, what would Anne see in this small-framed lad with the dirty face anyway?

Mary had come to Providence when she had heard of the new governor, hoping to find employment. She stood in front of the governor as Mark and boldly requested to fill any position in which he deemed necessary. Mark found favor, and he was assigned to run errands for the governor. Mary was so proud, except she still couldn't don ladies clothing, because she feared if the governor found out Mark was a Mary, he would dismiss her of her position immediately. So she continued as a man, and the close friendship that she and Anne had already developed during their journey from Jamaica appeared as though Anne was fond for another man. John's jealousy gnawed at him as Mark left John's place and rented a room from Pierre, which Pierre thought was grand. It wasn't long after that when Anne discovered Mark's gender.

Back in Charles Town, the chancellor was pleased to hear that his plan was in motion, as he had been informed of the wonderful progress of the Royal Governor Woodes Rogers. He was delighted at the reports of how the governor was able to surrender the pirates of Providence and in such a short amount of time. Although the chancellor was content with the good news and especially the accounts of the massacre of Edward Teach, he would still not rest until he saw the capture and hanging of Captain Vane.

In Jamaica, Sarah Lawes was now the official sister-in-law to the governor, as Nicolas Lawes had been sworn into to office as Royal Governor of Jamaica. As Sarah Lawes gazed in the looking glass, she practiced her smile, and although her prosthetic was somewhat believable, it still was not the smile that she once proudly displayed, as she had lost her charm. She continued to seethe, and as far as Sarah was concerned, she could care the less about Charles Vane and Edward Teach, for her only intent was to see the capture and hanging of Anne Bonny.

CHAPTER 14

THEY GAVE ANNE'S first kill to Pierre who had marvelous intentions to turn the hog into palatable bliss. Anne had shared some of her knowledge with Pierre about Cuban cuisine, and he was thrilled to experiment. Anne was pleased to have presented Pierre with such a gift, as he had been so eternally generous with her. In fact, Pierre was the most generous individual that Anne had ever met. She was somewhat puzzled by his feminine range of emotions, but besides his generosity, the revealing of his heart through those emotions is what Anne relished most about him.

Pierre never did disclose his yearnings for masculine companionship to Anne, as he felt that in her innocence, she would never be able to comprehend his natural tendencies, and he definitely did not want to disturb the glorious relationship that he and Anney had developed. John, however, knew of Pierre's longings and told him that there was not a single man on the island or probably in the whole world that was worthy of Pierre's love, which brought a bit of a tear to Pierre's eye.

One evening, John and Anne decided to visit the tavern as there were so many new men on the island that Anne dressed as one in a crowded saloon should go unnoticed by James Bonny without effort. In fact, it had almost turned into a game of sorts, as a few days earlier, John and Anne had crossed his path while they were returning from a hunting excursion.

Anne had just killed her first hog, and she was proud as John complimented her on her excellent aim and handle of the musket. While they toted their pig, they were thrown off when their paths crossed James Bonny, but he hadn't noticed a thing as he forged by. John and Anne fought to contain their laughter as they continued and were in agreement that it was a rather fun sport taunting James unaware.

On that particular evening, Anne and John sat at the bar enjoying conversation with Pierre. Anne listened as John told Pierre of a plot that Captain Vane had revealed to him before he lost favor in which Vane planned to sneak onto the island and assassinate Woodes Rogers in his sleep. They also talked about the demise of Edward Teach as John ordered another cup of punch, but Anne declined, as she was only resigned to wine ever since her ordeal with the rum. As she finished her drink, Pierre asked a favor of her. He had baked some bread and had whipped some butter and wanted Anne to deliver it to Mark's room as a gift, thinking Mark may delight in an evening snack. Anne, of course, was more than happy to greet her friend, and John thought nothing about the situation, since he had given up his jealousy for Mark, knowing that he and Anne had a solid relationship.

Pierre instructed, "Mark's room is the very last door in the corner, the one isolated from the others."

Anne ascended the staircase with Pierre's gift and located the room. Anne lightly knocked at the door, but there was no reply.

Mary, completely naked, had been bathing from a porcelain bowl when she heard the rap at the door, and she was horrified for she had not secured it, as Mary was not accustomed to using a locked door.

Anne decided that Mark must be sleeping, and she slipped the door open, figuring she would quietly place the bread on the chest and leave, but she was aghast when she opened the door to a nude Mary and beheld her gender.

"Mark, you have breasts like me!"

Mary, in a state of shear panic, grabbed a blanket and concealed her nakedness and began to sob violently.

"You must not tell anyone. You have to promise me that you will not tell anyone!" Mary managed to choke out the words.

Anne was adamant. "Of course I won't. It can be our little secret, and I'm so sorry that I entered your room without permission. I thought you were sleeping, and I was going to leave this gift that Pierre had sent. I thought it would be a pleasant surprise when you woke in the morning. I'm ever so sorry."

Mary was a beautiful woman with just a hint of freckles over ivory skin. She wore her auburn hair short, and it framed her big blue eyes and full pink lips marvelously. Her body was lean and toned from years of hard work, and her skin was ever so smooth with Pierre's beauty cream.

Anne's sincere apology eased Mary's tears somewhat, and then Anne craved more information.

"So you're not a man at all."

Mary conceded. "No, I am a woman as you are."

Anne inquired gently, "So why do you ardently conceal your gender? Is it that you prefer a woman?"

Mary was shocked at Anne. "No, I definitely prefer a man!"

Anne smiled. "Well, don't you think that it would be a little more difficult to fall in love when you always don men's clothing?"

Anne was remorseful for her humor, as she saw Mary's countenance fall. "I dress as man so I can eat."

"So you can eat?"

Anne had never been in want of food a single day in her entire life, so she couldn't understand, but Mary had. When Mary's grandmother died, and before her mother had set her out to be the footboy for the French woman, she and her mother practically starved to death.

Mary was actually relieved that Anne had walked in and discovered her gender, for she would never have gained the confidence to disclose her vulnerability to anyone. But now she was free to tell Anne the entire story, which opened her heart and let things emerge that she was unaware that she had harbored.

Downstairs at the bar, John had just finished another cup of punch, and his imagination, being unrestrained by his excess of strong drink, began to play tricks upon him.

"Pierre, what could be taking Anne so long?"

Pierre was encouraging. "Oh, Mark probably started talking, and Anne can't get away. She and Mark have become wonderful friends." Pierre recognized the concern on John's face. "You're not worried about Anne's affection toward Mark are you?" Pierre lowered his voice, "Personally, I think Mark has a fancy for men, so you need not to worry."

Pierre was able to ease John's mind for the time being, and up in Mary's room, Anne held Mary in her blanket as Mary had emotionally decompensated in the middle of her story.

"Mary, you will never ever be hungry as long as I am alive. I promise with all my heart!"

Suddenly, a loud knock was heard at the door. The two women scrambled and communicated through breathless whispers, while Anne thought a quick plan.

"Here, get in here!" Anne pointed at the wardrobe.

John drew his rapier as he heard the hushed whispers and commotion in the room through the closed door, and he could not believe what he was hearing. He forced his entrance and gritted.

"Where is he that I may cut his throat?"

"John!" Anne was in utter shock. "What are you doing? Have you lost your senses? Replace your rapier at once! I am thoroughly disappointed that you would think that I would ever do such a thing!"

Anne turned to the wardrobe.

"Mark came out of the wardrobe that we may clear the dregs out of this muddied pond!"

Mary emerged wrapped in her blanket. Her clean face glowed of feminine youth. She addressed John.

"You need not slit my throat for I am no threat to you, John Rackam."

John stood dazed for a second and then turned his head out of respect for her privacy.

"I'm so very sorry that I disrespected you in such a way." John replaced his rapier and very humbly left Mary's room.

John was on his best behavior for days after his grave mistake in which he was then horribly embarrassed. Anne eventually used the event as fodder to tease the brave pirate, and John allowed her to have her fun as he too eventually found the whole ordeal to be quite hilarious. They firmly decided to keep the matter a secret, as they did not want to compromise Mark's position with Governor Rogers. John, however, did decide to confide Mary's gender to Pierre, as he knew Pierre was very trustworthy, and Pierre had also mentioned his whim for Mark. John didn't want to see Pierre get his hopes up only to be thrashed to the ground again.

John had arisen early that morning for his appointment with Governor Rogers and had taken extra care in his appearance. He had heard that the governor was recruiting men as privateers against the Spanish in response to the War of Quadruple Alliance in which England, France, Austria, and the Dutch Republic had declared war against Spain. Although Anne was reluctant, she finally gave her blessing, for she knew of his ardent love of the sea.

John had gotten high hopes of securing such a position, as he was sure of his qualifications, but he was sorely disheartened when the governor declined his offer. Woodes Rogers believed that John lacked the experience necessary to captain a ship against the Spanish, although he said he would consider a land grant on behalf of John and any other position for which John may be qualified. John accepted the rejection from the governor with grace, and Anne was secretly relieved.

The couple spent the next few weeks hiking the entire island of Providence, as there were so many places where John desired to show Anne. The island of Providence is only twenty-one miles in length and seven miles in width. Anne took a rapier in case she ran into another boa, and of course they did, but it was John who chopped off its head, so he could prepare a special dinner for Anne.

The first site to where John took Anne was the secret place where he kept his treasure. It was about five miles inland, heading in a southwesterly direction away from Nassau. The treasure was concealed in a deep cavern, which resided next to a pool of seawater that surfaced in the inner part of the island. The island was known for such pools called blue holes.

Anne marveled at the pool, and John cautioned her not to drink of it, as it was salty, but it was an excellent source to gather and collect the sea salt.

He removed the foliage from over the cavern, and Anne was astonished as she had never seen so much gold and silver in her entire life. She wondered if her father, in all his wealth, had ever witnessed such.

Anne was puzzled. "Why are you showing me this?"

"I want you to know where it is, in case something should ever happen to me."

"Nothing's going to happen to you, silly, but now I can gain access when I fall in love with the next young man who comes along, such as Mark, and we can run away to Cat Island and live lavishly on your behalf."

John offered a hearty laugh, then recited, "And you and your lover have my complete blessings to build you a grand home upon Mount Alverina, which looks out over the ocean. My only wish is that you find happiness forever on my behalf."

John's smile always did something magical in Anne's heart, and she caressed his majestic face. "No, I've decided that I fancy a house in a tree as long as I'm with you."

John lavished her attention and then added, "I wanted to show the treasure, so you may come and take as much as you want, whenever you want."

John wanted to make his treasure available to Anne, because Nassau had grown to a thriving community with many markets in which to purchase all sorts of items that would provide a comfortable life.

Anne kissed John with passionate affection as their tongues glided sensually over each other enjoying the taste of the mint, as Pierre had taught Anne how to freshen the mouth with sea salt and mint leaves.

John returned the foliage to the cave and never worried about its security. He had always stored his treasures there and had never been robbed. He figured if some rogue came along and took it, then the cheat must need it worse than John as there were more valuable things in life than gold and silver. It was the next site that John desired to show Anne that excited him even more than where John hid his treasures, and the place was in close proximity.

A bench had been crafted out of pine in the middle of a clearing with shrubbery forming a hedge about them. John offered Anne a place on the bench as he surveyed the trees and called out,

"King Henry, are you there? King Henry, I've brought you some bread."

Suddenly a pig emerged from the bush, and Anne jumped upon the bench in terror. John quickly added,

"It's all right, that's only Catherine."

Anne chided, "Catherine?"

Anne watched as the pig ran to John wagging its tail like the overseer's dog used to do. It offered affection and was obviously overcome with joy to see John who graciously rubbed behind the pig's ears. The hog looked like any other pig in Charles Town, except that it was covered with course hair with a soft-brown hue. John talked to the animal,

"I brought you some bread as well."

Anne remained speechless as she watched the pig jump up and receive the offering from John who explained.

"I found her when she was just a pup and kept her out here for all these years. I was afraid that if I took her back, she'd be hunted in a moment, so I wait until she's sleeping and slip away. My only fear has been that she'll follow my scent, but she hasn't so far."

Anne retorted, "I cannot believe the sight before my eyes"—and she began to laugh. "You keep a pig as a pet." And she laughed even more.

John smiled grandly and then added,

"They make fine pets. Oh, and wait until you meet King Henry. You'll truly get a good laugh. You'll see why I've named them such. Henry and Catherine make a glorious couple, except they get along much better than the king and his wife did."

The pig rolled over as John rubbed her belly, and she half closed her eyes, lavishing the attention just like the overseer's dog. As Anne enjoyed the display, suddenly, a horribly unfamiliar sound resonated from a nearby tree, and she ducked her head. John laughed.

"There you are, King Henry!"

He took a piece of bread and offered it to the parrot perched on a limb. The parrot proceeded to talk, which left Anne's mouth ajar.

"Damnation to the queen."

John reproved. "Now, King Henry, that is no way to speak in front of a lady. You must mind your manners."

The parrot continued, "Would you like some rum?"

"Why, yes, I would, thank you very much."

The parrot then whistled a clever tune.

John placed his hand horizontally toward the bird, and it perched on his wrist. John offered him to Anne.

"Would you like to pet him?"

Anne backed away. "No! No thank you very much. I'll just watch this time."

Anne, still aghast over the whole ordeal, observed the peculiar scene with much delight. It was a circus of sorts. The bird could dance to John's command by bobbing its head up and down, and he would shake John's hand for more bread.

Anne asked. "How long did it take him to learn that?"

John was proud. "Not long at all. He's a very fine student. Much better than I was growing up." John smiled.

Anne replied, "We should teach him the Lord's Prayer."

John chuckled. "I don't think it would work, as he would follow it with damnation to the Queen and ruin the whole thing."

Anne did indeed get a good laugh form King Henry as she marveled at how amazing John Rackam truly was. He continually mesmerized her with his interesting life, his pure heart, and his gracious soul.

When the pig had fallen to sleep, John and Anne slipped out and headed back home. Anne felt certain that she may never be able to shoot another pig again, but John reassured her that if the feral animals were not hunted, they would breed to such a degree that the whole island would be overtaken by pigs, and therefore, they should kill and enjoy the meat. However, Anne still resolved in her heart that she could never do it again. That evening, the couple decided to remain at home instead of patronizing the tavern, as they desired their complete solitude.

After a bath in the hot springs, Anne and John held each other bare-skinned by the light of a candle. John's body was fit and healthy; Anne's body had returned to the youthful tone she had been blessed with prior to her childbearing. The couple had not made love since the birth, but Anne was ready. By the light of the candle, John lightly stroked Anne's face with his fingertips as he spoke tenderly.

"There's so much more I want to show you, but we'll have to sail in order to see it all."

Anne whispered, "Sail to where?"

John took his time. "Oh, there's Andros Island to see the most amazing orchids that grow in the wild."

John envisioned the orchids and then continued,

"Let's see, there's Abaco Island to watch the horses run free. And of course, Eleuthera, where the Atlantic Ocean meets the Caribbean Sea underneath a magnificent rock formation. I can't even describe the water for its beauty, but you'll see it for yourself and then you can describe it to me."

His words were like poetry, and Anne began to kiss his neck and down onto his chest and over his belly. The tingles she experienced were more intense than she'd ever felt, and she enjoyed the swollen warm wetness of her private areas, as her tongue swirled on his skin.

That night, John and Anne spent hours exploring each other bodies and discovering ways to create intense pleasures for each other—pleasures in which they had never encountered.

It was in the light of dawn when Anne awoke and put on her undergarments, for she didn't want John to wake to her nakedness in the daylight. He apparently had risen during the night, because he lay sleeping in his breeches.

Violently, the door to their room slammed open, and Anne collapsed in terror, as James Bonny and several English soldiers stood armed and ready to subdue. John had arisen and grabbed his rapier, but James entered the room unaffected. He addressed Anne,

"Oh, there you are. Wasn't Chidley Bayard good enough for you?"

John rebuked, "Leave her alone, James Bonny."

In his smugness, he faced off John.

"What are you going to do, gut me like you did Hawthorne after you've slept with my wife? What kind of man are you, John Rackam?" John was sorely outnumbered as his weary eyes scanned the soldiers behind James, and John dropped his rapier.

James sneered his command, "Lock em up."

James Bonny was an extraordinarily clever young man, and he had seen Anne, despite her disguise; it was foolish for her to think that he would not. James had let her have her folly and then he had waited for the right moment to strike, catching them in the very act of adultery.

John solemnly accepted the cuffs and bludgeons that he endured by the soldiers. Anne's eyes were glazed over as she disconnected herself from the humiliation of James placing her in cuffs and taking her from her room only clothed in her undergarments. They were escorted in silence to the governor's chamber to wait for His Majesty to try their case.

CHAPTER 15

THE BOUND PRISONERS stood before the Royal Governor Woodes Rogers, while James Bonny attended and loathed the very sight of Anne in her undergarments and John Rackam shirtless in his calico breeches. The governor ordered the guards to have John removed from the room so he could interrogate his captives separately to see if their stories would conjoin. John submitted as he was forcefully shoved out of sight, and the door was slammed shut.

The governor was gracious to Anne and offered her a woolen blanket to conceal the shame of her nakedness. He then gazed at the delicate young woman from behind his oversized desk.

"So I hear that you are the daughter of Chancellor Cormac of South Carolina."

He had been well informed as to who she was by James who had bragged about his marriage to the chancellor's daughter.

"Yes, my lord, and I sincerely regret to have caused him such shame as I appear before you in such a condition."

The governor had yet to meet the chancellor, but he was aware of his grand reputation. He sighed at her humble appeal and then continued.

"Is it of truth that you are married to this young man?" He pointed to James Bonny whose arrogance sickened Anne.

"It is of truth, my lord."

"And is it also of truth that you have defiled your marriage bed in the arms of John Rackam?"

"It is of trust, my lord, and for that I am grateful to have done—"

"Do you understand that I have to the power on this island to hang you for such an offense?" Anne had horribly provoked the governor, and James relished in seeing the governor's anger flared toward the despicable creature.

"Yes, my lord, I do understand that you hold utmost authority in Providence."

The governor chose not to reply as he marveled inwardly at Anne's brazen character, and he preferred rather to address James.

"Would you like to comment on your wife's behalf?"

James clenched his jaw. "I would delight to see them both swinging from a noose for what they've done to me."

The governor addressed Anne.

"Do you feel you are worthy of such judgment?"

Anne, still standing erectly, gently replied, "I will accept whatever punishment your honor deems fit because I perceive that you are a fair judge. But my prayer is that you will not succumb to the venom that this man spews on my behalf, for he was not a husband at all—"

"I object!" James shouted, and the governor immediately rebuked him harshly and ordered him from the room. James glared at Anne as he instantly heeded to the governor's demand.

Woodes Rogers seemed to relax a bit, and the tension in his chamber was eased after James was removed. The governor gazed at Anne in thoughtful consideration.

"What has he done to you that you would disclaim him as your husband?"

"He hates my father with a vengeance and entreated me unkindly by striking me in the face when we first arrived on the island. After that, I fell out of love, and I can't bear the thought of him."

The governor pondered Anne's words as she resolved to tears.

"So then, you simply fell in love with John Rackam?" The governor's cynicism reminded her of her father.

"Yes, my lord."

"And you had no concern that your marriage decree was with another man?"

"Of course I did. I regretted horribly that I had made such an error in my judgment to enter into such a decree in the first place. My lord, can't you please intervene on my behalf?"

The governor was humbled in his heart, as he too lived separately from his wife.

"You realize, Anne Bonny, that I don't have the authority to simply pardon your marriage decree. And if I should be so foolish to attempt, I would be relieved of my position at once and go down into history as the governor who did not uphold the views of the Church of England and who flagrantly condoned adultery on the island of Providence. Do you think that I should display such lack of wisdom?"

"No, my lord." Anne lowered her face.

The governor thoughtfully considered for the moment as he pondered the chancellor's daughter.

"Have you considered returning to the house of your father and living out your days separately from James Bonny?"

"I've given it a great amount of consideration, my lord."

"Because, Anne Cormac, I could arrange to put you on a ship bound for South Carolina this very day if you desire."

Since Anne had met John, she had relinquished all thoughts of returning to Charles Town as she couldn't bear the thought of leaving him now, so she stalled the governor.

"My desire would be to remain in Providence and live separately from James Bonny."

The governor was wise to her tactic.

"I don't believe that you would stay away from John Rackam if you were to do that, Anne Bonny."

"That is probably of truth, my lord."

The governor was slightly amused. "And do expect me to turn to a deaf ear to your screams of pleasure as you blatantly commit adultery right under my very nose?"

"No, my lord, I would not expect that."

"Anne Bonny, I truly do not know what to do with you, and I'm sure you gave your father a similar chase as you were growing up," the governor sighed in his bafflement at the strong-willed young girl.

Anne could discern that Woodes Rogers had a good heart and that there was truly nothing he could do to set her free from James. Although, she sensed that he would have done so if he hadn't been bound by the Church.

Suddenly, her mind raced to the plan that she had heard John discussing with Pierre about Vane's plot to assassinate the governor, and she couldn't bear such a thought, so she divulged the information.

"My lord, this is completely off the subject of my adultery, but I want to warn you." The governor returned his full attention to Anne.

She disclosed the plot by Charles Vane to sneak onto the island and assassinate him in his sleep. The governor thanked Anne for her gracious revelation, and he would heed her admonition, as Charles Vane had still not been apprehended. Then he sentenced Anne to the prison overnight, so he could deliberate her punishment.

After Anne was taken from the governor's chamber, he brought John Rackam into his presence, and it was quite sometime before he addressed the prisoner, as he was drafting a letter. When the governor granted his attention, John broke eye contact out of respect as the governor pondered the bare-chested man, which stood before him. Finally the uncomfortable silence was broken by the cynicism of the governor.

"Ah, Mr. John Rackam, so we meet again. Would you like a shirt? Or perhaps you'd like a blanket like we offered Anne Bonny to conceal the nakedness of her adultery?"

"A shirt would be welcome, my lord."

John could barely button the shirt as it fit a smaller frame, but he managed to attempt to conceal his chest, as he did not delight in standing before the governor in such a way. The governor showed consideration and turned his head while John struggled with the last of the buttons, and then Woodes Rogers continued with his interrogation.

John's questioning went similarly to Anne's, and John had also found favor with the governor. John expressed his willingness to purchase Anne's marriage decree from James Bonny, and the governor thought that his plan may be feasible, of course, if James Bonny would agree. The governor also listened carefully without rebuttal as John was allowed to express his views about how he didn't believe that a marriage decree credentialed one to be a husband. But rather a husband was one who would nurture and care for his wife, and John felt that James Bonny had abused and neglected his place and didn't deserve the title. John expressed the unfairness by using the letter of marque as an example.

"England can issue the marque, which is a simple piece of paper, and that document will condone you to be a pirate as long as you can turn revenue for the crown, and if not, it will be rescinded. However, the marriage decree is treated as if it is written in marble and can never be rescinded, even if one fails miserably as a husband. My lord, can you glean any fairness from it at all?"

The governor was moved in his heart but concealed his regard with impassiveness, although it was difficult, as John had also shown concern to spare his life from Vane's scheme.

"Mr. John Rackam, nevertheless, you have committed adultery, and I am forced to address your sinful behavior, so you will be taken to prison to remain overnight until I decide what in God's name to do with the two of you."

That night in prison, Anne thought of baby Jonathan and wished so badly that she could hold him in her arms again. She thought of her father and returning home to Charles Town. Then she thought how much her desires had changed ever since she had met John. She knew that she had found her true love, and she envisioned him by her side and felt comfort as she drifted off to sleep.

John was in a cell far from Anne's, but he could feel her presence in the musty darkness. He repented in his heart for the trouble that he had caused her, as he took full blame for the fact that she now lay in prison. He wished he could take the punishment for her and set her free. He wondered if he would hang from the noose the next day, and he relished the thought, as it would be better to hang than to live without the hope that he and Anne could be together again.

From his bedchamber, the governor felt secure as he had ordered guards to protect his door, but he was far from achieving peaceful rest, as he contemplated the case. He repented in his heart that he had turned John Rackam away when he attempted to enlist as a privateer against the Spanish, for he could see that John Rackam would have made him proud, but now it was too late. He couldn't possibly employ a man whom he'd just tried for uncontested adultery. And once again, the governor was displeased with himself that he had shown such a lapse in character judgment to ever have coupled with James Bonny in the first place.

He dismissed the thought and recited in his mind as to what he would include in the letter he was drafting to Chancellor Cormac. He also planned to pen one to the governor of Jamaica to inquire about the relationship of the chancellor's daughter and Chidley Bayard when they attended the royal ball, as James had told him of her illicit affair with the womanizer, and the governor wanted to dispel the myth. He did not believe that Anne was capable of such but wanted to know the uncut truth about her. Nevertheless, the governor did not sleep at all that night, as he knew what he was obligated to do the next day.

The pangs of guilt pierced Pierre's heart, as he heard James Bonny bragging about Anne and John in prison that night at the tavern. James's tongue always got loose when he drank rum, and he had a healthy portion that night to attempt in easing his hatred of Pierre's dearest friends. Pierre was barely able to put on a pleasant front as he served James the rum, and Pierre would never forgive himself, because it was he who had told James about Anne's lover's retreat with Chidley Bayard to Jamaica to attend the grand ball.

Upon Anne's departure, Pierre had convincingly acted concerned for poor James, lying in order to taunt Anne's husband, figuring that Anne was safely in Charles Town. Concocting the lie was Pierre's attempt to drive a stake into James's heart at the thought of his wife running off with the gentleman who had an eye for the ladies, who was wealthy enough to embellish her with all precious gifts, and then carry her to the ball in Jamaica. Pierre's contrivance was rooted in his grudge against James for the mistreatment of Anne, and now he had caused James to despise Anne to the bitterest degree.

Pierre inwardly cringed as James Bonny boasted that he would see his revenge at the hand of the governor the next day. Pierre hung his head, as he had to be tormentingly honest with himself, because it wasn't only James's ill treatment of Anne that had caused him to develop such contempt for James Bonny. Pierre left the bar to weep, as he abhorred himself for what he had done.

That morning, in the governor's chambers, Anne and John had been brought before Woodes Rogers together this time to receive the final resolve of his deliberation. Anne thought of her father, as the governor reminded her of the way that he had looked the day she told him that her name was Anne Bonny, for the governor had dark circles outlining his eyes. James Bonny was not present as he had been sent on a mission to pursue the capture of Charles Vane, but the governor's real intent was to get him off the island, so he would not take pleasure in what was about to occur. Mark and two other men stood in his place. The governor had requested his assistant and two guards to witness the punishment, as he did not ever want to be accused of unfair treatment of a prisoner.

The governor disregarded the couple's presence for quite a lengthy space as he completed penning the details to Anne's father with sincere regret. John and Anne pondered their punishment but weren't aware that Woodes Rogers had also acquired another reputation from when he had taken his grand voyage around the world. The captain was known to flog the men upon his ship when he perceived that they were disobedient, and not all sea captains believed in such punishment, as some thought it to be inhumane. Since then, the governor had changed his position toward the doling of torture, and in his deepest heart of hearts, he would have released the couple to run away and enjoy the rare love that they had happened upon. But the fires of hell would be extinguished before he would ever mouth such a confession, so he kept his lips pursed, making himself appear rather angry.

Pierre awoke that morning and chose not to get out of bed, and although he felt sympathy for his cow, he could not muster the energy to relieve her swollen utters. He just lay there alone in his sorrow, pondering his vile heart. He was bitingly aware as to why he had developed the resentment for James Bonny.

When Pierre and James had spent the night together, James was a fair young man at the time and Pierre had actually fallen in love with him. After their evening of pleasure, Pierre had hoped that he and James could continue to develop a commitment, but James, upon arising, went from the bedchamber and drank his rum. Pierre was horrified to learn that James Bonny had smeared his name to the fellow pirates, proclaiming that Pierre was worthy of the punishment in which God had rained upon Sodom and Gomorrah, as Pierre had violated him against his will. Isolated in his thoughts, Pierre rolled over in bed and covered his head with his blankets, and a sector of his heart had died that day as he thought about Anne and John in their chains before the governor and the part that he had contributed toward the situation.

The governor completed his letter and addressed his convicts.

"Anne Bonny and John Rackam, you have openly admitted committing adultery in my presence and worse, without even a hint of remorse. I, Royal Governor Woodes Rogers, upon accepting my commission have sworn to King George that I would uphold English common law to very best of my ability. The law demands for anyone caught in the act of adultery to receive punishment ranging from a simple fine to death by hanging."

The governor paused in thoughtful consideration. "If I fine you, John Rackam, you would simply deliver a tiny portion of your hidden plunders and not even flinch at the minuscule loss, disregarding it as punishment at all. Anne Bonny, if I fine you, your lover would simply pay on your behalf, and there would be no consequence for you at all."

The eyes of his prisoners confirmed to the governor that he had discerned correctly.

"Therefore, I have condemned you both to be flogged for your unrighteous behavior." The countenances of John and Anne were unchanged, as they bravely accepted the deliberation, but then the governor continued,

"Anne Bonny, after you have received your punishment—since you choose to remain in Providence—I must demand that you return to your rightful husband, James Bonny."

Anne broke at that moment, as her mental anguish overwhelmed her, but the governor offered immediate comfort. "Anne Bonny, be not disheartened."

Anne was able to somewhat compose and listen to his words.

"Young lady, I grant you full access to my presence any time of the day or night in which I encourage you to take full advantage. For if James Bonny should lay the slightest hand upon you with the intent to harm, he will rot in my prison, and I shall firmly admonish him as to that fact."

Anne closed her eyes as the governor addressed John.

"John Rackam, after your punishment, you are never to touch or even speak to Anne Bonny again, and if you choose to disregard my judgment, I will make certain that you are hung immediately. Do I have an understanding from the both of you?"

"Yea, my lord," they said in hushed unison as their necks slowly fell limp.

The flogging actually wasn't so terrible. The governor chose to be present in order to direct the punishment, which was delivered by a guard with a cat-of-nine-tails. The guard was firmly instructed not to swing the whip above the head. By swinging the whip above the prisoner's head, the torturer is allowed more momentum upon completing a figure eight with the lash, allowing for more painful force to be applied upon the victim's back. The governor also allowed Anne to retain the cover of her blanket. However, the governor, not wanting to appear weak, ordered John to remove his shirt.

During Anne's, flogging Mark was somehow able to keep his composure while he was commissioned to witness, as she had too much at stake to break down before the governor, but Mary's heart felt every lash, and she wept inside. John turned his head and didn't even care to wipe his cheeks as the tears openly streamed down his neck. Anne received her five lashes, and although they bore an awful sting, even with the protection of the blanket, they were nothing in comparison to the pain she had endured giving birth to Jonathan.

While John bravely endured his flogging, Mark stiffened to constrain his agony, and his tears flowed backward, causing his nose to drip. Anne pleaded with each swing of the whip for the torture to stop on John's behalf. The two guards had to restrain her to keep her from rushing to the aid of her lover and throwing her body between his raw back and the cruelty of the thrashing device. John endured his ten lashes with composure, as it was nothing compared to the beating that he had received which caused him to finally take courage and leave the African Royal Company ship when he was only sixteen.

Pierre's cow had turned her head to stare at the dainty French man, who offered such relief to her fullness.

"I'm sorry, Jezebel, I was in awful state this morning, but I'll make it up. I will give you an extra portion of grass today and tomorrow and maybe even the next day." The cow turned her head back to grab a clump of grass from her trough and chewed her cud, almost as if to disregard his swelling promises. Pierre continued to collect the valued milk and purposed in his heart that he would never lie again in his life unless he had to.

The sport of avoiding James Bonny hadn't lasted long, for John and Anne were flogged in February of 1719, only a month after their return to the island from Cuba. Directly after their punishment was awarded, Woodes Rogers released his prisoners and admonished them both. In James's absence, he honored Anne's request to be delivered into the care of Pierre, as the governor had a great amount of respect for the owner of the tavern. Although the governor had some concerns about Pierre's loyalty to John Rackam, he knew that Pierre would never allow anything to compromise John's safety. And he figured with certainty that Pierre would not develop a love interest toward Anne, for which she seemed to have a propensity in which to attract. John was ordered to walk in the opposite direction of Anne and to go wherever his heart led him as long as it did not circle back to Anne Bonny.

Anne was completely resolved to never talk to John Rackam again for fear of his demise at the end of a rope, but they discovered with delight that Mark and John could openly display an inseparable friendship in which Mark would carry the lovers' messages back and forth without constraint. It was during those many encrypted moments that John Rackam, Anne Bonny, and Mary Reed would together devise a plan that would launch them into the history books forever, inscribed as the famous pirates who chose to valiantly sail despite the jeopardy of hanging from the gallows.

CHAPTER 16

THE GOVERNOR SENT Mark to the dock to deliver the letter that he had drafted to the governor of Jamaica in attempts to ascertain the nature of Anne's relationship to Mr. Chidley Bayard. The letter was to be transferred into the care of a reliable captain whose ship was bound for the royal colony. Woodes Rogers was anxious to hear a reply, as he was certain that it would confirm his hunch that the whole ordeal was all a vicious rumor, probably conjured up by James Bonny.

John walked in the opposite direction of Anne as ordered by the governor, and he shunned Pierre's bar after that. He spent the majority of his days fishing with old friends who had given up pirating and now only drew their living from the shallow waters off the shoreline of Providence. John was handling the governor's judgment to refrain from Anne quite well, as long as he consumed healthy quantities of fine rum distilled from the West Indies molasses. It was during one of his fishing adventures that John had heard the details about the torrid death of Edward Teach.

Apparently, since the conniving governor of North Carolina decided not to harness Edward Teach, the governor of Virginia took it upon himself, as he was wearied of Teach's antics interfering with the Virginia economy. Governor Spotsworth, using his own money, hired Lieutenant Robert Maynard to coordinate the endeavor, providing Maynard with two sloops, the *Jane* and the *Ranger*, in which the governor had employed from civilians. Maynard was not a large man but was well known for his excellent skill and bravery.

Blackbeard had been located by Maynard's spies in the Ocracoke Inlet, one of Teach's favorite spots, where he regularly set anchor. On the day before the attack, Maynard's spies reported back that Teach had twenty-five men on board of his ship, the *Adventure*. Maynard was relieved, as he had thought that Teach had at least forty men according to the pirate's boastings. The pirate was outnumbered, as Maynard had thirty-three troops on board the *Jane*, of which he was the captain. A Mr. Hyde was named captain of the *Ranger*, and he had twenty-four soldiers armed and ready in addition to some civilians who chose to remain on board their ships.

When the day had barely broken, Maynard planned to enter the inlet with both sloops after sending a smaller vessel first to test the depth of the water with a line and lead. Teach fired upon the sounding vessel, which had found the water to be shallow, but the boat retreated and escaped unharmed. That is when Maynard and Hyde entered the inlet. As they moved in on Teach, the pirate slipped his cable and hoisted his sails to turn his ship in order to fire upon the sloops with his starboard guns. Hyde was positioned to the port side of Maynard, and the two approaching ships manifested an intimidating force that was further magnified when they hoisted their flags revealing the king's colors.

Blackbeard chose to retreat instead of fight, so he turned his ship with the intent of slipping away through a narrow channel, which proved not possible, as the tide was low, and his ship ran aground, tipping the vessel to its port side. The *Adventure* wedged in such a position that Blackbeard's guns had a perfect aim of the coming sloops, so Teach unloaded a battery of ammunition upon Maynard and Hyde. After a brutal assault, Blackbeard had killed Hyde and all his commanding officers, leaving nine men mutilated on the deck of the *Ranger*, and although he had suffered casualties as well, Maynard himself survived.

Hyde's sloop was demolished and was no longer operable, so its sails were surrendered, leaving it to sway in the surf. A reprieve in the arsenal allowed Maynard to board Hyde's remaining troops. They were swift, as they knew the pirates were merely gathering shot for the next round.

With Hyde's men aboard, he forged ahead but directed his ship toward the port side of Blackbeard where his guns were no threat. With the exception of a few men at the stern, Maynard ordered all others below deck to prepare themselves, as they were about to incur a vicious fight. *Jane* was run ashore in close proximity to the *Adventure*, and only Maynard and his few men remained visible.

With the amount of deceased men oozing their blood upon Maynard's deck, it appeared that the ship had been virtually unmanned by Teach's cannon storm. Maynard was openly displayed on his deck, but Blackbeard was not to be seen. The pirate's raspy voice echoed as he taunted the lieutenant.

"Damn you cheats. Who in the hell are you and from where did you come?"

Maynard rebutted, "Blackbeard, we are no knaves. For look at our colors and see from where we've come."

Blackbeard sneered, "Come aboard my ship you coward, so I may behold the weak man with whom I speak."

Maynard replied, "I choose not to desert my few remaining men, but we will board your ship when we are well ready."

Blackbeard took a healthy gulp of his gin from his confines and retorted, "Damnation will seize my soul if I give you and your men even a speck of quarter upon my deck."

Maynard retorted, "Well then, if you will not allot me such hospitality, then I too shall deprive you of quarters upon my ship."

Infuriated by the insult, Blackbeard's rage began to ooze from the core of his being. An eerie silence followed as Teach below deck began to weave the hemp into his beard. He breathed, "I'll teach that damned fool not to mess with the devil himself." Teach lit the hemp and inhaled the fumes. He gulped his gin and signaled to his men.

With smoke arising from his beard and with the calmness of a serpent, Teach ascended to his deck. Maynard remained unmoved by the demonic display, and he and his men opened fire. Teach was hit several times but appeared unaffected as he strolled forward, unloading his pistol in Maynard's direction.

To shield their captain, Blackbeard's men threw bottles filled with powder and shot lit with short fuses onto Maynard's deck. The smoke of the bombs filled the air, depriving Maynard's sight, and Blackbeard took advantage to board the *Jane* and rushed to the Lieutenant Maynard, who had retired his pistol for a cutlass.

Blackbeard, with cutlass drawn, faced off Maynard with all determination to brutally slaughter him singlehandedly. Maynard focused on his target, and his eyes beheld the wickedness manifesting from Blackbeard's core. He truly was a force of evil with which to be reckoned. As their cutlasses collided with vicious strength, Blackbeard's men stood ready to devour the lieutenant at the very word of their captain. That is when Maynard gave the command, and suddenly, all of his men surfaced from the hold of the vessel.

Surprised by the emergence of Maynard's crew, Blackbeard's small gang of men willfully defended themselves against the swarm of soldiers, succumbing to the slippery blood-filled deck, which allowed Maynard's men to advance toward the lieutenant virtually uncontested. They arrived upon the tenacious duel of Teach and Maynard just at the right moment as the lieutenants cutlass snapped, and he was left with half a blade, rendering him unarmed. Teach sneered and moved in for the final thrust, and one of Maynard's men, with perfect timing, interceded Teach's advance by bringing his cutlass down hard and slicing a deep gash in Blackbeard's neck. Even so, Blackbeard did not fall. He only spewed vile cursing.

Weakened by the blow, Blackbeard swung his cutlass toward Maynard, who was able to avoid the blade, and the lieutenant uttered his command, as he did not want to deprive his men of such a satisfaction of finishing the kill for their unarmed lieutenant. The men responded by synchronously plunging their swords into the pirate, who slowly sunk to his knees and finally fell to the deck; all the while, he was spewing insults, and blood splatter through his lips.

It was November 22, 1718, when Blackbeard lay motionless upon the deck; all his remaining men readily surrendered, even the man hiding in the hold, who had entered it after Maynard's men surfaced. His intent had been to blow up the ship by igniting the powder room. Maynard inspected Teach's dead body in order to assess the damage that he and his men had done. He counted at least five bullet holes, and Teach had been cut no less than twenty times.

At Maynard's command, Blackbeard's body was dragged to a suitable plank, and his neck was stretched across the board. The soldier handed Maynard his cutlass and offered, "You may have the honors, sir."

With the swift motion of an axe, the cutlass was brought down, and Blackbeard's head was removed by a single blow.

After the tide had risen and allowed the *Jane* to become afloat once again, she sailed homeward. Maynard paraded Blackbeard's severed head on the bowsprit of his ship as they returned to Virginia to inform Governor Spotsworth that his money had been worth his effort.

John and the men had reached the shore just as the talebearer was finishing his story. When John would return from the sea every evening, he and Mark would take walks along the harbor or sit on the bluff and watch the sunset, which splashed across the horizon. Its deep reds faded across the complete spectrum to pale yellow and then slowly succumbed to darkness. Springtime was approaching, and often it would rain, but John and Mary took no notice of the weather, and often they would retire soaked.

Mary told John all about her military experiences, which rather impressed John. He complimented Mary for her many accomplishments, which rendered Mary proud. When they would conclude the evening, John would always tell Mary to tell Anne that she was forever in his heart.

Anne impatiently waited in the confines of her room, and Mary could always find her there for it was where Anne had been spending all of her time. It had become a prison of sorts. Lately, Anne hadn't even felt like accompanying Pierre out and about with his daily chores, as she was in a terrible way. She even became jealous of Mary because of her ability to see John. Anne was starting to wonder if maybe John and Mary were beginning to develop fondness for one another. Anne's cynicism was getting the best of her as she thought, "Wouldn't that surprise the governor? Now John is lying with the governor's male assistant."

But developing fondness for Mary was the last thing on John's mind, as he was desperately in love with Anne. Like Anne, John was also in a bad way, as he was losing his will for life. But he was thankful for Mary, as she had a good ear for listening, the ability to encourage, and the wisdom to advise. Mary worried about John as he told her that the two things he had ever really loved had now been seized from him—Anne and the sea. It was becoming difficult to find any reason to continue with his mired existence. He had tried his best to find a new passion, but in his attempts, he felt as though he were being drawn down further and further into the depths of the abyss.

After her meetings with John, Mary would go to Anne's room and spend hours talking and listening some more. Mary was in a tough spot, because if she told Anne how desperate John had become, Anne's mood would decline even further. If she lied and told Anne that he was having the time of his life, Anne would become indignant, because Anne certainly wasn't having the time of her life, having suffered the loss of John and being plagued with the thought that her husband could return at any moment. So Mary, in her desire to comfort, was pondering a plan.

One evening, after Mary had already left him, John decided to go to the tavern, knowing that Anne was directly upstairs, and there was a risk of being caught, but he had resigned to apathy. He was on the verge of risking it all to hold her one more time, but the only thing preventing him was his fear that he would compromise Anne by his rash behavior. John sat at the bar and glanced at the stairway, following it up with his eyes.

Pierre was sharp. "Don't even think about it!"

John rebutted, "How about another cup of punch then?"

"No! If you have another, you will find yourself prancing up those stairs, and you will swing tomorrow. I'm telling you!" Pierre lowered his voice, "The governor has spies everywhere. These men used to be proud pirates, and now they've become nothing but spineless snitches. Providence is not what it used to be, John."

John faced the harsh reality. "That's right, Pierre, it has changed drastically. Gone are the days when you could take your rapier and settle a dispute, and may the best man take the prize. Now the island is crawling with English common law. Pierre, wasn't that the reason we came here to begin with was to get away from that filth anyway?"

Pierre sighed, "That's right, John Rackam, we certainly did." Pierre never did address John by his nickname of Calico Jack, as he knew how much John despised the term.

John took Pierre's admonition and didn't visit Anne's room that night, but before he left, John asked Pierre for some sewing supplies and two different types of material. He told Pierre that he had gotten an idea the other day while fishing and wanted to try his hand at crafting it from his own imagination. He went home that night and cut out the material and stitched a pirate flag that would become one of the most famous flags throughout history.

The very same plan that Mary had conceived had been developing inside of John, but they had not yet discussed it during their evening visits. Some of his fishing mates, who also missed the sea and longed for the days of pirating, expressed their desire to sail under him again if he would captain his ship, and it had planted a seed in John Rackam.

As he walked along the harbor's edge, John had seen his brigantine that George Fetherston had surrendered to the governor of Providence when he accepted the king's pardon. The vessel was anchored, sitting alone and calling for John. He noticed that the governor had made a grave mistake. Woodes Rogers had not assigned guards to assure it. While he pondered his ship, John figured that it was worth the risk of the gallows, because he wasn't living anyway, and although he would certainly long for Anne, she'd been taken away from him already. Without Anne, he could find no reason at all to settle into an honest living, so he chose to return to piracy in attempts to acquire his life again.

Mary was also getting restless, as she had an insatiable obsession of the sea. She had heard so many men brag about John's abilities as a pirate, and she fantasized about being part of a grand crew that was captained by John Rackam. Mary thought, "If he would sail again, I would obtain my dream, and if Anne came, John and Anne could be together again." It was the only solution that Mary could find that would restore their lives to all of them. Mary finally got the courage to confront John about her desires, but John was in stern disagreement.

"No, Mary, I can't take the risk that you and Anne will be tried as pirates if you sail with me. I plan to go, but it will only be with a handful of men."

Mary was earnest. "But, John, I gladly accept the risk of death by hanging. I wouldn't choose any lesser judgment for a pirate. Because it's the fear of dying that separates the cowards from he who is courageous enough to call himself a pirate. And I'm bringing you this message. Anne Bonny feels exactly the same way that I do. We want to sail with you, John Rackam."

John left Mary that evening, telling her that he needed time to consider, and Mary's heartfelt pleas must have struck a chord with him, because the next evening, he met with her and that is when John outlined the plan.

"If you both come, you will present yourselves as men, and you will not allow the crew to know that you are women. Can you imagine pulling up to plunder a ship and how ridiculous it would appear to have two ladies running about in their gowns upon the deck? It would appear as a joke." John chuckled at the thought.

Mary was at attention. "I completely agree, sir."

"And furthermore, the men can't be distracted by the hopes of lying with the ladies. Pirating takes a captain with a focus and men who work as a solid and unifying team. It's almost as if you're reading each other's minds and that sense of camaraderie. It's why we do it. And I don't want two women to compromise the course."

"Yes, sir."

John pondered his decision.

"You will remain as Mark Reed and tell Anne that she will be Adam Bonn."

As Mary turned to leave, John jested,

"Mary, tell my little bastard that I'm taking her on board for good luck."

"John, I too am a bastard.

John laughed. "Well then, I just doubled me luck."

Mary left with a grin and returned to relay the message to Anne, who quickly replied, "Well, you tell Calico Jack that—" Anne's smile turned wry. "Never mind, I'll tell him myself." Anne entertained herself with her thoughts of jesting toward John as she beamed at Mary. From that day forward, Anne donned her men's clothing and was known as Adam Bonn to the men on the island.

Pierre had outfitted her in his most manly clothing, as he did possess a few prime pieces in his wardrobe. Mary schooled Anne on the art of lowering her voice to match the part. Anne, however, could only speak believably in short phrases, so the two decided that Anne should remain silent the majority of the time. Adam and Mark entered every dueling match for which they had opportunity, with the intent to hone their skills.

Since the soldiers had come to the island, the sport of dueling was even more prevalent, as the governor welcomed the activity as a means for his men to combat the pirates and keep sharp their battling abilities. There were still contests on the hardened sand by the harbor, but only the victorious contestants were allowed to duel in the town square in front of the governor's chambers. Adam and Mark had won the honor of becoming daily contenders in that arena. In fact, they won every match in which they set their hand, except once when Mark's rapier had snapped due to the sheer force of the beating to his opponent's blade.

John's crew would consist of nine men whom John had once sailed with on Vane's ship. They had been some of the men who had voted him as captain over Vane. As a group, they chose their positions. It was agreed that George Fetherston would be master under Rackam. Then Richard Corner was named as quartermaster. John Davis was the first mate, and James Dobbin the second. John Howell was named as the sailing master, and Patrick Carty the boatswain. Thomas Earl took the position of carpenter and surgeon, and then there was Nicholas Paige as the master gunner and Noah Harwood as rigger.

His men were surprised that John was able to secure two more souls for the journey as he introduced Adam Bonn and Mark Reed. John was pleased at how well Adam and Mark seemed to fit into his crew, and he was thankful that he had decided to offer them a place on board. Adam and Mark were given the title of able-bodied sailors, but all agreed that with such a small crew, it would be necessary for each man to play a double role. They would have never expected Adam and Mark to pull such weight, being that there were only two of them. It was a much smaller crew than to which John was accustomed, but with the surrender of all the other pirates on the island, it was impossible to recruit more help. Therefore, John planned to make due and recruit men along the journey outside of Providence.

The brigantine, once named the *Ranger* by Vane and armed with its six cannon, was renamed the *Anne Bonny*, which amused John's men for they had heard of the woman who had once taken down a crazed pirate in a match along the harbor's edge. Only one man on board the ship had actually witnessed the match, but he didn't seem to make the connection between Anne and Adam.

Since John and his men were familiar with the brigantine, its preparation seemed effortless, as he sent Patrick Carty on board at night without a lantern to prepare it for its mission. John feared that Carty would be discovered by the illumination of a lamp, so the mate, only by the light of the moon, groped his way from the bow to stern taking inventory of the necessary supplies. Carty was pleased to report that many of their reserves had been untouched.

There were soldiers commissioned at the harbor's edge but presented no threat as they had become complacent after having had such an easygoing time disarming the pirates of Providence. John had also noticed that after midnight, the guards were virtually absent. So the ship was loaded each night in the wee hours before dawn, and when it was well stocked, John and his crew were ready. With exception, John had to wait for the moon and tide to be in his favor. In the meanwhile, he tied up his loose ends on Providence, as he knew that he would never return to the island again.

Before he left the island, John retrieved his treasure in order to have means to buy any extra supplies that would be necessary. But what was most difficult for John was the evening he spent saying his goodbye to King Henry and Catherine. That night, he actually wept, but then turned his pillow over to find a dry spot as he drifted off to sleep. He was thankful that he was alone in his home in the tree, as he would never have allowed his men to see even the speck of a tear in his eye.

The next night and well after midnight, the moon was absent and the tide was low, as it was springtime. John was thankful that the rainstorm had stopped when he and his eleven accomplices boarded the ship and slipped anchor. The brigantine, without its sails engaged, was allowed to drift in the current, as the low tide slowly pulled the ship out of the east end of the harbor. It was the same exit in which Vane had made his escape the night that Governor Rogers arrived on the island. As they cleared the exit, the speed of the current increased, and they were thrust from the harbor. Once they were out in the open waters, John had Noah Harwood hoist the sails, and they headed in a southerly direction.

CHAPTER 17

AFTER HAVING STOLEN his brigantine from Nassau's harbor, Governor Rogers figured that John Rackam had returned to his old trade of pirating, as only a pirate would steal a ship. Also Anne Bonny was nowhere to be found, so Woodes Rogers knew that she had been taken away by the man whom the governor had strictly warned against any contact with the married woman. Therefore, John Rackam was to be sought out and apprehended immediately.

Not long after their escape, the governor received a reply from the Royal Governor Nicholas Lawes of Jamaica confirming Woodes Rogers's hunch about Anne Bonny. His royal governor outlined the details of the investigation of Chidley Bayard in regard to the chancellor's daughter. It was reported that Anne Bonny had sailed to Jamaica with Chidley Bayard in order to flee the oppression of her violent husband and had hoped to reconnect with her father. As far as Nicholas Lawes could ascertain, there was no inappropriate conduct between Chidley Bayard and the chancellor's daughter, as Mr. Bayard had simply been acting in the steed of her father, who was in Carolina battling a fire on his estate. Governor Woodes Rogers was comforted inwardly that he had correctly judged Anne Bonny in that particular affair, although it didn't matter now.

The governor stopped reading the letter to ponder on how he was not surprised at all by John's escape with Anne, as he too had felt the irresistible passions of love at one time for his wife Sarah Whetstone, but only until her heart had callused toward him. The governor did, however, think it strange that his assistant, Mark Reed, had found company with the couple but disregarded Mark's irrational behavior, as he knew how much Mark had gushed about his love for the sea.

As he continued to read the letter, his jaw dropped, leaving his mouth agape. The final paragraphs detailed Anne's behavior toward his sister-in-law, Sarah, and Woodes Rogers was left dumbfounded, as he had not even suspected that Anne Bonny would be capable of such.

Governor Rogers immediately sent a reply thanking Nicholas Lawes for his response and asked a favor from the Jamaican governor. In his letter, he informed Nicholas Lawes that Anne Bonny was no longer on the island of Providence, as she had disappeared with her lover, John Rackam, who had appeared to have returned to piracy. His special request of Nicholas Lawes was such that if they were to apprehend the outlaws in Jamaica, Governor Rogers would sincerely appreciate it if His Excellence would kindly extradite them both back to Providence for their judgment, and Woodes Rogers sent his letter out that day.

Governor Rogers wanted to be the man who dealt with John Rackam for John's rebellion toward him, and he gravely feared that Anne would be sentenced as a pirate because of her association with John. Even if she had not participated in any pirate activities, the noose would surely be applied to Anne as a means of gaining revenge for the loss of Sarah Lawes's two front teeth. The governor ran his fingers through his hair as he hovered above his desk. He felt sorrow in his heart for the chancellor of South Carolina, whose daughter was spiraling out of control, for he could relate, as he too was a father.

The chancellor had received the letter from the Royal Governor Woodes Rogers that had been written the day he tried Anne for adultery, and the chancellor sailed to Providence as he had planned, but he arrived on the island two days after Anne had escaped with John. The governor didn't want to be the one who broke the horrible news, but the chancellor was a gracious man and thanked the governor for his attempts to bring Anne into line. The two men got on very well, and despite the discouraging report of Anne's departure, the chancellor thoroughly enjoyed his time with the infamous Woodes Rogers, who purposefully failed to mention a word about his employment of his son-in-law.

James Bonny was never able to complete the governor's commission to capture Charles Vane, because Vane was no longer at sea. After being demoted as captain, Vane's sloop had been shipwrecked during a hurricane. As the sole survivor of the catastrophe, Vane managed to drift to the shore of a deserted island and that was where he was residing during the time that James was hunting him. Vane was able to survive because of the benevolence of a few small-time fishermen who would frequent the island. Besides attempting to ensure his survival, Vane would spend his days scanning the sea and hoping to be rescued by a passing ship. Unfortunately, while James Bonny was desperately searching for Vane's whereabouts, he encountered the same dreadful tempest out in the North Atlantic Ocean and perished when his ship was capsized in the raging waters.

The governor held a memorial service for James Bonny when the news returned by crewmembers of the other ship in James's company that had miraculously survived the storm. Pierre was solemn as he attended, and afterward, the governor stopped to chat.

"Isn't it a shame, Anne Bonny is now a widow and free to marry whomever she chooses. If she'd stayed on the island and minded her manners, she and John Rackam could have been together forever, but now they'll surely be separated by death. What a pity."

Pierre lit a candle in his room that night and resolved in his heart to forgive James Bonny. He also lit a candle for John, Anne, and Mary, and he spoke a blessing over them, praying for their safety wherever they were. Pierre truly loved his three friends, such that he would have gladly laid down his life for any one of them. He envisioned them sailing free upon the open waters as he lay in his bed, and he knew that if he had even an inkling for the sea, he would have been right there with them.

Word quickly spread throughout Providence, Jamaica, and the American colonies that the notorious John Rackam was on the loose, and it wasn't long before accounts would trickle in confirming that he had indeed returned to pirating. Except for this time, instead of sailing under Captain Vane, John Rackam was reported to be captain of his own ship, and his consorts were only a handful of men and a woman named Anne Bonny.

For the first time ever, the chancellor was thrilled that Anne's surname was Bonny. While the citizens of Charles Town were shocked at the reports of the woman pirate Anne Bonny, they delighted to hear the chancellor's stories that Anne Cormac was having the time of her life touring Europe. The chancellor was also pleased to hear of the demise of James Bonny, as he still harbored ill feelings toward the lad and figured it was God's judgment for the agony that James had caused him. He and Woodes Rogers kept a steady trail of communication after his visit to Providence.

John knew that he could not remain in the Bahamas for fear of Woodes Rogers, so he headed toward the Caribbean Sea. His small crew performed their assigned tasks with proficiency. They would gather knowledge from each other when necessary in order to hone their abilities. Anne was determined to learn it all, as she was truly fascinated by the workmanship of the team and the operations of the ship. Mary, however, was focused on doing a good day's labor, and John was pleased with the performance of both of them.

Although John was confident and unbending in battle as well as highly skilled in his navigation and seamanship, he chose to be somewhat top-heavy on the leadership aspect of his ship, especially for such a small crew. It was uncommon to find a master and a quartermaster on a pirate ship, but John had assigned both. Maybe he had contemplated allowing his master to act in his steed, so he could steel away privately with Anne at times, or perhaps, he inwardly had reservations as to his abilities as a captain, seeing that he lacked the essence of time in the position. One would never know.

The master on a ship was virtually an equal position to that of the captain, with the only difference being that during times of engagement, the captain had the ultimate authority. During all other times, the crew was liable to the direction of the master, and it was his responsibility to protect their well-being. It was also his duty to maintain order and settle disputes. He could punish minor offenses, but a jury of the men tried the major offenses, and the captain doled the punishment.

The quartermaster, on any other ship, would have included the master's duties as described prior as well as other tasks, but John chose to divide the duties between the two titles. John's quartermaster was responsible for distributing the booty and keeping records of each crew's allotment, as well as the accounting ledgers for the ship. He also divided the food and other basic supplies among the men. If they had a successful heist, it was the quartermaster who decided what value to extract from the prize. If they decided to keep the captured vessel, it was he or the master who would take direction of the ship to form a company with the *Anne Bonny*.

The sailing master was in charge of navigating and the sailing of the ship. He was skilled with map and compass and would guide the vessel to the destination determined by the captain.

The man appointed as the boatswain would maintain the vessel and its inventoried supplies. He was responsible for the care of the sails, and he inspected them along with the rigging daily and gave an account to the captain. Lastly, he coordinated the weighing and setting of the anchor.

The carpenter was directed by the master and boatswain and was responsible for maintaining and repairing the hull, mast, and yards. He was to check the hull regularly and seal the seams with pitch and tar and place wooden plugs into holes to keep the ship leak-proof. When there was a bullet wound or crush injury, the carpenter had the tools to extract the bullet or amputate a limb, and he would most likely be the one who performed such a surgery.

The man called the master gunner was responsible for all the weaponry and ammunition upon the ship. He would properly care for the gunpowder, maintain the cannons, and repair any of the firearms that malfunctioned.

The mate was a man appointed to apprentice under the masters, boatswain, carpenter, and master gunner. It was his responsibility to learn every aspect of all the operations of a ship. His job responsibilities included equipping the vessel with rigging, overseeing the repair of cables and anchors, taking inventory of the tackle. In addition, he would manage the sails, yards, mooring, and the surfacing of the anchor.

The rigger was the man who hoisted and released the sails. This was by far the most dangerous of positions, as he often had to scale the tall masts and slick spars high above the swaying deck.

The rest of the men aboard a ship were entitled as able-bodied sailors, and they were the workforces of the ship. They had to have a broad body of knowledge concerning the rigging and sails, operation of the helm, as well as the intuitiveness to interpret the skies for star placement, cloud formation, and winds. They were at the bottom in the chain of command, with the exception of the cabin boy, powder monkey, and swabbie.

The journey to the West Indies took some time, as they were dependent upon the deep current to propel the brigantine while sailing obliquely against the trade winds, but they had no worries for they had no schedule to uphold. As they neared St. Kitts Island, they plundered several vessels, and the John Rackam that his men had all known and loved so well was back to the trade of pirating. Except for one difference, John would not be taking on any man-of-war ships with so little crew and few weapons. Adam and Mark had proven their skills of dueling and marksmanship to the men, and they were welcomed to join the forces that were necessary to secure the prizes.

On the first plunder of their journey, John was perched in his casual fashion on the bulwark, as he watched the small-time captain of the seized vessel with his passengers cowering behind him. The prisoner took a shaky aim at John with his pistol, and John offered a hearty laugh at the quivering man.

"Put down your pistol. Are you raving mad?"

The captain fired and missed by a good length. John spread his arms to provide a larger target.

"Here, I'll give you one more shot, but you might want to reconsider because you are sorely outnumbered." John's men rose from behind the bulwark with eleven pistols precisely aimed at the trembling captain, who dropped his weapon immediately.

"Oh, much better. Now lower your boat to the other side of your vessel and assist your passengers, ladies first, and please be on your way to the shore. And for god's sake, don't allow this to ruin your day."

John and his men ravaged the ship and took ample supplies and only a small amount of tender, but the supplies and trinkets were the items that intrigued John more so than the gold and silver. Anne was simply intrigued by John, as she had never seen him in this light before, and she loved it, although she was wondering how they would ever get to be together as a man and woman when she was clearly a man. It wasn't until they arrived to the Windward Islands that a crewman discovered Anne's gender, and in her rage, she had killed him, which caused John and Anne to experience their very first lover's quarrel.

It was during one evening when Adam had been standing alone at the bow of the anchored brigantine. He couldn't sleep, so he decided to enjoy the serenity of gazing out upon the moonlit waters. All the other crewmembers were sleeping, with the exception of Nicholas Paige and James Dobbin in the crow's nest. Nicholas had been watching Adam all evening. In fact, he had been for the entirety of their trip, for Nicholas was the one who had witnessed Anne take down the pirate during the match in Providence, and he knew who Adam really was. He approached her from behind and startled her. Instantly, she went for her rapier but stopped when she realized it was only Nicholas and reproved him,

"You sneak, I could have killed you!"

Nicholas took on a sly grin. "You wouldn't kill me, now would you?" He made a move, assuming that Anne would reciprocate. Anne was at a loss for the element of surprise as Nicholas proceeded to feel of her breasts. She moved back, but he had a grip of her shirt and forcefully ripped the buttons from their holds, revealing her bare breasts. He chortled,

"I knew it. You are a woman!"

Anne's breath was beginning to heave as she closed her blouse, and her vision turned to red. She couldn't make out what the sailor was saying as her hearing clouded, but she was fully aware of his forceful groping of her chest. Instantaneously, she flashed back to the time she was only fifteen and the overseer had fondled her tender young breasts. The same emotion that she had experienced back then was rushing to the surface, but to a much greater degree. Next thing Anne recalled was Nicholas gurgling blood from his mouth over the bulwark into the water, and she was retrieving her rapier from his pierced, twitching body. Anne then lifted his legs, and the weight of his body pivoted him over the edge, where he splashed into the water and slowly sank, as Anne watched without emotion. Her only witness was James Dobbin, and the next day, the crew was lined up and questioned by John Rackam who was furious.

"Who in the bloody hell killed Nicholas Paige last night?"

Not a single person replied.

"If I don't get a confession, when I find out which one of you did it, I will render the same treatment to you as well."

John waited as he eyed each man in the lineup one at a time. He could see that James Dobbin was fidgeting, so he faced him off.

"James, did you kill Nicholas Paige?"

James was shaken. "No, sir, I did not."

"Did you see anything, being that you were in the crow's nest last night?"

"Yes, sir, I did, but I was waiting for Adam to confess, so he wouldn't be put to death."

John glared at Adam, while he asked his men.

"Is there anyone here who demands the death penalty of Adam Bonn for the killing of Nicholas Paige?"

The men were disheartened by the crime, but unanimously voted against Adam's demise, so John, with his anger brewing, commenced,

"Adam, you come with me."

The crew remained solemn, knowing that the only righteous punishment should have been death, because it was taboo to kill a crewmember upon a pirate ship without consent of the captain, and although they would long for Nicholas, killing Adam wouldn't offer his return. John was thankful for his men's decision, for he was at a loss for how he would have handled the situation if the majority had voted against Adam.

John rowed to the shore with Anne and disappeared behind the tree line with her trailing him and her head lowered. The men sat on the deck, straining to hear the punishment. After a while, John could be heard clearly as he was shouting. They couldn't hear Adam's replies, as Anne spoke in hushed phrases to John, which didn't surprise the men because Adam had been a man of few words.

When they reached the clearing, John was so angry with Anne that his words were robbed, and he finally settled enough to compose a slur.

"What in the fuck has gotten into you?"

Anne was incensed at the foul word used toward her, and she chose not to reply.

"You killed my master gunner! Now if we have to engage in battle, there's not a man for the position! And who even cares about the goddamned position. Anne, it is never allowed to kill another crewmember on a ship, especially mine!" He hushed his voice, "I wish I'd never brought you along, Anne Bonny."

Those words were like daggers and struck her hard as she replied through gritted teeth.

"Damned you John Rackam—"

"No, this time I won't allow it. I took it in Cuba because I deserved it, but I don't deserve it now!" His anger had mounted. "You killed one of my men!" He grabbed her by the blouse and so wanted to strike her. Anne seethed.

"Get your bloody hand off me!"

She pulled away to a safe distance and chided.

"Are you the kind of captain that condones one of his men to forcefully feel the breasts of a lady, all the while she's opposing him? And only because you need to keep him around to shoot your cannon?"

John had just been skewered by Anne's verbal sparring that entailed the harsh reality of Nicholas's misconduct toward John's woman, and he wished he could have been the one to slice the throat of the vile figure. John was unable to find a word to reply, but Anne was able.

"Maybe you should have asked me why I killed him first before you laid it into me, don't you think? So you know what, John Rackam? Go fuck yourself."

Anne walked away, and John took his insult like a gentleman. He was sorely disappointed within himself that he had jumped to conclusions without gathering all the facts, and he purposed in his heart that he would not make the same mistake again. He so desired to captain his ship with wisdom as he had witnessed from the captain of the Dutch ship who fathered him in his youth.

John's men were getting concerned as it was taking quite a while, but finally, from behind the tree line, Anne had accepted his apology for berating her without hearing her case. And only when Anne asked for his company, John thrust her so hard that the men assumed Adam was bellowing from the vicious beating he was receiving from John. They were glad that John had chosen a beating rather than death, as they didn't want to lose another crewmember. One thing was for certain, each one of them had resolved that they were not going to mess with Adam Bonn, as he was obviously the silent type with a deadly temper. Mark contained his smile, as he knew the reason for Adam's howls of misery, and thankfully, James Dobbin never saw Anne's breasts that night, as Nicholas's back had blocked the view.

When they returned to the ship, John was appeased of his anger, and Adam was subdued, as it had completely released all the sexual tension that had built in both of them over the past few months. The crew was found to be tending their positions, and everyone agreed that they would all rotate into Nicholas's vacant spot until they could gather more men. The position of master gunner was the job that Anne enjoyed most, and she even used profanity to emphasize her enthusiasm.

Concerning the foul language, there were four major words that were used in that era to display irreverence, the worst being *damn*. It was thought to be blasphemous. And believe it or not, there was *fuck*. It has been around since the fifteenth century, in which it started off as *fukkit*. Then there was *cunt*, which was a disdainful reference to the female genitalia. Last but certainly not least, there was *prick*, which was in reference to the elongated and hardened state of the male genitalia.

After the whole ordeal had blown over, the crew operated with clarity even more so than prior, and they returned to their jesting as they diligently tended their positions. Initially, Adam and Mark would cringe as the men would jokingly call one another cunts if they perceived a crewmember was slacking in his duties or just wanted to playfully rib at him. Sometimes, the men would call each other pricks, and that was taken as a great compliment, as they were all proud of their manhood. Eventually, Adam and Mark joined in the folly, and their mouths were just as filthy as the rest, for they didn't want to appear to be different in any way. John complimented them as being two of his best mates on his ship but let them know that it wasn't necessary to use such foul language all of the time, and so Anne and Mary cut down on the usage and were very proud for John's compliment.

So far, their journey had been a pleasant adventure, as the scenery was magnificent in the West Indies, and the weather was milder than in Providence. With exception of Anne's altercation with Nicholas Paige, the operation was flawless until they reached just off the coast of Jamaica, and John killed his first man ever outside of self-defense.

CHAPTER 18

ONCE THEY HAD cleared the Windward Islands, the journey sped along, as the surface tides and the trade winds were in their favor. Anne loved the rush of the ship under such conditions, as they swept by the Leeward Islands. With the full force of the wind behind their sails, they headed west toward Jamaica. John was anxious to see the island, as he hadn't been back since his youth. He figured it was too dangerous to go ashore, since he knew that the royal colony was the infamous site where pirates found in the area were tried and hung, but John preferred the waters off its coast, as he was well familiar with every cay and inlet. Notwithstanding, it harbors sent out a countless number of small-time ships, which were ready for the taking.

One of the reasons he had not been back was that Vane had not been a fan of the area. But Vane wasn't preventing him now, as he was still stranded on the deserted island somewhere off the coasts of the North Americas, waiting to spot a ship to aid in his rescue.

John thought about Providence and wondered if Pierre had taken him up on his offer to enjoy the house in the tree. Of course, Pierre had indeed done so, because it was the perfect place to get away with his new lover, Benjamin Smythe. Benjamin was a British soldier whom Pierre had served at his tavern. He was the perfect specimen of a man in every way. His eyes were dark and piercing. He was tall with a healthy build of hearty, well-defined musculature. Nobody would ever suspect that Benjamin would have affection for Pierre, but he most definitely did, for if there were ever two souls more attracted to each other, it was Pierre and Benjamin.

In John's tree house, they partook of their fill of love, taking over where John and Anne had left off. Pierre was glad that he had waited for a love like Benjamin and had not whored himself out to all the casual advances that had come by way of the pirates and British soldiers. Pierre and Benjamin kept a very discrete relationship. As far as the eye could tell, they were merely two men who had found a great friendship, as they did not want to be tried by the governor for sodomy.

While Anne enjoyed the journey to Jamaica, Mary picked up the slack for Anne as an able-bodied sailor. Mary didn't resent her friend's temporary reprieve, as she loved feeling the burn of her muscles from the hard physical labor. However, she did jest at one point, calling Anne a cunt for her slacking, which made Anne chuckle. As Mary had envisioned, she was having the time of her life sailing under John Rackam, and she delighted in the knowledge of the love that John and Anne had found in each other, hoping to find a similar love for herself one day. For the time being, she was content as she served in her position well.

It was Mary who had brought the limes for the crew, as Woodes Rogers had told Mark that it was the secret he had used to keep his men free from the deadly scurvy when he had sailed around the world on his grand voyage. Coincidentally, it had been Woodes Rogers who had discovered that bit of wisdom before its time when others scoffed at such a notion.

Governor Rogers was planning his trip to South Carolina where he would be staying with Chancellor Cormac, and he was informed that Chidley Bayard would also be arriving for his annual trip to receive his deer hide. Woodes Rogers was looking forward to meeting the man and hearing his accounts of sailing to Jamaica with the chancellor's daughter. He hoped that the subject would not be too raw for the chancellor.

The Royal Governor Woodes Rogers had been asked to speak to the council about his victory in sequestering the pirates of Providence, and the chancellor hoped that he would bring news of Anne's whereabouts. However, the only information the governor had was that Anne had probably been taken to the Caribbean, as there had been some accounts of piratical activity reported in the area by a captain that matched the description of John Rackam, although no lady was reported to be on board. The chancellor was disappointed, but he let Woodes Rogers and Chidley Bayard know that his daughter, Anne Cormac, was enjoying her grand European tour. The men laughed out loud, commending the chancellor for his brilliant idea, as they all sipped their brandy and enjoyed their fine Cuban cigars.

After a good laugh, the governor read the latest reply written by Governor Lawes to the chancellor, in which Nicolas Lawes declined to agree to extradite the convicts if found, as he planned to hang them in Jamaica. Of course, the royal governor of Jamaica let Woodes Rogers know that he would most certainly be invited to such an occasion. Governor Rogers extended the invitation to the chancellor, as he figured that perhaps there was something they could contrive in order to intervene on Anne's behalf to prevent her hanging.

Being hung was not in the forefront of John's mind when they took a vessel off the coast of Jamaica. In fact, John wasn't even present during the seizure of the ship, as he, his master, George Fetherston, and his sailing master, John Howell, were below deck discussing the details of where they should land in order to clean, repair, and restock the ship. John had ordered Richard Corner, his quartermaster, to serve in his steed, as it was common on a pirate ship to delegate such responsibility to the position. John dismissed all concern, as he knew that Corner would summon their assistance if needed.

With their black flag displayed, the grappling hooks of the *Anne Bonny* took a firm hold of their capture. Corner relaxed his crew as the prize had displayed a white flag to signal their submission, and Corner was not expecting a fight.

The ship belonged to a small-time merchant who was set to sail to Cuba in order to trade some slaves for cigars; Jamaica had a ravenous appetite for the fags, and his profit would be grand. The captain was David Plant, and in his company was a tavern keeper named Hosea Tisdell. Hosea had asked to sail with Mr. Plant on his journey simply for his own pleasure, being that it was a short distance. The only other souls on board were a cabin boy and a handful of Negroes.

When the two ships were locked, Plant took Rackam's crew by surprise by firing his pistol and sinking his shot into the thigh of Thomas Earl, the carpenter. Rackam's men, under the direction of Corner, retaliated and easily subdued the belligerent captain, as Mark had wounded him in the right shoulder, disabling his firing arm. John could hear the exchange of gunfire, but he was unaffected, as he knew of Corner's abilities. While Mr. Plant was being bound, the cabin boy climbed over the bulwark and onto John's ship. Rackam's men surrounded Mr. Plant with all intent to bring the death penalty in payment for Earl's thigh, and the old man pleaded parley. *Parley* was a piratical term used in order to summon the captain of a pirate ship to stay an execution with the hopes that the captain may show mercy.

Stephen ran downstairs in attempts to hide below deck. John and George, hovering over a map, were taken back by the young boy as he raced for cover. John firmly addressed him,

"Halt!"

The boy stopped immediately and turned to listen.

"Who are you, and what are doing on my ship?"

The boy was humble. "Sir, my name is Stephen, and I'd like to stay on board this ship instead of with Mr. Plant. I make a fine cabin boy!"

John offered a hearty laugh, as the little fellow was as cute as he could be, and George chuckled at the kid who was now grinning.

"May I, please?"

The nine-year-old had the face of an angel, almost feminine, like many boys do, long before they reach puberty. He had large blue eyes that begged for leniency from the two men, as if they were viewed as some kind of gods.

John inquired, "Why would you want to stay on board a pirate ship and give up your grand position as cabin boy to Mr. Plant?"

Stephen's countenance fell. "I don't like him. He's an evil man."

George interjected, "Has he hurt you?"

Stephen stepped forward. "He hurts me all the time."

George looked at Howell and then John replied, "Would you like to tell me just how he hurts you?"

Stephen hung his head. "I can't tell anyone"—and tears filled his eyes.

John's words were soothing, "It's all right, you don't have to tell me if you don't want." John could feel the boy's pain, as he too had suffered unspeakable abuse when he was a cabin boy on the slave ship at the young age of thirteen.

John concealed his anger, as he didn't want the boy to think that it was directed at him.

Stephen pleaded, "Can I please stay?"

John smiled. "Of course you can." Stephen's grin returned but even larger this time, and then the boy wrapped his arms around John's neck. After a good hug, he let go and John looked at his delicate face.

"Stephen, what kind of punishment do you think God would dole to Mr. Plant if he were to do so?"

Stephen replied. "I think God would rain down fire and brimstone, like he did on Sodom and Gomorrah."

Suddenly, Adam descended the staircase to alert Captain Rackam that Captain Plant had called for parley.

John chided, "What perfect timing for Mr. Plant to hope for my mercy." He mumbled under his breath as he arose. "Goddamn him."

John, George, and Howell surfaced from their meeting, and Adam was commissioned to assure that Stephen remained below deck.

John stood with his arms folded before Mr. Plant.

"What may I do to assist you, Mr. Plant?"

John interrupted him, as he surveyed the scene.

"Hold on. Mark, go comfort the Negroes and let them know that we mean them no harm."

John addressed Hosea who stood submissively out of the way.

"And who are you?"

"My name is Hosea Tisdell, and I am tavern keeper from Jamaica."

"Oh, a tavern keeper. One of my dearest friends owns a tavern. He's an amazing fellow."

John returned his focus to Mr. Plant.

"Now back to you." John studied the weathered man who was attempting to harness his tremble.

"What can I do for you, Mr. Plant?"

John's men were intrigued as if beholding a grand performance upon a stage.

Mr. Plant humbly replied, "I was hoping for you to spare my life."

"Why would my men want to kill you?"

Mr. Plant stalled. "I injured one of your men out of self-defense."

John inspected his crew and could see the blood saturating the pant leg of Thomas Earl and then returned to Mr. Plant.

"So Thomas took a shot at you first, and you were defending your life?" John looked at Richard Corner to verify the report. "Is that correct, Richard?"

Richard corrected, "No, sir, Mr. Plant fired the first shot out of the element of surprise."

John looked up at the white flag displayed on Mr. Plant's main mast. "Do you always attack your opponent after a show of surrender, Mr. Plant?"

Mr. Plant remained silent, which angered John.

"Well, do you?"

Mr. Plant looked down. "No, sir."

John clenched his jaw. "Look me in the eye when you address me, Mr. Plant, because I have more questions for you."

Mr. Plant had given in to a slight tremble, and he started to heave his breath.

"Why would your cabin boy want to take refuge upon my ship?"

Mr. Plant seethed. "The boy is incorrigible and is a formidable liar."

John kept his composure. "That's strange, I would have never known that, because he seems like such a well-mannered child to me."

John surveyed the man who had debauchery smeared all over his face, and John continued,

"And why would he say that you are worthy of punishment by fire and brimstone?"

Mr. Plant remained silent.

"I will spare your life if you truthfully answer me just one question."

Mr. Plant looked John in the eye.

"Do you have a fancy for little boys?"

Mr. Plant retorted, "What kind of a vile question is that?"

John kept his composure. "Are you such a fool to use an angry tone with a man who can take your life this instant?" John was stern. "Now answer me the question!"

Mr. Plant closed his eyes and shook violently as he clenched his jaw, and he refused to confess or even attempt to deny the sickening truth. John addressed his carpenter,

"Thomas, would you like to take the honors, seeing that you're the one who's bleeding?"

Thomas replied, "No, sir, I prefer that you carry out the judgment on my behalf."

John ordered Hosea Tisdell to join the slaves, and he had Mark turn the passengers in the opposite direction so they would not see the gruesome scene. Then John's cutlass came down upon Mr. Plant's head, the force splitting it clean in two and down into his spine. His men saw a side of John Rackam that day that they had never seen, and they were all certain that they would not ever cross their captain after witnessing his display of wrath on behalf of the cabin boy.

Before he could lose the entirety of his blood supply onto the deck, Mr. Plant's body was dumped into the sea, and the area was mopped. Stephen never heard a thing, while Adam entertained the boy below deck.

Stephen studied Adam closely.

"You're not a man at all, are you?"

Anne asked, "Why do you say that?"

Stephen studied her further.

"I can just tell."

Anne was at a loss, as she did not want to lie to a child, and she did not want to be discovered, so she stalled, but Stephen was insistent.

"Well, are you?"

"Stephen, I am a woman, but nobody's supposed to know, so can you keep that to be our little secret?"

Stephen nodded and then asked,

"What's your name?"

"My name is Anne, but you are to always call me Adam. Agreed?"

Stephen nodded, and Anne rustled his hair.

"You are a very smart young man."

Stephen grinned at the compliment, and Anne thought it humorous that a little boy could be on board for less than hour and figure out her gender, yet she could work alongside grown men for months, who still have yet to know. Anne and Stephen became inseparable, and it was Anne who would teach Stephen how to read, using a plundered Holy Bible.

The young boy, orphaned early in his life, was raised by slaves in Jamaica until Mr. Plant had taken him to be cabin boy of his ship. It was surprising to Anne how much Christian training the boy had received, and Stephen told her that his knowledge of the Bible had come mainly from Mr. Plant. Stephen was given a hammock below deck right next to Mark, and he slept securely from that night on.

After the deck was cleaned of the blood, John allowed Hosea to sail home to Jamaica, and Hosea did just that, but not until he had offered John all the liquor that he had brought along that he had planned to trade in Cuba.

Upon his arrival to Jamaica, Hosea told a tale of how Mr. Plant and Stephen had fallen overboard and perished in the sea. He even managed to work up a tear to make his story more believable. The slaves never spoke of the incident, as they were thankful for the kindness that the pirate had shown on their behalf, so Nicholas Lawes was not privy to the knowledge that John Rackam was right in his backyard.

Thomas Earl was thankful that the shot was only under the surface and was easy to retrieve. In fact, he extracted it himself with the same pliers with which he used to repair the ship. After scrubbing the wound with sea salt, he wrapped it, and the healing occurred with difficulty. Thomas was given an extra share of the liquor to compensate for his troubles.

The crew adored the cabin boy, as he was entertainingly full of life, and his position was invaluable. Before his arrival, the men spent much energy scaling the stairs leading to and from the lower deck, but with Stephen on board, he was able to run for supplies, and it made the team operate so much more efficiently.

John's ship had been at sea for six months, as it was now October of 1719, and the ship was in dire need of cleaning and maintenance. John Rackam and George Fetherston had decided during their meeting to go ashore and remain until after Christmas, and they headed for the Cayman Islands.

The Caymans consisted of three islands. The largest island was called Grand Cayman and the two smaller islands were known as Cayman Brac and Little Cayman. Christopher Columbus named the smaller islands in 1503, calling them Las Tortugas, meaning "the turtles," for the islands were known for the abundance of sea turtles laying their eggs on the land and swimming their shorelines. The Cayman settlers were an eclectic group consisting of pirates, shipwrecked sailors, slaves, and, best of all, Spanish refugees.

Cayman Brac was chosen in order to give his men a reprieve, as the young Spanish women were more than delighted to trade a pirate's plunder for womanly favors. Also, the patrons of Cayman were friendly folks, and there were ample supplies on the island, as it was a hub for trade in the area. The onshore time was a holiday of sorts to allow the men to take a break from their arduous tasks, with exception of Patrick Carty, the boatswain, and Thomas Earl, as they had their work cut out for them. The rest of the crew would scrub, wash, and clean during the day, but at night, they would enjoy their pastime.

A bonfire was lit on the beach every evening, and the people of Cayman would gather to boil pots of flavorful dishes consisting of turtle meat, drink of fine rum, and socialize. That was John's favorite part of their visit in Cayman, as he delighted in the characters that he would meet. Stephen enjoyed the gatherings as well, for he was able to play with other children as they wrestled and ran through the sand. John, Adam, and Stephen had become a family of sorts, and they were never happier, except that John and Anne were not able to display their affection openly, which was beginning to present somewhat of a discomfort. John feared that their secret rendezvous in the captain's cabin would be discovered by one of his men, who would think that he and Adam were closet lovers, for which they were.

At one of the gatherings, John met a man named Daniel Woods, and he expressed the desire to come aboard with the crew. The man was an artist without fencing or skill of a musket, so John was reserved as to what place he would hold on the ship, and Daniel wasn't keen on the idea of being hung for his adventure.

Daniel was a tall lean, but muscular man. His face was chiseled and gentle to the eyes. He had the heart of a child and a wonderful sense of humor. Although Daniel didn't intend to be humorous with his innocent comments, he evoked grins from those who allowed themselves the pleasure to get to know such a unique individual. From the first encounter with Daniel, John was intrigued by the young man's uncanny ability to instantly see details that others completely missed, and John knew that Daniel possessed the gift of a visionary. It was for that trait alone that John chose to take him aboard.

John liked to think that he had extended the offer for only Daniel's rare gift. However, the fact that Mary was completely smitten by the young fellow had pulled at John's heartstrings as well and had definitely swayed him in his decision. Mary had attended the beach gatherings every night, and Mark and Daniel had developed an inseparable friendship. John chuckled to himself at the thought of the look that would grace Daniel's face if he were to find out that Mark was really a Mary.

CHAPTER 19

THE SHIP WAS beached on Cayman Brac during high tide and secured with ropes. The booty was unloaded and divided among the men. After the tide receded, the ship tipped to its side upon the shore, allowing the boatswain and carpenter to inspect and repair its hull. During the next high tide, the process was repeated, and the other side was exposed for repair. The process took a couple months, and they remained on the island until after Christmas. John planned to take his crew on the long voyage to Bermuda after they left the Caymans, being that the threat of hurricane would have subsided. Bermuda is located out in the Atlantic Ocean in the same latitude as North Carolina, and its surrounding waters have the potential to be quite fierce, for it is in the southern part of the North Atlantic where hurricanes develop.

Their stay in the Caymans was a pleasant retreat, except for a few days before their departure when Daniel got into a verbal dispute with an older pirate who had become jealous of Daniel's opportunity to join John's crew. The older man had pleaded for a position from the day that John first arrived on the island, and John was certain that he did not want the pirate on board, as one cantankerous fellow can spoil the harmonious fulfillment of an entire crew.

When John wasn't present, the old man would release his mean streak toward Daniel in the form of vile slurring. Daniel attempted at verbal negotiations, but one night after a bit too much rum, Daniel agreed to a duel the next day at high noon to settle the dispute. Mark was practically hysterical with the idea that Daniel would surely not win a fight with a seasoned pirate and thought a quick plan. Mark would meet the old man at an earlier time to subdue him. Mark knew that old man would be there anxiously waiting and anticipating a vicious slaughter of his opponent, for Mark knew the temperament of that type of a pirate.

About two hours prior to noon, Mark was ready for pistol or cutlass to stand in the steed of Daniel, which made the old man angry, as he had wanted to see Daniel suffer a horrible death. However, his anger was quickly diverted toward Mark, as the young man slung the same vile slurring upon the old man as he had used toward Daniel.

The duel began with an agreement that they would only use the cutlass, as the old man said he didn't own a pistol. To provide for fairness, Mark surrendered his pistol to a crewmate who stood in attendance. When they began the match, Mark instantly could tell that old man had a lively skill, as he presented a challenge even for Mark.

While they fought, Mark focused intently upon his opponent, anticipating his every move and striking when the old man was at the end of impose, which the old man was able to block. When the pirate was tiring and beginning to lose ground with all swiftness, he leaned away, dropped his cutlass, and brought forth his concealed pistol. He drew a quick shot in Mark's direction, and the young man, with amazing speed, was able to avoid the bullet, as he always considered a shot to be nothing more than an extension of a rapier. Mark's eye-to-body coordination was so honed that he could anticipate the area of strike and avoid being its target. Mark instantly retaliated by swiftly bringing his cutlass around and down to completely sever the old man's firing arm. The pistol flew from the fingers of his tremulous arm, as the arm fell to the earth with a thud. Mark stood poised as he watched the old man sink into unconsciousness while he lost the entirety of his blood supply into the thirsty sand. By the time Daniel showed up for the duel, he was surprised by the whole account but very thankful for Mark, as he would have foolishly died that day due his loose lips caused by the excess of rum the night before.

The next day, the *Anne Bonny* departed from Cayman Brac, but John decided to remain in the region surrounding the island to let the storms die down, as the Atlantic was experiencing unseasonable weather, and the waters were said to be treacherous. The report had come from some sailors who had just sailed through the tempest. While in the Caribbean and over the next two months, John's crew seized nothing but one ship full of thieves being exported out of Jamaica. John and his men decided to free the prisoners to the shoreline. He chose not to keep even the heartiest of the men to work on board, as he had grown leery of strangers. Unlike Vane, John was a nurturing father figure for the nine men, two women, and a child sailing under his care, and he didn't want to subject them to any unsavory fellows.

He did, however, decide to keep the ship that had carried the thieves. The ship would be used for its wood in order to refurbish the *Anne Bonny*, and George Fetherston captained the vessel until an English man-of-war was spotted in the distance approaching the company with the king's colors displayed. George quickly joined John Rackam, and the pirates made their escape, abandoning the prize to the man-of-war as they sailed toward Bermuda.

The Bermuda islands were a prime location to apprehend ships en route to the American colonies. John knew that he could reward his men lavishly with the excess of tender that was readily available surrounding the triangulation of islands. They sailed eastward below Cuba and planned to round its northern coast and head west, cutting past the Florida Keys in order to avoid scaling up the chain of the Bahamas. It was much too risky to be in the Bahaman neighborhood of Governor Woodes Rogers.

It was during the morning inspection that Patrick Carty noticed that water was collecting in the lower part of the inner hull. He had informed John in Cayman that the ship was in need of oakum in order to seal the seams, but Cayman did not have the supplies necessary. Patrick had been fairly certain that they could make it to Bermuda where there were ample provisions to pitch and tar, but his judgment had failed as the leak was such that it forced them to land at Andros Island, which was only forty-three miles from Providence. Thankfully, Andros had the necessary provisions in order to complete the task, and once again, the ship was beached for its repairs.

The island of Andros was one of the islands that John had wished to take Anne in order to show her the orchids that grew in the wild. So while the men worked to repair the vessel, John led an expedition to get provisions, but his main objective was to show his company the magnificent flowering plants. He took with him Adam, Mark, Daniel, and Stephen.

After a good hike inland, they located a small grove of the most amazing pale blue and lavender orchids that any of them, besides John, had ever witnessed.

Stephen asked John, "May I pick one for Anne?"

John was at a loss for words and shot a glance at Daniel to assess if he caught the error. Daniel replied, "It's all right, I already knew. You can't fool everyone."

John was actually surprised by his relief of the truth. Daniel didn't let on about how he knew, but it was Stephen who had confirmed it to him. Stephen was a well-mannered child but could not keep a secret to save his life. In fact, Stephen had befriended all the men on the ship. Each one had taken to him as a big brother of sorts, and Stephen had let it slip to every last one of them about Anne. The men actually found it to be endearing, and they were somewhat refreshed to know that John wasn't finding his fancy with Adam, as they had lately suspected. Besides, Adam had more than proved himself to the men during the past ten months in which they had been sailing, so the myth of having a woman on board to be bad luck had been long dispelled.

Daniel continued, "No, I think it's wonderful, the love you two share is very inspiring, and I've admired it from the start, even with Anne dressed like a man. I only wish I could find such passion."

John placed his arm around his lady and drew her close for an embrace. "Thank you, Daniel Woods, your sentiments are liberating." He held Anne while Stephen grinned at the sight, and then he kissed her tenderly.

That night, Mary thought up a plan, as she had found a great bit of courage by Daniel's passionate words. Mark had invited Daniel to a secluded place on the island with the intent to show him something. To Daniel's pleasant surprise, Mary found the bravery to let him discover that she too was a woman, as she unbuttoned her blouse.

It was completely out of Mary's character, because she was far from a promiscuous woman, and Mary was even taken back by herself, as she stood there with her breasts bared, breasts that had never even been exposed to the sunlight. And now, as Daniel's jaw dropped, they were in plain view being illuminated only by the lantern. As she stood there in her vulnerable state, it was clear to Mary that Daniel's approval was very apparent, and he embraced her tenderly.

Daniel was for certain that he had found a rare love that he planned to cherish forever. Mary could not believe that her dream of longing to be held by a gracious man such as Daniel had actually come true, as she melted into his chest. Daniel had known all along that Mark was a woman, as he felt that no man could ever be so beautiful. Well, it wasn't just Daniel's superior intellect that solved the mystery. He had help from Stephen who eagerly confirmed his hunch.

That night, they spent the duration in each other's arms. Daniel was allowed to caress Mary's soft breasts, but she wasn't ready to consummate. Daniel understood, for he was a patient man, and he knew her love would be worth the wait. Just to hold her and feel the passion was enough for him, and they drifted off to sleep wrapped in their blanket, lying in the hammock that Mary had made among the trees in their secret spot.

During their walk to see the orchids, John hadn't allowed Stephen to pick the flower, as he explained the reason to just allow them to remain in their untouched beauty. For if Stephen picked the flower, it would wither, but if he left it, the flower would remain strong and glorious to grace the vision of the next person who wandered upon its path.

While Mary and Daniel took their fill of love that evening, John had chosen to spend his time in solitude as he pondered his crew and the way that things were transpiring. John was content and would not have had it any other way, but now his concerns for capture were more daunting than ever, as he felt the overwhelming responsibility for so many souls on board that he had come to cherish. His life as a captain of his ship was turning out to be more of a pleasure cruise rather than a serious pirating adventure, like he had experienced when Vane had captained the ship. John wondered about Vane's destiny, and although he didn't know it then, he would eventually discover the fate of the man who was still stranded on his island somewhere off the coast of the North Americas.

Charles Vane had finally spotted a ship and summoned it to the shoreline. His rescue seemed assured, and Vane was delighted to discover that the captain of the ship was an acquaintance of his named Henry Holford. Henry was an old buccaneer who had encountered Vane numerous times along his journeys and knew of Vane's character and reputation. After what seemed like a grand reunion, Vane was sorely disappointed that Mr. Holford had refused him a place on his ship unless he took him in chains as a prisoner. Mr. Holford expressed his belief that Vane would most definitely attempt to sway his crew and then knock him in the head, leaving him to die, while Vane stole away with his ship to go a pirating.

Vane pleaded to the point of tears that such a case would never occur, and he offered his oath of complete loyalty, but Mr. Holford knew Vane all too well. Before he left, Mr. Holford suggested that Vane should steel a fishing boat from one of the usual patrons of the island to make his escape. Vane replied,

"So you think I should steal a boat from fishermen who are keeping me alive?"

Mr. Holford chided, "What? Do you suddenly have a conscience that bothers you to steal a mere fishing boat, when you have been a wretched thief, stealing ships and cargos and plundering all mankind that fell in your way? Vane, stay here and be damned, if you are too squeamish to go with me in chains."

Besides being removed in shackles, the only offer Mr. Holford rendered was to leave Vane on the island in hopes that another ship would rescue him. If not, Mr. Holford would be back in one month, and if Vane was still there, he would for certain be subdued and taken in chains to Jamaica to be delivered up for his hanging, and Mr. Holford left the island and sailed away.

As John pondered his thoughts in his solitude, he planned to have Anne and Mary remain dressed as men, as he didn't want to change the dynamics of the work aboard the ship. He also thought about the repairs that needed to be made and planned to have all men assist with its restoration first thing in the morning so they could get far away from Providence as John feared the discovery from Woodes Rogers.

The ship was upright at last, and Patrick was pleased to report that there was no sign of water in the inner hull. The crew was loading the final provisions. One would never have discerned that Mark and Adam were two wistful women in love as they worked diligently lifting and carrying the supplies, exerting as much energy as any man. John ordered his men to bolster their efforts, while he worked by their sides. He saw the two sloops approaching in the distance and recognized them as belonging to Woodes Rogers. He had seen them many times before in the harbor of Nassau. His fears were confirmed as the two sloops displayed their British flags upon the main masts and drew nearer.

By the time they had loaded and the ship was set to sail, the sloops had positioned themselves in formation with ten cannons precisely aimed at John's ship. Governor Woodes Rogers had indeed sent the sloops, as he had been informed that John Rackam was in the vicinity.

The soldiers proudly displayed their numbers by lining the bulwark of the sloops, and John, being sorely outnumbered, wondered if this would be their final day. He ordered Stephen to bring the powder from below, and he positioned his men at his six cannons with the hope that luck may prevail as he anticipated his small return over their great exchange of artillery. However, John was puzzled as the British troops did not fire upon the pirate ship, although John knew that they were aware that it was clearly his ship.

Woodes Rogers had sternly commissioned his men to bring the pirates in without using the heavy artillery, because the chancellor's daughter was on board, and he did not want to be the one responsible for killing Anne Bonny. They were to only use the cannon for their defense and only if they were fired upon first, but firing his cannon was the last thing on John's mind as he thought a plan.

The sloops had to remain at a distance, as they feared being grounded by the numerous sandbars surrounding the island of Andros. John knew the sandbars well and saw a channel to the west in between the island and the governor's sloop. He had his crew go below deck, because he would be sailing dangerously close to the opponent, and if they were to fire their cannon, John's crew would be fucked. He sailed past with ease, being puzzled as to why they would position and not discharge their weapons, and then he remembered how fond the governor had been of Anne and Mark. The two women had truly proven to be his good luck charms that day.

Once they were at sea and after John, George Fetherston and Richard Corner had devised a new plan; the crew was jubilant, and John allowed the men to be at ease and enjoy his company. They sat around the grand table below deck drinking rum and jesting. The men let John know that they knew about him and Adam.

John laughed out loud when Noah Harwood told his story of his utter shock the first time he saw Adam sneak into the captain's cabin, and he couldn't believe in his wildest imagination that fiercely bold John Rackam was sweet for a man. The crew all bellowed with laughter as they drank their rum and smoked the fine Cuban cigars that were plundered from the captain of the ship full of thieves. As Daniel had been, his men were also inspired by the passion in John's eyes for his lady, and they had all been relieved when they found out that Adam was really an Anne. They saw the passion on the first day of the journey, because John was never able to conceal the way he marveled at Anne Bonny.

Anne told the story of why she killed Nicholas Paige, and all agreed that he deserved his judgment. Then they took turns reminiscing about Providence and laughed even harder when some told their stories about Pierre and his antics. They all missed Pierre desperately and wished him well.

Benjamin returned from being commissioned on the governor's sloop and informed Pierre that his friends had escaped with ease. Pierre was delighted, and as usual, he lit three candles for John, Anne, and Mary before he retired that night. He made Benjamin laugh out loud as they lay in John's bed in the tree house, and Pierre told him of the adventures he had incurred with Catherine the pig and King Henry that day.

John, his master, and quartermaster had decided that sailing to Bermuda would be too much of a risk at that time, so they planned to take refuge in a place where John had always been safe. They continued west toward Cuba to hide for a while with Elias and Avala.

CHAPTER 20

Anne was thrilled when John told her of his plans to return to Cuba. He had broken the news directly after the celebration while Anne was spending her daily ritual with Stephen. Anne would school Stephen every evening by teaching him to read from the Holy Bible, and after John had told her of the good news, Anne replied, "Listen to this, John."

She beamed at Stephen who read,

"Yea thou I walk through the valley of the shadow of death, I will fear no evil for thou art with me, thy rod and thy staff they comfort me."

Stephen grinned at John with pride.

John doted. "Stephen, that is wonderful. You are a very intelligent young man."

Stephen humbled. "Well, I don't know if I'm actually reading it, as I've memorized it by now."

John defended, "No, I believe you are truly reading. I can tell good reading when I hear it."

Stephen's pride returned as he grinned at John who addressed Anne.

"Why don't you have him learn the story of Stephen in the book of Acts. That was always one of my favorites."

Stephen interjected, "No, I want you to tell me the story."

John sat down with the boy and told him the story of the brave man named Stephen, who had the face of an angel. The daring Stephen had stood up against the religious council who had become jealous of him for his pure heart. The council had gathered false witnesses against Stephen and had condemned him to death because they interpreted Stephen's faith as blasphemy. Then they took him out and stoned him, but he didn't even take notice of the punishment. There was no fear or pain in his death, as Stephen hadn't felt a thing, because he looked up toward heaven and saw God receiving him into his comforting arms, all the while the religious council were throwing their boulders.

When John had finished his story, Stephen was already on to the next subject and asked him. "John, can I call you father?"

John laughed. "Of course you can, but not in front of the men, as they would all want to call me father. And how can I be a grand pirate if grown men are getting soft on me?"

Stephen grinned even larger, and Anne smiled with contentment, as she realized what a wonderful father John Rackam truly was to Stephen, and her mind drifted as she was anxious to show Mary baby Jonathan's grave in Cuba.

Although Stephen couldn't keep a secret, he did keep one, as he never spoke of the gruesome violation that had occurred while he was in the care of the vile sea captain. Stephen would always bear the scars, but he was able to put it behind him, as John's love had healed his gaping wounds. The torrid nightmares had even vanished the very day that John Rackam gave him permission to call him father.

When they arrived in Cuba, John had John Davis moor the ship in a safe harbor just south of the peninsula where Avala's family kept their plantation.

The crew was thankful for the freedom of Cuba, as they were still a little shaken by their narrow escape of Woodes Rogers's sloops. Besides, Cuba was one of their favorite stops, as there were an ample supply of beautiful women for which to lavish their plunders, and that was foremost on their agendas. The men were eager to search for the passion that they observed in their captain, and the ladies of Cuba reaped the benefits for the grand treatment that was bestowed upon them by John's men.

Anne's reunion with Avala, Ester, and Miriam was filled with tearful embraces. John heartily greeted Elias as always, and everyone thoroughly enjoyed the fellowship. Anne went with Mary and the other women to the grave of Jonathan. Although it was a tearful moment, Anne had resolved that she would see her baby again one day in heaven. She was glad that he was safe in the arms of God, as their destiny was not quite as certain.

For the first time, since their journey had begun, Anne clothed herself with a dress that Avala gifted to her, and she was able to openly display her affection as John's lady. John had not seen Anne in a dress since the day they had left Cuba and sailed for Providence, and his eyes were truly delighted as he marveled at her magnificence.

Avala had also given Mary a beautiful dress, and Mary donned it while she could not stop gazing at herself in the mirror, for it was the very first time she had been in feminine attire since her husband, Peter, had died.

Daniel swooped Mary off her feet and twirled her around while he asked for her hand in marriage.

John and Anne didn't see the need for a ceremony of their own, as Anne was already married legally to another man. Besides, they both felt somewhat of a disdain for religious rituals. However, they were sincerely happy for Mary and Daniel, who had a strong desire to say their vows before God in the company of their friends, so Elias acted as minister, and they were married in the grand home of Avala's parents on the coffee plantation. The marriage wasn't legal like Anne's to James Bonny with an official stamp, but they sealed their hearts together that day to prevent any guilt that would plague Mary, as Mary had a very sensitive conscience.

That night, Mary was ready and let destiny carry her to where it would. Daniel was well endowed, and Mary allowed herself to relax, giving herself completely to him. She took pleasure in the searing stretch of the skin in her private areas as he entered her, and she heaved to the deep penetration of his love until both had obtained their fill. Daniel had been correct that is was certainly worth the wait.

Stephen enjoyed being big brother to Raphael, Cordula, and Michael who were all getting so big. It had been two years since Anne had seen them, as Anne had only been on the verge of eighteen when she had visited Cuba, and now she had just turned twenty on the eighth of March.

It was in that same month that Charles Vane had found the fortune of being rescued by a ship off his deserted island. He was taken aboard by Captain Mathew Chandler and allowed to tend the kitchen for his crew. By pure circumstance, Mr. Chandler was a good friend of Mr. Holford, the man who had refused Vane aboard his ship. One evening, the two men anchored their ships and dined together. After Mr. Holford boarded Chandler's ship as a guest, he happened to peer below deck and noticed that Vane was alive and well, working as the common help. Mr. Holford returned to his friend and inquired,

"Do you really know who you have working on your ship?"

Mr. Chandler was puzzled. "Why? I have just rescued a shipwrecked trade sailor, but he seems to be a good worker and a straightforward individual."

Holford replied, "Well, he's not, because he's one of the most notorious pirates that ever lived. If I were you, I wouldn't keep him. I would sail straight to Jamaica and surrender him."

Mathew Chandler was a little taken back by the brashness of Mr. Holford and quickly changed the subject, because he saw no harm in the man.

When Mr. Holford returned to his ship, he could not rest for the sight of Vane and the potential for his friend to lose his ship and his life. He sent his first mate with a pistol to bind Vane and bring him in chains aboard Holford's ship. The first mate accomplished his assignment without any opposition from Vane, and Mr. Holford directed his ship toward Jamaica, where Vane was delivered to the authorities and sentenced to die on March 20, 1720. However, the Jamaican authorities, having been informed as to the vile crimes in which Vane had committed, didn't execute him immediately as was typical. They kept him alive in the dungeon only to torture him for his wicked behavior and the abuse he had doled toward humanity.

In Cuba, John was getting restless, as it had been five months since they had landed. Although it had been a refreshing haven, John had relaxed enough, and they had stayed longer than John had wanted. He had probably given in about four times to Anne's pleadings for just one more week, but this time he was firm.

"We are going. If we stay here any longer, we will be discovered. We are outlaws. Don't you remember?"

Anne replied, "Yes, and we will hang if we are caught and so on and so forth. But can't we just stay one more week?"

John was stern. "No!"

Anne rolled her eyes. "Yes, sir."

Anne loved the family environment at Elias and Avala's, and she was getting a bit tired of the constant travel. She wished that she and John could have gotten the land grant and settled in Providence and filled their home with children like he once had dreamed, but she figured that as long as she was with him, it really didn't matter where they were. And to her pleasant surprise, as soon as she had set her foot on the ship, she was as excited as the next man that they were setting sail. She was also excited for the child that now grew in her womb.

It was in the afternoon when James Dobbin had pulled the anchor, and Noah Harwood had just engaged the sails, Thomas Earl was in the crow's nest, when he noticed the Spanish man-of-war coming closer to the shore. He alerted John, and when the ship came closer, it hoisted its bright colors and began to position itself to attack; John mumbled under his breath,

"We're fucked."

He alerted everyone else, and they lined the bulwark as the man-of-war began to fire its cannons in their direction.

The Spanish *guarda de la costa* had been informed by an English sloop who had scouted the pirates some days earlier during a short excursion where John and his men had hoisted the black flag. Being that the English had no jurisdiction in Cuba, they were forced to turn it over to the Spanish authority, and the man-of-war had been circling the island ever since in search of the infamous fugitives.

John and his men were able to watch the barrage of cannon fire make a splash onto the land and into the water, being a safe distance from their ship. The man-of-war was too great a vessel to enter the inner cove where John's ship rested and to position itself in a way to fire upon its target. In addition, it was nearing evening, and the winds were low, so they lacked the force in order to propel such a large ship.

The Spanish had attempted to fire beyond the small peninsula that shielded the harbor, but they could only get so close to the shore, so thankfully, their shot could not reach John's ship. After the failed attempts, the Spanish moved perpendicular, leaving their cannons without the target, but their move completely occluded the exit of the main. The Spanish troops were confident that there was no way out, and they planned to hold the prisoners in the harbor until morning, hoping for favorable winds in order to make their entrance and position for attack. Another ship from their company blocked a potential lesser exit. It was a sloop manned with twenty-five men, who rejoiced, as they were certain that they had conquered the most notorious pirate left from Providence, because there was absolutely no way of escape.

John and his men surveyed the scene. John had always excluded Daniel from all pirating activities, and he firmly insisted that if they were captured that Daniel was to boldly lie to save his life. He was instructed to look them in the eye and tell them that John Rackam had taken him as prisoner. Besides, it wasn't really a lie, because he was not pirating. However, it was somewhat of a lie, because Daniel was definitely on their ship of his own accord. It was Daniel standing on the bulwark with the crew that had sparked the idea for the plan against the Spanish, as he peered through the telescope. Daniel noticed that the sloop was not heavily manned. He counted only twenty-five, and he had faith that John could probably overpower the soldiers with only John's team of eleven men—or twelve, if Daniel were allowed.

John retorted, "Well, you must think we're immortal." John chuckled at Dan's innocent show of faith. "They outnumber us more than two to one. What do think we are, some type of fucking gladiators?" Then he chuckled at himself, and everyone had a good laugh except Daniel as he had not said it to be humorous, and he defended his case,

"I think you and your men are pretty amazing, actually."

That exchange of words was followed by an epiphany, and John pondered. Then he outlined the plan to his crew as it was developing in his mind.

"Okay, here's what we're going to do. The *Anne Bonny* is doomed, so our only hope of escape is to sneak aboard the sloop after midnight and subdue the crew by the element of surprise and steal their ship." He followed his plan with a bit of sarcasm, "God bless Vane. He did one thing for me. He imparted a bit of a fiendish nature." John's suaveness made each man grin with pride. Each man felt in his heart that if this was their final showdown, they were honored to have had the opportunity to have sailed with John Rackam.

Well after midnight, John and his crew lowered the boat and loaded what necessities they could take and rowed to the sloop. They climbed aboard with all care to be silent, and they placed Stephen and Daniel in a safe place upon the ship. John was pleased when they only found ten men aboard sleeping, as the rest must have rowed ashore for the night.

One at a time the Spanish soldiers were awoken to a gag and a cutlass to their throat only to hear the hushed speech in their own language, "If you utter a word or make a noise, you are a dead man." John was thankful for all the time he had spent in Cuba, for he had learned the language, and at this particular time, it came in handy.

Once all the souls on board were bound, they brought the boat up and retrieved their supplies. John had Davis hoist the anchor, and after Noah had set the sails, they headed out to sea. Once they were at a good distance from the shore, only one prisoner was released from his ties for rowing, and the entire bound crew was loaded into the boat to be taken ashore.

By morning, the men were still rowing to the shore, and the men on the Spanish man-of-war ship didn't even take notice that the sloop was missing, as they were so intent on the prize of John Rackam's ship. The winds were in their favor, and they found a way to maneuver in the harbor to allow their cannon to rest on the target and in close proximity. After the ship was stabilized, they unleashed a furrowing attack onto the *Anne Bonny* and shredded the ship to mere splinters. The men rejoiced as the bow broke free and plunged into the harbor. They were sorely disappointed when they discovered the ship had been gutted and was absent of John Rackam, not to mention that their sloop was missing.

Governor Rogers had heard of the sighting in Cuba, and he figured John would head south toward Jamaica. The Royal Governor Nicholas Lawes had horribly criticized Governor Rogers for not being more aggressive when he had John Rackam pinned at Andros. Woodes Rogers let him know that it was out of respect for the chancellor of South Carolina that he had ordered his men to refrain from artillery, as to not kill the chancellor's daughter. Governor Lawes did not reply, but as far as he was concerned, Anne Bonny was to be considered a pirate and was worthy of the noose. Woodes Rogers hoped that being an uncle would soften the old goat's heart a bit, as Sarah Lawes was now with child.

Woodes Rogers, in attempts to repair his relationship with Nicholas Lawes, assigned Captain Jonathan Barnet to command a sloop that was designated only to pursuit John Rackam. Captain Barnet was one of the finest, as he was well known for his amazing strategies. Governor Rogers had also provided Captain Barnet with a full crew of his best soldiers, and the captain was ordered to use artillery or any means necessary to capture and/ or kill John Rackam. The sloop would be stationed in Jamaica and would be dispatched by the Royal Governor Nicholas Lawes at his discretion. Governor Rogers hoped his generous gift would ease the tension that was caused by the fact that he had offered John Rackam the opportunity to escape.

Sarah Lawes didn't spend much time concerning herself with Anne Bonny anymore, as she was infatuated with the idea of having a child. And when she wasn't absorbing herself with herself, she was throwing up or craving some strange dish.

John and his crew were pretty solemn after their affairs in Cuba. John realized that there was really no safe place in which to hide anymore. They headed south to Jamaica to feed on familiar waters, as he knew that Jamaica had always been a treasure trove for men who wanted to pirate. John planned to bolster his crew in order to fight off any ship that would attack him. He was thankful that the stolen sloop was armed with sixteen cannon and was well stocked with arsenal, as the Spanish were greedy for their victories, even more so than their insatiable lust for gold.

John would've never taken his crew to Jamaica if he had been aware of the ardent determination of Governor Lawes to see him hang. John's reasoning had been tainted by the golden era when a pirate could roam the seas and go virtually unchecked, but now the era was coming to a close, and the awareness was such that pirating was turning into a grand annoyance filled with pursuits and conflict. At this point, John didn't have any option but to continue his journeys at sea, for there was no longer a safe haven, and there was no turning back, for he had long squandered his opportunity for clemency. All men aboard agreed that if they wanted to survive, it would be crucial to recruit more men in order to defend against the men-of-war ships, which seemed to be the flavor of the month. John second-guessed his decision to divert from Bermuda, but unbeknown to John, the weather had remained volatile throughout the spring, and chances are, they may have encountered great difficulties with the tempest at sea.

Back in Providence, Benjamin begged Pierre, "Just shoot me in the thigh."

Pierre was firm. "I'm not doing it."

Benjamin pleaded, "Pierre, if you don't, I will be gone in two days."

Benjamin had been commissioned to sail against the Spanish who were showing increasing aggression toward the royal colony of Providence. Although the War of Triple Alliance was no longer a threat, this series of invasions was in retaliation over England's blatant disregard for their trade agreement with Spain. English merchants had bought into a plan called the South Sea Company, and England upheld it with the sole purpose of eliminating their national debt. However, Spain most definitely was not in agreement. English merchants were somehow under the delusion that they now had the right to access the oversupply of gold and silver, which was extracted from Chili and Peru. The Spanish were furious, and the assaults on England's royal colony of Providence were relentless.

Pierre was stern. "I'm not doing it, Benjamin."

Benjamin chided, "Pierre, you're acting like a cunt."

Pierre returned, "And you're acting as if you have a larger-than-life prick." Pierre was smug.

Benjamin replied, "Pierre, this is not a humorous affair. If I don't get wounded during this hunting excursion, they will never discharge me from the naval forces. I've already been commissioned."

Pierre dealt a solution, "Why don't you petition the governor?"

Benjamin played out the part, "Oh yeah, Governor, I'd like to be discharged from the royal navy so I can remain in Providence, because I found my true love with Pierre." Benjamin continued, "The governor's jaw would drop, and he'd reply, "You've got to be joking me, right? Now get your ass on that ship and get out of my face, you despicable fuck.'"

Pierre and Benjamin chuckled at the thought.

Benjamin sulked. "If you're not going to do it, give me the goddamned gun so I can do it myself."

Pierre argued, "No! Have you lost your senses? The wound be too great at such a close range." Pierre finally conceded, "All right, I'll do it, but you must stand at a good distance."

Benjamin was poised and bravely awaiting his self-affliction. Pierre took aim and delayed, which caused Benjamin to become impatient.

"Come on, Pierre, what the fuck?"

In his quivering state, Pierre kept his eye on the target of Benjamin's left thigh, but due to his nerves, he missed the first shot, which caused Benjamin's impatience to surge even higher. "Goddamn it, Pierre. I know you can shoot better than that. Now stop fucking around."

Pierre defended, "No, I gave it my best shot."

Benjamin chided, "Yeah, right. Now shoot me in the goddamned thigh, and don't miss and castrate me, or I may as well get on that damned ship."

Pierre hit his second shot directly in the thickest part of Benjamin's left thigh and was commended for doing such a good job. Thankfully, it was a surface wound, which appeared as though it would heal easily with Pierre's sea-salt treatments.

The governor was disappointed to hear about Benjamin's hunting "accident," because Benjamin was one of his best soldiers. After Benjamin produced a horrible limp, the governor gave him an honorable discharge from the royal navy. The governor could not send out a soldier limping his way into battle to fight the Spanish who were well known for their impeccable combat skills. The governor suspected that Benjamin and Pierre have contrived the whole ordeal, but since Woodes Rogers had immense respect for the two of them, he chose not to even ask. Besides, he knew it would be futile, for the royal governor of Providence had a grain of wisdom in that he was certain that the two men would never tell anyway.

That night, after treating Benjamin's wound, Pierre lit four candles, one for John, one for Anne, one for Mary, and one for Governor Woodes Rogers. Pierre drifted off to sleep displaying his contentment upon his face.

CHAPTER 21

J OHN MISSED THE *Anne Bonny*, but he had no great disappointment for the exchange of the Spanish sloop, for it was well equipped with supplies to sustain twenty-five soldiers. It was actually a game of sorts to explore the ship and discover the essentials as well as the treasures that lay buried beneath her deck, mainly the ample supply of tequila. John never did name the new vessel, as he figured it was not necessary, as everyone just referred to her as the Spanish sloop. She was a well sailing vessel and in good repair, much more so than the *Anne Bonny* had been.

Anne knew that she was with child the first month that her blood did not come; however, Mary was not aware that the blood would stop when a child was developing in the womb. Anne was delighted, as Mary had confided that her blood had stopped two months prior, the same time that Anne's had stopped, so the babies were due to be born around the same time. Mary marveled at the thought, and Daniel was elated. Stephen was also giddy, as he would now be a big brother to two babies. John, however, was not so exuberant at the revelation that he was going to be a father, given the present situation. He drank an extra portion of the Spanish tequila that evening, and he decided that distilling the agave plant was a rather clever invention by the Spanish. However, he still preferred his rum.

John didn't divulge his trepidation to Anne about her condition, as he didn't want to rob her of her joy. Although it was almost impossible to hide his feelings when he found out about Mary, for now he had just lost two of his men, and they were already lacking of help from which to start. Although the weight of the world was beginning to light upon his shoulders, John stood strong, and he continued to nurture his crew like a wise father, and he was optimistic that they would find some way to continue in their journeys even without the help of Anne and Mary.

John would never even consider Stephen as part of his fighting crew, but he patiently taught Stephen how to fence and shoot a pistol at Stephen's insistence, as Stephen wanted to be just like John when he grew to be a man. John commended the boy for his excellent skills, and Stephen beamed with pride. He practiced daily with the other men, and it wasn't long before they were casting lots as to the winner of the match. Of course, the men went easy on the little guy, but Stephen didn't know, and to witness the young man's innocent jubilation and the thrill over collecting his coins brought much joy to the entire crew.

If they had simply been a band of gypsies, they would have been content to wander the seas forever, enjoying their adventures and harmonious company. However, they were not, as they were the most sought-out villains of the era, and their only hope of survival was to increase their numbers in order to fight their way out of each attempt by the authorities to succumb them.

It was now August of 1720, and John had scoured the coasts of the northern and western parts of Jamaica. They plundered several small vessels but were not able to find even one soul who desired to come aboard and join his crew, so they took what they needed and moved on. Gone were the days that the men of Jamaica were turned away in large numbers—men who had petitioned to come aboard and sail with the pirates.

John and his men thought another plan that they felt would be certain to increase their company. They would begin to target fishing boats, as they knew that the majority of fisherman had once made their way by pirating, and surely they would find some who missed the adventure. However, after plundering seven or eight boats off the coast of Jamaica, John was sorely disappointed to find that the men who once valiantly sailed with courage were now meek and shaken at the thought of punishment that had been openly publicized in Jamaica.

Anyone convicted of piracy was taken to Jamaica and chained in the town square. They were suspended, hanging by their shackled wrists, and the chains were held firm to a thick wooden beam. The public could see the men writhing in their agony as their wrists and shoulders would dislocate under the pressure of the weight of their bodies. After they had spent ample time in the chains, they were taken down and sent to the gallows. Not to mention the publicity by the Jamaican authorities of the capture of the infamous Captain Vane and the details of the torture that was being doled to him in the Jamaican prison. Those fear tactics had been quite successful, and the men who were once pirates from Jamaica and who had pleaded clemency would not even consider squandering their merciful opportunities.

Although they could not find men to recruit on the fishing boats, it was a fine opportunity to gather fishing nets and tackle from some and from others reunite with company they had kept in days past. The opportunity for a reunion presented on one such boat that was out turtling when John's black flag was unfurled against it, and to John's marvelous surprise, the men on board were crewmembers that had sailed with him on Vane's ship.

It was John Eaton and eight other men. The nine men now made a business out of fishing the turtles from the sea around the Caymans, as the meat of the turtle was in high demand. They had relocated to Jamaica after receiving their clemency and had kept their association with Vane an undisclosed mystery, so they wouldn't suffer repercussion from the Jamaican authority. John's men secured the boats together out at sea and greeted their old comrades. They had a grand time as they drank rum, while reminiscing about the good old days.

That is when John heard the stories of Vane's capture and torture in the Jamaican prison. After their tales of Vane's woes, the men told John that they so wanted in their heart of hearts to sail with him, but they couldn't take the risk as they were now in an honest business, and most had settled into a family way. John understood and wished them well, letting them know that he planned to sail to Hispaniola in attempts to recruit men, and when he returned to the area, he would seek them out for more fellowship.

Although the hope of recruiting men was his main reason for sailing to Jamaica in the first place, John also had an attraction for the area, for it was around those waters that he had spent his youth. He had fond memories of the island, and he thought about his family, wishing he could go home to a grand reunion, but he figured that his presence would never be welcomed. John put aside his sentimental yearnings and sailed for Hispaniola and landed on the shore of Haiti.

The island proved to be a more prosperous journey than Jamaica had been, as they were able to recruit three French men to come on board. The men had been scouted and approached while hunting hogs one evening. John's men also found cattle for which to butcher, and after salting the meat for preservation, they had an abundance of sustenance in which to nourish them. The Frenchmen were more than eager to join John's crew, as they were once sailors and missed the sea.

Not only was John limited by the lack of enthusiastic recruits that he could find, he had to be selective as to the character of the individual. In the days of Vane, men were taken as prisoners to work on board a ship and beaten into submission. However, John would not deal that way as he could not take the chance that some man being taken on board would rise up with resentment and threaten the safety of the women and Stephen.

The Frenchmen were endearing, and it was probably a subconscious allure, as their accents mimicked Pierre's.

After the Frenchmen boarded and were given their positions, John's crew plundered two sloops off the coast of Haiti. John and his men were pleased at the skill of the Frenchmen, and Daniel had also proved himself. Daniel was allowed to join in their plights after he had discovered a new talent besides his painting. His marksmanship was second to none. Adam and Mark donned men's clothing even in their weakened conditions and insisted, against John's will, on joining the pirating activities. John now had fourteen men in his crew.

John had discovered long ago that Anne Bonny was going to do whatever she wanted to do, and being that John was not the dominating type, he had learned to trust in her judgment. He knew that Anne had been correct almost every single time that she and John had been in serious conflict. It was Anne who unknowingly showed him the value of a woman's wisdom that empowered him and made him into a better man if he would humble himself to receive it. Mary, however, was simply a soldier, and she would never consent to be left out even with a child growing in her womb.

Even though they donned men's clothing when they pirated, the two women did appear differently than when they first sailed, as they no longer applied soot to their faces, and they allowed their locks to flow. Mary had not cut her hair since the day she accepted her position with Governor Rogers, and it was getting to a womanly length, but not nearly as long as Anne's. To look upon them, it was apparent that they were women in men's clothing, and John had actually found it to be a benefit, as the opposing side was often so distracted by the two ladies that it made it less difficult to suppress them. As far as Stephen joining the crew in pirating, he was strictly forbidden. Although it was disheartening to the little guy, he was gracious and submitted without an ill attitude.

After their plunders off the coast of Haiti, John and his crew returned to the coast of Jamaica, and for what reason, only God will ever know. It would turn out to be that foolish decision that would seal the fate of John Rackam and his crew of notorious pirates. Most likely, John was returning to Jamaica in hopes of reuniting with his comrades that he had crossed while they were out turtling. His decision was probably fueled by the hopes that some or all of the men had changed their minds and had decided to sail with him after all. If he could recruit the nine men, he would have twenty-four, and that was a decent number with which to sail. John would have fared better if he had turned his ship and headed to Bermuda, where the stormy seas had taken an abundance of sailor's lives, but not the entirety of them. However, all pirates who came near Jamaica were most certain to meet their doom.

Off the northern coast of Jamaica by Porto Maria Bay, John's black colors were hoisted in pursuit of a schooner captained by Thomas Spenlow. The seasoned veteran had in his company twenty men, but John's confidence was riding high by the addition of the Frenchmen who had shown even greater skill than previously detected. The schooner went to make its escape, but John's Spanish sloop was swift and closed the gap and entrapped it with its grappling hooks. The men expected a fight, as the victims had not set the white flag of surrender.

John surveyed the scene, and not one soul was on deck, so they expected a surprise attack of the twenty men, who had been spied through their telescope while they were gathering the information about their prey. Stephen was below deck, when the men were set in their positions. John's men took any solid object that they could find that presented no particular value to them and threw the objects onto Mr. Spenlow's deck, which sounded to the opposition as if the pirates had boarded. Suddenly, the men sprang forth from the hold armed with pistols and cutlass, and to their surprise, there was no one upon their deck. John stood behind the bulwark of his ship with some of his men crouched below. John firmly ordered for Spenlow's men to halt, but they disregarded him as they rushed in his direction, firing a barrage of bullets in their fury. John was grazed by a single shot as he went for cover with his men, and that is when Daniel, who had been placed in a sniper's spot, picked the men off one at a time as they rushed for John. James Dobbin, Noah Harwood, and John Davis stood behind Daniel replenishing shot and powder into each empty pistol that was handed to them, and they handed Daniel a loaded one every few seconds in order to create a rapid firing sequence. Spenlow's men were so confused by the hidden and armed aggressor that they retreated, leaving Spenlow alone on his deck taunting John, who showed no concern for the bullets as he had his eye on the prize.

"Looks like I shall be the man who shall take down the famous John Rackam."

John directed a stern order in Daniel's direction, "Do not fire upon him." John had not used Daniel's name in order keep him from being named by any potential witnesses.

Mr. Spenlow knew exactly who John was, as John was a well-publicized man on the loose, and the flag that John created had given him away on this particular occasion. He had brought the black flag from the *Anne Bonny* when they fled Cuba, and it was distinguishable from all other pirate flags. John's flag had two cutlasses crossed below the skull instead of the familiar long bones. Reports had gone abroad of the infamous flag, and ships everywhere searched in order just to catch a glimpse of it.

Mr. Spenlow drew his cutlass as a sign to challenge John to a match, but before John drew his, he spoke to the sea captain.

"First of all, I never duel unless I know the name of the man of whom I'm about to kill. Secondly, you don't have to do this, as you may escape unharmed if you surrender."

Mr. Spenlow spit, "I'll not tell you my name, and I will not surrender, because I want to reap judgment for the deaths of my honest men. But mostly, John Rackam, I want to be hailed as the man who butchers you."

John drew his cutlass and boarded Mr. Spenlow's ship. The men from both teams came forth and stood behind their captains in a show of support. Daniel remained alone in his concealed place with four loaded pistols ready to discharge at his captain's slightest command. John had fourteen men to Mr. Spenlow's fifteen, as Daniel had killed five of his men, so the playing field was equivalent, except for the fact that Mr. Spenlow was no match for John.

A vicious fight ensued between John and his opponent, as Mr. Spenlow was greedy for the win. His abilities were well above average with only one disadvantage. The man was older than John was, and his form was not nearly as honed as John's. Their cutlasses collided with brute force, and they continued for a good while, but it wasn't long before Mr. Spenlow was tiring, and that had been John's plan all along. He would exhaust the angry man and then let him choose his fate.

When Spenlow called for his first mate to intervene, George Fetherston stepped forward and fought the mate to keep him from advancing toward his captain. When that occurred, John knew he needed to complete his task rapidly, as he did not want to see the battle escalate to the point where all his men were fighting the opposing force, so he took Mr. Spenlow by surprise. John spun around and sent Mr. Spenlow's cutlass flying through the air with a sharp crack of his boot. George had already skewered his opponent, and Mr. Spenlow stood before John unarmed and seethed.

"You bloody cheat."

John replied, "Is it even possible to cheat when you are defending your life or the life of your crew? Now, mister whatever your name is, do you want to call it a day?"

Mr. Spenlow gave a shout for his men to retaliate, and not one stepped forward. In his rage, Mr. Spenlow reached behind his back for a pistol, and before he could even begin to aim it in John's direction, Daniel had emptied all four of his weapons into the irate captain, who sunk onto his deck, with his blood rushing from his body.

The ship was plundered and left at sea with the dead tending it, and the fourteen remaining men of Spenlow's crew were allowed to row to the shore of Jamaica. Upon their landing, they went directly to the authorities and told of their dealings with John Rackam. When he heard the news, Governor Lawes dispatched Captain Barnet and his troops to sail in the sloop that was designated for the sole purpose of apprehending John Rackam, the fiend that was now plaguing his island.

John left the area of Porto Maria Bay and sailed to Dry Harbor Bay, where he spotted John Eaton's ship. John fired his cannon high and into the air as a salute to his friends, and the men, being ashore, rushed to the water's edge holding up bottles of rum. They laughed with amusement by John's playful show of the pirate's honor on their behalf, and John motioned for them to come aboard. Without hesitation, they ran for their boat and rowed out to greet John and his crew. The nine men never considered that they would be charged, even if caught with John Rackam, because they were unarmed of pistols and cutlass.

The celebration was full of jolly merriment after John's buddies boarded the anchored, stolen Spanish sloop. John Eaton and his eight men supplied an overabundance of rum, and John supplied the tequila and salted meat that was grilled to perfection upon the galley fire. The men roared with laughter as they told their stories, enjoyed fine dining, drank the best liquor in the region, and smoked the Cuban cigars. They toasted to the Spanish while they lit their butts and took healthy gulps of the tequila. Best of all, they passed a pipe among themselves with the herb known for its quality of enhancing the effects of liquor. However, enhancement of their drunkenness was the last thing that they needed, and Anne reminded John of that often that night. It was common knowledge that the captain of a ship was never supposed to be inebriated. If a captain became impaired, he would not have the judgment to act appropriately in emergent situations; John just passed Anne off as being a bit of a nag, and he patted her on the rear and went back to his company.

While enjoying the men's companionship, John felt more liberated than he had since his days on Vane's ship. He realized that evening that the nine men as well as his men with whom he currently sailed were the reason he had remained so long with Vane. John had always harbored guilt and inwardly berated himself for remaining subordinate to a captain who had treated his victims so treacherously. That night, it was clear to him, as he dined with seventeen of the men whom he had overseen as quartermaster on Charles Vane's ship, that he had stayed because of his concern for them. John truly loved these men, and they loved him as well, for they had all voted him captain over Vane.

The night was actually a cathartic adventure, as John's conscience was cleared. The nine men had been given quarters, as John insisted that they should stay, for he didn't want them to capsize and drown while rowing ashore because of the influence of the strong drink. The party had lasted all night, and by early morning, the men were passed out below deck in a drunken stupor. Anne, Mary, and Stephen were the only ones awake when Captain Barnet rounded the corner of the island and unfurled the king's colors.

CHAPTER 22

PIERRE AWOKE THAT morning with an ominous feeling in his gut. He shared his thoughts with Benjamin who passed it off, blaming it on the wild mushrooms they had eaten the night before. Pierre feared something was not quite right with John, Anne, and Mary. He spoke a blessing over them and went to milk his cow.

If ever there was a time that they needed a blessing, it was now. Not only had Nicolas Lawes dispatched the sloop captained by Jonathan Barnet, but he had also sent two other sloops in their company. Fifty soldiers manned each ship. Upon seeing the armed forces, Anne and Mary ran below deck to arm themselves and wake the men. They had Stephen run to the powder room and prepare for a battle.

Anne slapped John in the face, but he only turned over and offered a groan.

"Wake up, goddamn it. British troops are upon us!"

But John was out, so Anne and Mary yelled and shook the other men in attempts that some would wake and help join them in the fight. A few of the men stirred, and it seemed like their pleas for help would not be heard. Anne and Mary ascended to the deck to see that two of the sloops were positioning to find their target. Mary, in a panic, fired her pistol down the stairwell to the hold, hoping the noise of gunfire would stir the men, but unfortunately, her bullet lodged in the first man who was responding to the alarm, one of the Frenchmen. He fell backward and bled to his death.

The sound of gunfire aroused the men and brought them to the deck where they viewed the horror surrounding them. Instantly, John was back in command. The only solution he could find was to move his target before they were set to fire. He did not have time to engage the sails, but the Spanish sloop could be rowed with the retractable ores with which it was equipped.

John remained composed and kept a clear mind. He ordered all men to the ores with the exception of Anne and Mary, and eighteen of the men rowed the ship with all the strength they could muster. The men rowing were John's eight men and Daniel as well as the nine men who had come aboard. John's only hope besides moving the target was the miracle of outrunning Barnet's rapidly approaching sloop.

Unbeknown to John, the Frenchmen hid in a cupboard as they had cowered. They had heard John tell the nine men who had come aboard, as well as Daniel, that if they were caught to lie boldfaced and tell the council that John Rackam had forced them to cooperate by using cruel tactics. John knew he himself was going to hang anyway, and he didn't care if the council thought he was a cruel man if it meant sparing his friends who never made an oath to sail as pirates.

Anne and Mary were instructed to remain on deck to survey the scene and keep them abreast of any valuable information. The women were to take cover if the troops began to fire. Although the women were armed with pistol and cutlass, John was firm in his orders that no cannons were to be discharged from his ship. John knew that if they did, it would most definitely provoke a gruesome onslaught. John chortled, "It would be like the little guy spitting in the face of a gladiator."

For the first time in John's life, he gave orders to hoist the white flag, but only if heavy artillery was engaged by the British troops. John knew that if they fired their twenty cannons that were positioning for their target, the ones he loved would face a horrible death of mutilation and be left mangled and strewn upon the waters of the harbor. However, if John Rackam surrendered, a fair amount of souls would have a chance to be saved. Stephen was placed in the captain's cabin and firmly admonished to remain. Then as John turned to leave, he looked back at the young man and told him, "Whatever happens, Stephen, just know that I love you."

While the British sloops were positioning, and as John was below deck, Anne disregarded her captain's orders and fired a cannon toward one of the ships. Thankfully, the target was missed, and the British were not in position to retaliate. John channeled his anger by grabbing an ore and assisting in the rowing of the ship, even though it offset the balance of the men.

John's plan of moving the target had been successful, and the two positioned sloops were left without a task. However, the men could not propel the ship fast enough to overcome Barnet's speed caused from the momentum of his approach, and John's ship was ensnared by the grappling hooks of the ship that represented a conjoined effort between the royal governors Woodes Rogers and Nicholas Lawes.

Anne and Mary poised themselves on the deck to combat as the troops prepared to board the ship.

John was firm. "Anne and Mary, drop your weapons!"

Mary dropped her cutlass and retrieved her pistol from her belt and let them both crash to the deck, but Anne spewed at John, "No! You arm yourself, you coward!"

John replied sternly, "Anne, look at their numbers. I would be a fool to pick up a cutlass right now. Now drop yours goddamn it!"

Anne disregarded John's command and remained armed as the men boarded the ship but soon released her weapons when she saw at least a dozen soldiers with loaded muskets take aim, as they had her in their sights. Anne was silent as they shackled her, and she refused to look John's way.

She harbored resentment for John, as he had not heeded her warning about the strong drink from the night before, and if he had, maybe this whole thing would not have occurred. The bitterness that flowed over from his binge caused her to criticize him in her heart. She viewed him as a coward for being drunk, but mostly for his unwillingness to take a stand against the opposition and fight. The two women on board were the only ones, and they had been more than willing to defend the ship even with their unborn children in their wombs. Anne purposed in her heart that she would never forgive John this time for how he had deserted her.

Captain Barnet had his men bind all the prisoners, including John and his original crew of eight men and the two women. They bound Daniel and John Eaton and the other eight men that had come aboard. After a thorough search of the ship, they discovered Stephen in the captain's cabin and the Frenchmen. They chose not to bind Stephen for his age, but he was shackled to an officer, so he couldn't escape. They almost chose not to bind the Frenchmen, as the Frenchmen insisted that they were no pirates but rather had been taken prisoner aboard the ship and had been forced into labor by the cruel tortures that were doled by the devices of John Rackam. Captain Barnet ordered the Frenchmen bound, after his officer had completed the search of the ship and found there was no cat-of-nine-tails aboard. John had dumped those devices into the sea when he had discovered them on the Spanish sloop. Captain Barnet decided to let the council be the judge as to if the Frenchmen had indeed partaken in any pirating, because he was not convinced.

To Captain Barnet's amazement, the prisoners were uncommonly polite and respectful of their authority. However, they truly appeared to be urchins upon the earth, as they were unmistakably unclean. The men, with their gnarled hair and swollen eyes, were barefooted and either shirtless or unbuttoned. The women, dressed in their men's clothing, had hair that fell in stringy strands, and their faces were scorched by the sun. Their bellies were swollen, which was presumed to be a sign of their malnutrition. But worse, they all had grime under their fingernails. Captain Barnet chose to focus on their good manners rather than their ill presentation, as he was a gracious man, and he never showed a sign of disgust toward his captives. That is why Governor Rogers had chosen Jonathan Barnet, as he knew of his character.

Woodes Rogers did not want the legend of John Rackam's last stand to be filled with the grisly accounts that were reported by Lieutenant Maynard as he boasted about his defeat of Blackbeard. Governor Rogers never revealed it to anyone and would have probably lied to refute it, but the governor actually had immense respect for John Rackam. He was relieved that Nicolas Lawes had refused to deport the last of the great pirates back to Providence, because Woodes Rogers knew deep in his heart that he could not hang John Rackam with a clear conscience. He honestly believed that John had not done anything worse than the royal governor had done during his lifetime. Woodes Rogers locked his chamber door and wept bitterly when he heard the news of John's capture. He sent out an urgent letter that day to Chancellor Cormac, and he ended his inscription with, "I'll meet you in Jamaica. Your comrade, Woodes Rogers."

Governor Rogers informed Pierre who tended his tavern that day with sadness, and then he knew that his unsettling wasn't simply due to mushrooms. As the day went on, Pierre was puzzled by the peculiar feeling of peacefulness that enveloped him, and he figured that it must be of truth, the passage in the Bible where it states that God is near to the brokenhearted, because his heart could not have been any more crushed. Pierre took a deep breath, and his tears fell with thankfulness that he had obtained the opportunity to know John Rackam, Anne Bonny, and Mary Reed, for they would always be considered as saints in his eyes.

The Spanish sloop was confiscated, and John and his crew were taken to Spanish Town, Jamaica, where they were imprisoned and left to wait. The Jamaican authority was in no hurry, as they needed time to gather their council and witnesses to make sure that they built a solid case against the notorious pirates.

The trial of John Rackam was anticipated to be the most substantial case ever tried in their courts. The people in the regions of the Caribbean, up through the Bahamas, and all the way up the coasts of the American colonies wanted to be present to observe Jamaican authority determine the fate of John Rackam and his crew. Word of the two female pirates on board heightened the people's curiosity to a near-frenzied level.

Although he too anticipated the trial, Nicolas Lawes was not distracted by the reports of public commotion. Knowing of John's history of miraculous escapes, he ordered John Rackam to be placed in constant chains with two guards securing his cell around the clock to make certain that he would have the opportunity to face off the pirate at the widely publicized trial.

Although Stephen had turned ten, he was still too young to be imprisoned. The officer to whom Stephen had been chained was commissioned to find a suitable place for the boy, but all his attempts had been fraught with difficulty. The officer cursed Captain Barnet under his breath for his assignment, as he knew that no decent family would want a filthy pirate child in their home. The orphanages of Jamaica were overwhelmed already, and attempts to place him were presenting a menace, and just when the officer's nerves were already spent, the boy started wailing for his father. When the words finally registered to the officer as to what the boy was actually saying, the officer immediately perked up and exclaimed, "Halt right there! Who is your father that I might go and find him?"

Stephen looked him in the eye and said, "My father is John Rackam." Stephen's pride showed through his tears.

The officer thought to himself, "Oh god, that's no solution to my problem."

Stephen grinned. "He's the best father in the whole world."

The officer murmured, "Oh, is he?"

Stephen offered a hearty nod, and the officer wondered how a pirate could possibly be a good father, but he passed it off as the little guy was only a child and didn't know any better. However, his conversation with the child was the impetus to offer a solution to his problem, as the officer allowed Stephen to reside in the cell with John Rackam. The officer boldly told his superiors that there were no other options available, and he couldn't turn the little guy out onto the streets. The officer hadn't truly exhausted all his options, as there were plenty more orphanages in Jamaica with which he could have inquired. Everyone was puzzled at the revelation of John's child, because not one soul knew that John had fathered anyone of that age. They figured that John must have picked him up from one of his delilahs along the way.

Anne and Mary, being women, were allowed to share a cell. They were placed in the dungeon, because it was the only isolated cell away from the men. It was damp and dimly lit, and the two women spent most of their time sleeping. Every time that Anne would wake, she hoped that it had all been a bad dream, but unfortunately it hadn't been. Mary would just wake and remain silent, and then she would hold her ears to block the sounds of torture that were being doled to the hardest of criminals. Anne didn't hold her ears, as she had been desensitized by the same sounds she had heard growing up—the similar groaning of the slaves as they were being beaten into submission by the devices of an evil overseer. The women weren't getting along so well in their tiny prison cell.

Mary rebuked Anne, "How can you sit there and listen to the horror of that?"

Anne was cold. "I don't know, I guess I'm just used to it. Why are you being so precocious?"

Mary asked, "Anne Bonny, are you really that hard-hearted?"

Anne was snide. "No, there's just nothing I can do about it, so I just ignore it."

Mary chided, "Well, I'll do something about it."

Mary started yelling and commanding for the noise to stop. Her voice echoed through the hallow walls of the dungeon. The guard standing by their cell turned to hush her, while Anne watched rather impassively. Mary sobbed as she asked the guard kindly to please make it stop, as she could not stand to hear one more sound of torture. Afterward, the dungeon was eerily silent. Anne and Mary lay there on their bunks, attempting to return to their sleep, and finally they drifted off. Thankfully for Mary, the governor consented to allow a stay on the doling of torture until after Anne Bonny and Mary Reed were hung.

When the women woke, Anne was still in a foul mood, and Mary reproved her, "What is your problem?"

Anne spewed her bitterness as she yelled. "I'll tell you what my fucking problem is, Mary, it's goddamned John Rackam. If he had fought like a man, he wouldn't be hanged like a dog!" The words echoed from the harrowed walls of the cold dungeon.

Anne began to weep for the first time since they were imprisoned, and she couldn't stop. Mary held her close like Anne had done for her the day that Anne discovered Mary's gender. Mary never defended John's choice to submit to the authorities, as she figured that Anne would come to the realization on her own over time. Anne just needed time to reflect, and she had all the time she needed in that tiny cell until the day of the trial, when they would most certainly be sentenced to hang.

Mary had heard the stories from the fishermen, and she wondered if they would have the courage to hang her dead body in the town square to make an example to any other women who may be inclined to go pirating. She hoped that if they did hang her out, they would at least keep her clothed.

After Anne's release of emotion, she was her old self again, and for that, Mary was thankful. The cell was much too small to be trapped with a contentious woman. The guard, who had overheard Anne's tirade, took those words of Anne back to the governor, and they would go down in history to support the view that Anne Bonny had never regarded John Rackam, but was rather was a hard-hearted woman who only used a man for what benefit he could provide to meet her selfish desires. That notion would form a picture in the minds of people as to the kind of woman Anne Bonny truly was, as her legend was set, branding her as a coldhearted and promiscuous woman with a vicious and vindictive temper.

As Anne lay in her bunk, she wept into her blanket for the guilt of her last words to John as she had called him a coward. She knew he wasn't a coward and that he was sorely outnumbered and would've even looked foolish for trying to fight. Anne also knew that she had a horrible temper, and she hated herself for it, but when she got angry, her words would fly out of her mouth like daggers toward her victim, and she truly had no control over it. And now because of her asinine mouth, the man that she was certain was her true love was going to die with her treacherous words echoing in his ears. She only had one wish. She wanted to be able to tell him that she was sorry before they were hung, so Anne asked the guard if he could allow her to speak to John Rackam one last time before the trial.

The guard laughed and replied, "Not unless you want me to be hung right along with you." He mocked out the scene, "I can see it now. Oh, I'm sorry, Governor, I didn't think you would mind that I released the prisoner, so she could talk to her adulterous lover one last time." He looked at her sternly. "Now be quiet and go back to sleep!"

Anne mumbled under breath as she turned over. "Cheeky old fuck." Anne and Mary giggled and then finally resolved to sleep once again.

John and Stephen had a grand old time in the cell, and the boy would have been content to stay there forever. Governor Nicholas Lawes was sorely displeased at the officer's choice of placement, but he had more pressing issues, so he let it be.

John was truly not afraid of dying. He knew it was a choice that he had made, and his conscience was clear in that he had made sure that everyone on board had honestly made the same vow to piracy for themselves. He told Stephen not to worry. Death was not necessarily a sad time. It was only a different time. He told Stephen that anyone could take your life from you, but they couldn't take your memories, and John asked Stephen, "And didn't we make some good memories on the ship while you were with us?"

Stephen grinned as large as ever before.

"Yes, those are my best days!"

John agreed, "That's right. You see? Those are your memories forever, and when I'm gone, you can think about those anytime you like, and I'll be right there with you."

John's words comforted him some, but then he asked, "But won't it hurt when they hang you?"

John was certain. "No, I won't feel a thing. I'll just think of you, and I'll be fine."

Stephen added, "Or you could think of Stephen in the Bible, 'cuz he didn't feel a thing when he was stoned."

John lit up. "That's right, a very good idea."

Stephen was proud for his contribution to the dilemma, and he hugged John Rackam, and John didn't think the boy would ever let go, and then John said.

"Stephen, I'm really sorry that I wasn't an honest man for you."

Stephen defended, "But you were."

John replied, "No, Stephen, I was a thief. I started when I was a younger man, and when I knew better, I didn't stop. I justified my sin by figuring that I was only stealing from someone who had stolen the goods from someone else, but that didn't make it right. My prayer for you is that you'll grow to be an honest man."

Stephen's countenance faded. "But, Father, if you had not been a pirate, you would have never found me."

John was rendered speechless, and Stephen held his chained father for a very long while. Afterward, Stephen lay down and slept, but John had no desire, for he wanted to be alone with his thoughts.

He hoped that Anne was faring well. He wished he could talk to her one last time before he hung, but he knew that would never be possible. He chuckled to himself at the scene that Anne had caused during their capture. John knew Anne too well to know that her mouth and her heart were in two completely different places, and he hoped she would not feel guilt for calling him a coward. John was thankful that he had bridled his tongue and that he had not called her what he had wanted to in the heat of their final confrontation, because if he had, he knew that Anne would have been livid.

John's men were all handling their situation with honor, and Daniel was a brave man. He thought of Mary and what an extraordinary lady she truly was. He was thankful for the short while that they had spent together, as they had found an uncommon love. He pondered in his heart if he could actually lie to the council and say that he had not been a pirate when he had indeed killed six men. John Rackam had ordered him to deny piracy, but even if he conceded to John's command, Daniel would absolutely refuse to say that John excised cruelty upon him, as John was the gentlest man that Daniel had ever met. Daniel relished his time on John's ship and had not a single regret, so if it meant hanging, then so be it. He felt certain that Mary would be all right, as his father was a lawyer, and Daniel knew that English common law would not allow a woman to be put to death when she was with child, but he wondered if Mary knew it.

CHAPTER 23

SARAH LAWES LOWERED herself to descend into the dungeon. In her wildest dreams, she would have never consented to such a vile place, but she wanted to make sure it was the actual woman who had caused her such grief. As she peered through the bars at Anne, Sarah wasn't quite sure if it was really her. The young woman who had once appeared as a royal debutante in her crimson gown was unrecognizable due to her filth and wretched condition. Sarah inquired, "Are you Anne Bonny?"

Anne gazed at Sarah's face and humbly replied, "I am, and I'm sorry."

Sarah's jaw was ajar, and her breath was robbed. She froze and could barely turn to leave, as she was sure that she was going to vomit for the stench of the dungeon and the scene set before her eyes. Sarah didn't understand what had happened to her during her brief encounter with Anne Bonny, but she was freed from the contempt in her heart for the woman who had retaliated against her for her wrongful judgments that night at the royal ball, and she was resigned to never think or speak about it again.

Woodes Rogers made it to Jamaica long before the chancellor, as it was of far less distance from the Bahamas than from South Carolina. After a victorious reunion with the Royal Governor Nicolas Lawes, Woodes Rogers went to the prison to see his captives, John Rackam, Anne Bonny, and Mary Reed.

Woodes Rogers found John with his head lowered in slumber and tightly shackled. He dismissed the guards so he could speak to John in private. As he scanned the tiny cell, the governor could see the boy sleeping upon the bunk.

Woodes Rogers reached through the bars and gently shook John awake. To John's amazement, he turned to see the familiar face of the man for whom John had immense respect.

John smiled. "Governor Woodes Rogers, what a pleasure."

Rogers replied, "No, the pleasure's all mine." John could see the fondness in his eyes. The governor turned to make sure that the guards were out of earshot.

John offered, "Governor, I apologize for letting you down."

Rogers replied, "No, John, I let you down. If I had been wiser and sent you out against the Spanish, you wouldn't be here right now."

John chortled, "Don't be so hard on yourself. Knowing my history, I would have sailed as a pirate in your man-of-war."

The men chuckled, and Rogers added, "Hey, but it would have made a grand story for the records, wouldn't it though?"

John's smile was wry, and Woodes Rogers added, "I wish I would have been able to spend more time around you, John Rackam, as maybe some of your bravery would have rubbed off on me."

John questioned, "Is that what I should call it, bravery—or damned foolishness?"

Rogers gazed at the subdued man and said, "John Rackam, I have utmost regard for you, and my only prayer is that you don't allow these proud people to make you falter. I know you're gonna walk to the gallows like you don't even care, because that's how brave you are, but I just want you to know that if I had any power at all, you would be walking a free man instead."

John reveled. "Governor, I'm honored by your presence."

Governor Rogers gazed at the humble man, knowing the governor wasn't worthy of such compliment, and he offered. "Would you like to see Anne one last time?"

John's face melted with sweet relief. "That would be more than which I could ever hope, and maybe you could set her straight, Governor, as her last word to me was coward." John chuckled under his breath.

Rogers was amused. "I don't think anyone could ever set that girl straight. Oh, and by the way, her father and I plan to petition Governor Lawes to release her into her father's custody. It will be a long shot, but certainly worth a try."

John added, "Governor, the very thought of it sets my mind at ease. Oh, and tell the guards to be careful with her, as she's with child, and so is Mary."

The governor was enlightened. "Well then, there you have it, they can't hang them because of English common law. It is strictly forbidden to impose the death of a woman with child."

John pondered on his words as the governor looked over at Stephen. "What should we do with the boy?"

John replied, "Maybe he could go with Anne."

Woodes Rogers mused, "We'll have to see what Chancellor Cormac has to say about it all."

John had heard so many stories about Anne's father, and he was certain that a man as brilliant as Chancellor Cormac would certainly take the boy and raise him as the son he never had.

The governor addressed the guards, "Now attend to your duties and make sure he doesn't escape, as he has been well known for it." John reveled as Woodes Rogers walked away, and he was thankful that he had gotten to make his peace with the royal governor before he was hanged.

Governor Rogers descended the stairs into the dungeon, and he thought, "How gracious of Nicolas Lawes to put the ladies in the most despicable place that the prison has to offer." After he had excused the guard, Woodes Rogers stood before Anne and Mary's cell, and sorrow filled his heart at the sight of the pitiful creatures. The women's greetings of Woodes Rogers were not as welcoming as John's had been, for the two could not look him in the eye for their shame.

Rogers replied, "Mark, how could I have missed that you were truly a woman." He smiled at her.

Mary blushed and then replied with a bow of her head, "Royal Governor, it's good to be in your presence."

He replied, "Governor Lawes tells me that your name is Mary."

Mary replied, "Yes, sir, it is."

He interjected, "I'll be back to talk with you, Mary. I just need to take Anne for a moment."

The governor marched Anne past the guard, and Woodes Rogers sneered to him, "I want her to see the torment of her adulterous lover."

He whispered to Anne, "Don't worry it's just a front. John wants to see you."

The governor stood away and kept guard as Anne stroked John's face through the steel bars. Anne spoke gently, "I can't believe that Stephen got to stay with you. That's wonderful. And can you believe that we got to see each other one last time, before . . ." Anne started to tear and couldn't say it.

John comforted, "Before I hang?"

Anne corrected, "No, before we hang."

John corrected her and let her know about the governor and her father's plan. Anne interrupted, "Oh my god, my father's coming?"

John chuckled at her response. "You don't think a good father would ever miss the hanging of his daughter, do you?" John chortled, and Anne reproved, "John, this is no time to be waggish, now stop."

John humbled. "All right, but listen to me."

He informed her of the plan of Governor Rogers and the chancellor to secure her freedom by pleading her belly and then to take her, and perhaps Stephen, home to South Carolina.

Anne was incensed. "And what if I don't want to go back to South Carolina?"

John sharply reproved, "Goddamn it, Anne Bonny, will you ever learn to purse your lips and just do what you know you need to do? You are the most stubborn woman I have ever met, and that is probably why," he huffed, "I have been so completely taken with you."

Anne looked down and began to weep.

"I don't want to leave you, John Rackam. And I'm so sorry for calling you a coward, because to me you're larger than life, and I don't know how I'm ever going to live without you." She concealed her face in her hands.

John was sure. "Anne Bonny, you're gonna be strong, and you're gonna do it. And every time you look into the eyes of our child, you're gonna see me. So dry your eyes and just be thankful. Anne, be thankful that we were able to find a rare occasion together in a world that's so fucked and brimming with heartless people."

It took all the strength she had, but Anne Bonny arose, as she knew the governor was starting to fidget. She gazed into the beautiful face of the man she worshipped, and she whispered, "Just think of Stephen when you . . ." She pursed her lips, as she couldn't finish her words for the agony of the thought, and she turned and bravely allowed Governor Rogers to escort her back to her cell.

John had made his peace, and he had found serenity in the presence of the only woman he had ever loved. He was thankful that the governor had allowed him to see his Anne one last time and gave him hope for Anne and Stephen's refuge with her father. He wished he could have said goodbye to Mary, but he knew that it wasn't necessary, as he could sense Mary's presence with her unending loyalty and admiration of her captain. He hoped Mary would plead her belly, but he was not convinced that she would. He relished the thoughts of the fellowship that he and his men had shared the night before their capture, and John returned his head to the bowed position in which Woodes Rogers had found him, sitting in his chains. He drifted off into peaceful slumber, being thankful and fully prepared for his walk to the gallows.

Anne went directly to her bunk, as the numbness from her emotional exhaustion had overtaken her. Mary gazed at Woodes Rogers through the bars as the governor addressed her. "I have good news for you, Mary. Your life will be spared if you plead your belly."

Mary dropped her head and replied, "I don't know if I will."

Governor Rogers fought bewilderment. "Why would you choose to die, Mary?"

Mary remained silent.

The governor gazed at the woman in disbelief and finally pleaded with her, "Mary please, you have to help me to understand your ill reasoning."

She finally conceded, "Governor, I am proud to say that I am a pirate, and I do not fear the gallows."

Their eyes locked, and Mary, filled with honor, continued, "For if it had not been for the threat of the noose, every dastardly rogue, who is now cheating the widows and orphans and oppressing their poor neighbors who have no money to obtain justice, would then rob at sea. And the ocean would be crowded with rogues, like the land, and no merchant would even dare to venture out, so the trade, in only a short while, would not even be worth following. Governor, I knew when I sailed with John Rackam that this day would eventually come, and I am fully prepared. And now you want me to watch John Rackam hang, while I go free just because English common law dictates that I don't obtain the same justice because I have a child in my womb? I think its rubbish."

Governor Rogers commended, "Mary, I understand your reasoning, but my prayer for you is that you won't let your bravery compromise the unborn child in your womb, and you will plead your belly. Think about your child, Mary." He reveled in the respect he held for her, and he whispered, "I must go now but just know that whatever you decide, I will uphold you, and I will be there for you at the trial."

Mary watched as the governor walked away, disappearing into the shadowy stairwell leading up and out of the dungeon. The governor was torn in his heart at Mary's words, as he realized that Mary would be loathed by the council for her views and would be sentenced by men who revered the vile members and all their twisted deeds of the ones of whom she spoke. Woodes Rogers marveled, as he considered Mary to be the noblest woman that he had ever encountered. He felt sure that he and the chancellor would be able to stay the executions of the two women, but he wondered if Mary would consent. He surfaced out of the dungeon a humble man and went to join Governor Lawes in preparing for the trial.

The doctor arrived early in the morning to assess the women. He gave each one a firepot with directions to fill the containers with their individual urines. Anne was more than willing, but Mary resisted, being resentful of the violation. However, she finally cooperated after Anne firmly shamed her for her selfishness. Anne had perceived the reason for the doctor's visit, and she reminded Mary that it was not only Mary's child that resided in her womb but Daniel's as well.

One at a time, the doctor saturated a ribbon in the pot and held a fire to its end. The flame crackled because of the wetness of the strand, and the doctor inhaled the vapors that were produced. Anne and Mary watched in silence at the peculiar scene. If the ribbon emitted a sweet aroma, the doctor would know that the woman had a wandering womb. He left the cell without ever saying a word, and he reported to Governor Lawes that the two women were indeed with child.

It appeared as though the chancellor would be prevented from attending the trial of his daughter, as the weather in South Carolina had been sinister. The hurricane was about to make landfall, and the captain of his ship had firmly insisted upon remaining until the storm subsided. Yet the Chancellor demanded that they sail despite the captain's better judgment of knowing that the swells of the water were much too great and that they thrashed the ship in rapid succession. After a harrowing entrance into the sea, the captain was relieved that the chancellor's foolish casting of lots with their lives had landed in their favor, as the great tempest eased once they had journeyed further south.

Pierre had dozens of excuses for not sailing to Jamaica as Benjamin pleaded. Pierre knew that he would be destroyed if he saw his friends, not only chained but also marched to the gallows. Pierre was adamant, and even got violently angry at Benjamin's urgings. After that, Benjamin resolved that he would make the trip alone, as he wouldn't miss it at any price. Benjamin had kept record in his journal of the accounts of the pirates of Nassau of which he had heard and had sometimes witnessed himself. He wanted to be present at the trial to not only show his support for Pierre's friends but to record the final chapter of the last great pirate from Providence, so he boarded a ship en route to Jamaica.

John's men were all standing sturdy with their positions and the determination that would be dealt by the council, but the nine men who boarded the ship to be in the presence of John Rackam one last time were not faring as well. John Eaton suppressed his tears, but his heart was ripped in two at the thought of his wife and two children suffering on his account.

He sorely hoped that the council would be wise and discern that they were no pirates, for if they had been, they would have come aboard armed and ready to defend their positions. He comforted the other eight men with his words for which he hoped, but inwardly, he knew the council and their insane hatred of the mention of the very word *pirate*. John Eaton knew deep in his heart that they would probably be found guilty by association, and he whispered a prayer for his family.

The Frenchmen conspired in their own tongue together, and they were determined at all cost to escape the noose and walk as free men, despite their willingness from the start to conjoin with John Rackam. They were firmly set to lie boldly in the face of the council, and they recited their twisted script to make certain that their stories would be identical, for they knew that out of the mouth of two or more witnesses, all truth was established according to English common law.

As by miraculous intervention, the chancellor arrived the day of the trial, but he chose not to visit his daughter after Woodes Rogers had warned him that her condition would overwhelm his emotions. Governor Rogers needed the chancellor to retain his strength, as he knew that they were in for a grand battle to even suggest the favor from His Honor, Sir Nicholas Lawes, as there was nothing in the universe that the royal governor of Jamaica loathed as much as a pirate. Governor Rogers knew that the chancellor would possess the wisdom to conduct the rest, as the chancellor was unmatched in his abilities as a lawyer, and his reputation was supreme to all the statesmen of Jamaica. Governor Rogers chose to take a subordinate role, as he didn't want his involvement to sour the plan, for he knew how he was perceived in the eyes of Nicholas Lawes.

The witnesses had been procured, and the harbors were filled with moored ships of the guests who poured onto the island of Jamaica. The commerce of the English royal colony had never seen such a rise, as the gold and silver rained upon its merchants. It appeared to the patrons of Jamaica that God was truly smiling upon them, that justice would be served at the hanging of the notorious pirate and for the wealth that the event had generated on their behalf. They rejoiced, as it was a very good day to all.

Benjamin had also arrived the day of the trial, and he had gotten the epiphany on his journey from Providence to format the stories that he had gathered and was about to gather into publishable material. He was deeply inspired, as he planned to set out a book about the great pirates, and he would use the pen name of Captain Charles Johnson. He hoped Pierre would share in his vision, but he feared that Pierre would contend, because Benjamin would have to feed the public's insatiable hunger to gnash their teeth at the promiscuous woman Anne Bonny, for it was she who obsessed the people to such a degree that they were practically foaming at the mouth.

CHAPTER 24

T HE COURTROOM WAS set in array and more grand than the chancellor could ever imagine. Inwardly he shuttered at the immoveable persona of the Royal Governor Nicholas Lawes in his long powdered wig and pure black robe made from the finest silk that the Orient could provide. His Majesty was seated in the center and at the highest position behind his grand rostrum and his council, consisting of the noblest commissioners of Jamaica, aligned his sides. They presented a supreme force for which to be reckoned.

The audience had been carefully screened and represented only those who had firsthand accounts of the pirates, as they would be utilized as witnesses if deemed necessary. Thankfully, Benjamin fit the criteria. He was readily welcomed to take part after he informed them that as a British soldier, he had witnessed the escape of John Rackam from the harbor of Andros the day Woodes Rogers had dispatched the sloop to which he was commissioned. Hosea Tisdell, the Jamaican tavern keeper was also allowed, as he had witnessed the killing of his captain, David Plant, at the hand of John Rackam. The only other exceptions in the courtroom room were Governor Rogers and the chancellor, who sat near the back in a discrete location.

The prisoners were not allowed to bathe or don fresh clothing the day of the trial. They were to be presented in their shameful conditions, as to not sway the opinion of their judges by more tamed appearances.

The men were to be tried first, and the women were to be held for the widely anticipated grand finale.

It was clear cut to the council by the reports of many witnesses that John Rackam and his eight men were guilty of piracy, none of whom disputed the accusations but rather confirmed their verdict by speaking nothing but dedication to piracy. The council was infuriated by John's men who were unmovable and spoke words of honor toward their captain, which caused the council to writhe in their seats. Nicolas Lawes gloated inwardly when the sentence of death was handed down, which would forever choke the breath that propelled their vile speech filled with devotion to sail as pirates and to their absurd allegiance to the contemptible John Rackam.

The judgment was set for John Rackam, George Fetherston, Richard Corner, John Davis, and John Howell to be executed at Gallows Point in Port Royal the very next day. Patrick Carty, Thomas Earl, James Dobbin, and Noah Harwood would be transferred to Kingston and executed the day after.

John Eaton and his eight men all testified the words that John Rackam had ordered them to proclaim, and they did so boldfaced in front of the council. They each told the judges that John Rackam had forced them to row the ship through the doling of cruel tactics and they were merely victims of the pirate. However, they faltered in their testimony, as they didn't quite know how to give answer to the council as to why they were on the ship in the first place. Nevertheless, the council had a difficult time with their deliberation, as there were no witnesses. They hoped the testimony of the Frenchmen would help shed some light, and it most certainly did.

Just when John Eaton had a glimmer of hope for their redemption, what he had gravely feared was handed down, and the council found the nine men who had come aboard to honor John Rackam also guilty of piracy and sentenced them to the gallows. The two Frenchmen had lied to divert attention away from them and toward the direction of the nine men. The Frenchmen told the council that the men were heavily armed and had made a pact with John Rackam the night before their capture, and the report of the show of cannon that John Rackam fired as a salute to the fellow pirates sealed the men's fate.

The Frenchmen were shown much appreciation for their testimonies, and the council found it an honor to proclaim them as innocent of all piratical activity. In addition, the council bestowed a great deal of sympathy toward the Frenchmen for enduring their supposed torturous journey as captives of the vile John Rackam, and they were freed even before the women were tried. However, they were required to remain as firsthand witnesses, if needed, to testify as to the character traits of Anne Bonny and Mary Reed in order to solidify the case.

Daniel's father was a well-known attorney in Jamaica with a good reputation, and Daniel was released from prison before the trial was ever held. It was his father's convincing story of Daniel's capture by John Rackam that swayed the royal governor to release the young man. Whether or not a cruel mean was exacted was never even asked, and for that, Daniel was grateful. Daniel was commissioned to be present at the trial if additional witnesses were necessary in order to ensure that a verdict of guilt was handed down for all the pirates involved. He was never asked to testify, and it was all he could do to keep his composure during the proceedings, especially when it came to Mary.

Stephen was not allowed into the court room and had been turned over to the officer to whom he was first chained. Upon hearing about his commission, the officer was disconcerted and murmured to himself, "Oh god, not again." Stephen gave the officer an awful chase as the child could tell that the man was insincere in his dealings with the little guy. It was a very bad day for the officer.

Mary Reed was awoken, chained, and marched to the courtroom by two guards. She stood in the presence of Nicholas Lawes, and he gazed upon her for some time in silent contemplation. Mary kept her eyes cast to the ground out of respect for His Majesty. Finally, the silence was broken by the royal governor. "Are you Mary Reed?"

Mary was humbled. "Yea, my lord."

Governor Lawes continued, "Do you know what charges have been brought against you?"

Mary replied, "Yea, my lord. I am a pirate."

Governor Lawes was rendered speechless as he peered at the brazen woman, but then addressed the obvious.

"Mary Reed, where is your husband, being that you are with child and no marriage decree may be found on the records?"

Mary was bold. "I have no marriage decree, and I will not name my husband."

Governor Lawes was firm. "How do you say that you have a husband with no marriage decree?"

Mary looked him in the eye and proclaimed, "Because my husband and I made our vows before a higher judge than an English court, and our judge does not issue a piece of paper in order to validate our marriage."

The commissioners writhed in their seats and Governor Lawes spewed,

"There is no higher judge than this English court, Mary Reed, and you are not only a fornicator, but you are also in danger of blasphemy!" Nicolas Lawes gloated in the power that he held over the young woman as he stared her down.

"Mary Reed, although I would delight in it, I cannot sentence you to death because of the child that resides in your womb, but I have the mind to let you rot in my prison until your child is born. And then you too will walk to the gallows."

Daniel's heart was breaking at the words of the judgment spoken toward his wife, and it took all his strength to keep his composure and not rush to her side, but he realized the futility of such. Mary bowed her head and closed her eyes. In her solitude, she could feel Daniel's presence in the courtroom, and she began to weep. Because of her fervent love for Daniel, she humbled and pleaded with the governor. "My lord, I ask your mercy on behalf of the child's father. He is no pirate, as he is an honest man. I vow that if you will relent on your judgment, I will obtain a marriage decree, so I am considered no fornicator, and I will live an honest life for the rest of my days. I swear to you." She could not see the governor for the tears that clouded her eyes. "My lord, I never knew a father, and it is my earnest desire that my child will have a mother as well as a father." Mary wept openly and crumbled to the floor in her weakened state.

The governor softened a bit at Mary's humble plea. "Mary Reed, you will be returned to your cell, and I will weigh your case, but let's not forget why you're here in the first place. It's not to try you for your fornication—you have been found guilty of piracy, which holds the penalty of death." The governor addressed the guards to remove her from the courtroom and called for his last defendant, which was Anne Bonny.

Anne was brought in her chains into the courtroom by the soldiers, and her father almost gasped audibly at the sight of his daughter. It had been four years since she had eloped with James Bonny, and he had to strain in order to connect the vision of the pitiful being to his recollection of his Anne. After studying the young woman for some time, he began to notice familiar features. Her current state reminded him of the time when Anne, in her younger years, had refused to groom for a lengthy period simply out of protest, but he couldn't remember the particulars about what she was protesting during that precise occasion. He relished the memory of his strong-willed child, while the glimmer of tears filled his eyes.

Anne stood before the Royal Governor Lawes and cast her eyes downward in her humility. She knew her father was present in the room, and she loathed herself for the embarrassment that she had caused him. The governor addressed the woman accused of piracy.

"Are you Anne Bonny?"

Anne looked him in the eye. "Yes, my lord."

The governor continued, "Do you know why you are here today?"

Anne replied, "Yes, my lord, I am being tried as a pirate."

The governor asked, "What do you have to say in your defense?"

Anne answered, "I have no defense, as I truly sailed as a pirate under the command of—" Anne began to break and couldn't utter the words for her anguish.

The governor asked, "Under the command of whom, Anne Bonny?"

Anne's breath was seized, but she managed to whisper the words, "John Rackam."

Governor Lawes inquired, "Why do you weep at those words, Anne Bonny? Was it not you who shouted that if John Rackam had fought like a man, he would not be hanged like a dog? That leads me to believe that you had no regard for the man you call your captain."

Anne tried to suppress her tears and replied, "I was angry, and I regret those words, because I have the utmost respect for John Rackam."

The governor was exhausted. "Why do you people have such loyalty to a thief and a murderer? Name one honorable thing that John Rackam has ever done."

Anne was bold. "John Rackam rescued a boy from the vile affections of a perverse man who used the child for his fiendish delights, my lord. I believe that is most honorable."

Governor Lawes asked, "Do you have any witnesses to back your story?"

Hosea Tisdell arose and stated that he could validate the story, and he proceeded to tell the governor the details of the entire event. Afterward, the governor was subdued but chose to focus on the righteous victims that had lost their possessions and some their lives by the hand of John Rackam. The governor was determined not to be swayed into thinking that John Rackam was some type of a hero.

Governor Lawes continued, "Anne Bonny, I find you guilty in that you have uncontestably admitted to being a pirate. However, I cannot sentence you to death because of the child in your womb, and I assume the father of the child to be John Rackam. Am I correct?"

Anne answered, "Yes, my lord."

The governor let out a sigh. "You will be sent back to prison until I can deliberate your judgment, but one thing is for certain. You will be present and you will watch John Rackam hang from Gallows Point tomorrow morning."

Anne fell to her knees and sobbed violently at the cruelty of such a punishment. For the first time, Anne wished that she was not with child, so she could be hung with John, for the misery that swelled inside of her was far too great for her to bear, and she hoped that her broken heart alone would take her life. As Anne crumbled to the floor, the royal governor ordered the guards to remove her back to her cell, and the trial of the last notorious pirate that sailed from Providence was now over.

After the trial, Daniel went to his father's home and was welcomed with loving arms by his family. He planned to remain in Jamaica until Mary gave birth, with hopes that his father could intervene on her behalf and then perhaps the young family could return to Cayman Brac to live an honest life, as he and Mary had dreamed. While he was with his father, he assisted in the law practice to earn his way. In the evenings, he spent his time painting, and his artistry was far greater than it had ever been before he sailed with John Rackam. He told his father all about their adventures, as his father had an empathetic ear and took pride in the bravery of his son.

Governor Rogers and the chancellor left the courtroom and went directly to the officer who was commissioned to watch over Stephen. They found them at the water's edge, as the officer had discovered that on the beach was the only place that the boy would behave. Stephen had befriended other children, and they ran through the sand playing pirates, using cane poles as their rapiers. Governor Rogers and the chancellor relieved the officer of his duty for which he was grateful, and the two men kept Stephen in their company. Stephen looked up at the governor and the chancellor with pride as if they were gods of sorts, and there was never a more well-mannered child.

That evening, they went to the home of Governor Lawes, as they had been invited as guests during their stay in Jamaica. The Negro house servants bathed Stephen and dressed him in fresh clothing. The shirt and pants were a perfect fit, because Nicholas Lawes had a son who was also ten years old. Stephen had never worn such grand clothing in his life, and he took pride in that he appeared as the perfect gentleman.

After dinner, the three men sipped their brandy and puffed their cigars as they discussed the details of the trial. It must have been Anne's story of the rescue of Stephen that touched the governor's heart, because he was a humble man to such a degree that Woodes Rogers had never encountered. The royal governor agreed that Anne had probably learned her lesson in following strong men like John Rackam, who would lead her down a wrong path. However, he would not relent upon her witnessing the execution of her captain, as that would make certain that she would never go down that path again. The royal governor consented to allow the chancellor to take Anne home to South Carolina, and the governor would make sure that all records of her exit from the prison were never recorded.

Nicholas Lawes was pleased to hear that the chancellor would also take Stephen into his home and raise him with the dignity that the boy deserved, for it was the one soft spot in the royal governor's heart. He loved his own son fervently, and he held the solid belief that whoever would harm a child, it would be better that a millstone be tried around his neck and that he be dumped into the depths of the sea rather than to meet the wrath that the royal governor would dole on the vile subject's behalf.

Anne and Mary found refuge in their sleep that night in their prison cell. Although she didn't believe that she could bear the pain of her judgment, Anne found a strength that she never could have imagined. Anne was truly a courageous woman who had not one regret for her journey to Providence and the discovery of her true love in John Rackam. He was forever knitted into the fabric of her heart, and she would cherish the memories of him forever.

She arose the next morning, being thankful that John had left a part of himself with her in the child that resided in her womb. She hugged Mary and didn't want to ever let go, as she figured that it might be the last time that she would ever see her dear friend.

It was on November 17, 1720, that the Royal Governor Nicholas Lawes had turned John Rackam and his men over to the executioners to accomplish their job. Anne watched as John walked to the gallows as if he humbly welcomed the occasion. She was never more proud of anyone, for she knew that John was a rarity upon the earth, in which it was not even worthy of his presence. Anne reveled in the thoughts of the unmatched qualities of John and her unending love for him. No one could ever take his place in her heart—the man who was truly a gentle man and had opened his heart to her without reservation.

Through her silent tears, Anne watched as the hood covered his regal face and the noose was applied. She so badly wanted to run to his side, but for the first time in her life, Anne realized that she was completely powerless. Governor Lawes had accomplished his mission. The brazen spirit of Anne Bonny had been broken, like a wild mustang yielding to the authority of its trainer.

When the pedestal was released, John's body relaxed as if his death had occurred in an instant. A rush of wind swept over her body, and Anne could feel John's presence. She basked in the moment as she closed her eyes, and she resisted the guard's hand on her arm, as he had arrived with the commission to deliver her to her father.

She could feel the crushing pain in her chest, and she welcomed it as the reality took hold. John had been extinguished forever from the earth, and his tender arms would never hold her again. Her pillar of strength was now lifeless, and his soothing words had been choked from existence by a force that was far greater than any man could ever hope to conquer. Anne blocked her ears as the crowd rejoiced at the demise of the last of the great pirates from Providence. They were jubilant because they were sure that their commerce would now be restored.

The next day, the executioners took the bodies of Captain John Rackam, his master, George Fetherston, and his quartermaster, Richard Corner, and hung them in chains, one at Plumb Point, one at Bush Key, and the other at Gun Key. They were displayed as a public reminder to warn anyone who dared to call themselves a pirate of the awful fate that they too would have in store.

The nine men who boarded the ship to fellowship with John Rackam were detained in prison and finally sent to the gallows in the middle of February of 1721. The Frenchmen were never seen or heard from again, and hopefully they enjoyed their freedom, but doubtfully because their hands were filled with the blood of innocent men.

In March of 1721, Mary was delivered of her child by a midwife while she remained in prison. The midwife was not able to place the child on Mary's breast, as she had developed a high fever during her confinement. Mary's body succumbed to the infection, and she was laid to rest soon after the birth of her baby.

Daniel's heart was completely crushed by the death of his wife, but he was thankful for the beautiful son Mary had given him. One of the Negro women on his father's plantation was nursemaid to the child, and Daniel returned to his home in Caymen Brac after the child was weaned, where they lived a peaceful and serene life.

Governor Nicholas Lawes finally surrendered Charles Vane up to the executioners after a year of torture and not even one sign of repentance for the horrid crimes against humanity for which he had committed. On March 29, 1721, he was hanged. His body was then hung in chains at Gun Key at the entrance to Port Royal as a harrowing omen to anyone who would consider piracy.

CHAPTER 25

H ER FATHER MADE sure that Anne and Stephen were below deck when they exited the harbor, for it was either the body of John or one of his men that hung from the chains on the pinnacle that protruded out into the harbor. Whomever the body had belonged to, it was used as an emblem that had been deprived of all dignity in order that the Jamaican authority could flaunt their position with utmost supremacy.

The chancellor watched the grim sight from the bulwark, and he breathed a deep sigh of sadness over the whole situation. Governor Rogers had filled him in as to the character of John Rackam, and the chancellor was certain that under different circumstances, he would have delighted to know the man. He was proud that his daughter had followed John rather than James Bonny. As for James, the chancellor was only glad for one thing. His daughter no longer had a valid marriage decree.

Anne slept most of the way to South Carolina out of pure exhaustion from everything she had endured. When she was awake, she scrubbed her body with sea salt and moisturized with what oils she could find. She also managed to remove the snarls from her hair, but whatever she did, she wept incessantly for John.

Her father didn't press Anne to talk, but he longed for the day when they would, as he wanted to explain the details surrounding his love affair with her mother. He so wanted to tell Anne that he never considered her to be a bastard child, and he would never consider her child to be one as well.

The chancellor was a pillar of a man. He never gave up on Anne despite the immense pain and suffering she had caused him, as his love was pure and immovable for his daughter. Although he was not a perfect man and would bend the truth at times to save face, his dedication for Anne covered a multitude of sin. He was a much more humble man than he had ever been and a better man for it.

He promised Anne on their journey home that he would never judge her or use anything in her past against her. He took full responsibility for her bold adventure, for it was he who had raised her to be the powerful woman she had become. Anne was grateful that her father delighted in the adventure stories that she herself had lived out, and the more the chancellor heard about John Rackam, the more he honored the last great pirate of Providence.

It was December of 1720 when they entered the harbor of Charles Town. Standing at the bulwark, the chancellor could see the Court of Guard, and he thought to himself that there was no better place to hide an unmarried daughter, who happened to be with child, than a four-hundred-acre plantation.

Anne's reunions with Samuel and Ahyoka were exhilarating, and Anne was grateful to be home once again. She hugged Samuel first and then stood back to take a good look, and she said with glee. "Samuel, you haven't changed one bit. Look at you!"

Samuel replied in his broken accent, "I missed Anne." He offered a huge smile.

Anne was in awe. "Samuel, you've learned English!" She lowered her voice, "And don't I have a few new words to teach you, but you can't say them around children or my father, but we'll talk about it later."

Anne turned to the Indian servant, who was patiently waiting her turn, and held onto the old woman for a long while. "Ahyoka, I can't tell you how much I've missed you. I know you will understand everything I've been through, and I can't wait to tell you all about it."

After Anne had settled in, she assumed her position as the mistress of the plantation, and she planned to use the wisdom that she had acquired during her journeys in her dealings with the help. Anne tried to restrict herself to the mansion or the garden, so she wouldn't be discovered in her expanding condition, but one day, she compromised her hiding.

While sitting in the garden, Anne could hear a slave being chastised. She went to the smokehouse and grabbed her rapier. As she marched to the stable, her presentation as a young woman in her very pregnant condition holding a rapier was a jaw-dropping sight. She sternly admonished the overseer, "If you ever touch one of these Negros again, you will suffer a horrible death at the end of my rapier. Do I make myself clear?" It was not certain who was more astonished, the overseer or the slave, but the overseer never doled his cruelty again, and Anne followed up to make sure of it.

The chancellor gave Anne the freedom to run the plantation the way she desired, and she made some necessary changes. First and foremost, her father would never ship another slave across the Atlantic again—end of subject. Although the Cormacs still kept slaves and purchased others, they did so because it was the culture in which they were bred, and they had not been enlightened to realize the injustice of the travesty. Even so,

Anne treated her slaves as indentured servants with the freedom to leave the Cormac Manor if they so desired, and none ever did. The help was given every benefit of a family member and cared for during their lifetime, and in their dying days, they were treated with dignity and grace.

In January, Governor Rogers came for a stay, as his health started failing after the trial of John Rackam. He hoped that a period of rest would do him well. His hopes for recovery were short-lived, for while he was in Charles Town, he met with an old opponent from Providence and attempted to settle the dispute with a duel. Instead of returning to Nassau with his health, he returned with an injury incurred during the fight.

On the eighth of March, Johanna was born on Anne's twenty-first birthday. Anne was relieved when she heard the baby cry and the midwife placed her daughter to her breast. Anne could not cease from sobbing inconsolably. All the emotions from her four-year journey flowed from her heart like a fountain. Although some were tears of sorrow, mostly they represented an eclectic mixture of feelings that she had encountered during her four-year absence from Charles Town.

She so wished that John could see his beautiful daughter, and as much as she missed him, she was thankful that she was alive. As she gazed into the face of his child, Anne could see that Johanna was the precious image of her father. She thought of John's words, "Every time you look into the eyes of our child, you're going to see me." It was of truth, and it gave Anne strength. She arose from her bed and was determined to be the best mother that ever lived, and she was, for she loved and nurtured John's baby with all tenderness.

Stephen was an amazing big brother, and he and the chancellor had developed an inseparable relationship. Stephen truly was the son that the chancellor had never borne, but for whom he had always hoped. It was well with the chancellor to be called grandfather, as he would never want to rob the boy of John's title. The chancellor took pride in teaching Stephen everything that a well-bred son should know, and Stephen found a rare talent on his grandfather's harpsichord. Stephen also honed his fencing skills with Chidley Bayard, who continued to visit every year for his deer hide.

After the baby was born and once Anne's shape had returned, she was presented to society as having returned from her grand European tour. Anne didn't have much interest in venturing far from the plantation, which was probably all the better, as she didn't know the answers to the questions about her European trip. The chancellor was hailed as a generous man for taking the responsibility of his deceased sister's children, Stephen and Johanna, and providing the orphans with a good life. Anne was given much credit as being a great help in his endeavors.

It was when Johanna was almost three years old that Anne consented to marry Joseph Burleigh, the gentleman whom her father had given his permission for her to court at the grand ball the night she disappeared with James Bonny. Joseph was a pure gentleman, and Anne counted him as a brave man, because he had the courage to betroth a colonial woman who had sailed as a pirate. Joseph did not shy at the discovery but rather was intrigued, and his pursuit of her was even more robust thereafter. Anne was thankful that she had consented, as he was a passionate lover and an amazing father to Johanna.

It was Joseph who took his young family on the grand tour, so Anne could tell the tales of her European adventure with pride instead of avoiding the subject when asked in public. Although her passion for John Rackam could never be replicated, she must have had some interest, for she had seven more children after Johanna, and it is safe to say that Anne instigated the spawning of each one. Consequently, Joseph died a happy man.

Woodes Rogers came to visit the chancellor one last time in 1731 with his ailing health. It had been Woodes Rogers who had supplied Benjamin with a plethora of information he needed to complete his book that was published in 1724, which had raised Rogers to a heroic level once again. However, his personal life was never set in order, as he was in debt well beyond his means. Woodes Rogers returned to Nassau after a five-month stay at the Cormac manor and passed away in July of 1732, six years before his comrade, Chancellor Cormac.

Anne learned in her lifetime that a heart is large enough to weave many into its fabric, and each person has a special place. She discovered one trait that Joseph had that John would never have consented. Joseph loved to court Anne to a grand ball now and then. Anne would dress in the finest gowns that England could provide, and the two would dance until the last note was played. Anne chuckled to herself at the thought of John surrendering up his calico breeches for a pair of velvet knickers to join a bunch of aristocrats in a stuffy ballroom. Then she laughed out loud.

From the garden, the two women had a good laugh at the thought of John in knickers, and afterward, the garden was silent, as the sun settled below the horizon. The women had exhausted their emotions, as they had laughed and cried many times throughout the day. Listening to her mother's story gave Johanna a sense that she truly knew the man who had conceived her. She marveled at the revelation in which her mother had unfolded, and she needed time to fully process it all, but she knew that she loved her mother even far greater now than she ever had before. In her eyes, her mother was a saint. She had always felt that way, but ever more so now. Johanna was thankful that her mother had insisted upon her company, for she wouldn't have missed this occasion for the world.

Anne was thoroughly relieved that she had finally told Johanna the truth. She chided, "Go ahead, Beaufford Johnson, spread your tales, because it doesn't even matter any longer."

Johanna smiled and replied, "That's right, go ahead and do your damage upon the earth."

Anne didn't hold anything against the queer old man, and she didn't hold anything against Benjamin either. Anne knew why he had vilified her character among the pages of the book, for a tainted heroine was the prey upon which society delighted to feast. Anne could see Benjamin's plan, and it had been successful, as he had sold more books than he had ever anticipated. Many copies were purchased solely because of the tales of her and Mary. The thought of female pirates in that day was absurd, which presented quite a temptation to learn more.

Anne's only concern had been that because of Benjamin's skewed accounts of her life, Johanna would be persuaded into viewing her mother as a once-promiscuous woman. And why it really mattered, Anne wasn't quite sure. It was probably because of her mother's gentle words of instruction throughout her entire life. From the time Anne could remember, her mother would encourage her to be a chaste woman and to save herself for the one for whom she had vowed to love forever. Whatever the reason was, Anne's mind was put to ease, because Johanna had been told the entire story. Pierre's mind, however, was not at ease.

Pierre was livid when he read the account of his Anney. He rebuked Benjamin and accused him of being a woman-hater. Benjamin rebutted with, "But Pierre, no one will even know who she is. She's Anne Cormac, remember?" It took at least a month for Pierre to stop fuming, but he eventually came around, because the two men loved each other deeply, and they both had a determination to always work things out.

Anne never lost contact with Pierre. Once a month, Anne would go to the harbor to deliver a letter and retrieve Pierre's package. He always sent a note, some more lengthy than others, and always a gift of his latest creation. The lavender cream scrub was Anne's favorite. She had attempted to make it herself, but no one made it as well as Pierre. It was Pierre who kept her abreast of the latest happenings on Providence throughout the years.

Anne marveled that Pierre was still among the living and that he and Benjamin had grown to a ripe old age together. Anne chuckled at her innocence as she had never once suspected that Pierre would fancy anyone but a lady, but as she got older, the truth of his love interest became so evident to her. Anne figured that Pierre and Benjamin would probably live forever in the paradise of Providence, as they both continued to have their good health.

Millie and Rebecca had done a wonderful job tending Johanna's tasks for the day. In fact, Anne and Johanna had not been interrupted even once with the exception to inform them that Stephen was setting anchor. The two women concluded their discussion and went to rejoin the family. All the women would be needed to prepare for the family gathering, as Stephen, John, and Jeremiah were home. Johanna's family always gathered when the men would return from the West Indies after delivering their flour.

Anne's other seven children never developed a sense of togetherness like Johanna's family. They were wonderful human beings who were involved in their churches, social functions, and their own families, and they would all gather with Anne for the holidays. However, they never formed the sense of community that came natural for Johanna, a community of which Anne was eternally grateful for the opportunity of which to be a part. It reminded Anne of life on John's ship, except Johanna's family had the privilege of living in a grand mansion on a wonderful plantation, of which Anne owed it all to her dear father, the chancellor.

The family was waiting as the men were expected at any time. It was Stephen who had taken over the chancellor's shipping business when he had grown into a man, and a few years later, his nephews John and Jeremiah had joined him. The three probably loved their livelihoods more than any of the others, and the family always looked forward to the grand stories they would tell upon their return.

That evening as they gathered around the table, Anne could see that Johanna was more affectionate toward her husband than usual, and his response was favorable. Anne took in the beauty of each one of Johanna's children and wondered if Johanna would figure out the mystery of the part of John that he had imparted to each one of them.

Charles Whitney wrote his beautiful poetry like John had written to Anne when they were first falling in love. The twins, John and Jeremiah, had a fervent love of the sea, as much as John ever had. Luke was an excellent marksmen who's aim was ever as precise as John's had been.

It's as if Johanna had perceived Anne's thoughts when Johanna drew her aside and asked, "Is it George who favors his appearance?"

Anne replied, "A mirror image." The two women smiled, and they glanced over in time to see George with his grand smile brightening the entire room, and he offered a hearty laugh at the story in which Stephen had just completed.

All the boys were accounted for, and of course, Rebecca was the exact replica of Anne when she was younger, but Sarah was still a mystery, and it wouldn't be until years later that Anne would make the connection for Sarah.

It was not until Anne's health had failed and she was resolved to a feeble state that Sarah revealed her side of John. Just like John had watched over Anne the night she drank too much rum, Sarah never moved from her grandmother's bedside during the time of her dying. Anne had always felt a bit of guilt for not possessing fonder feelings for Sarah, and she had her suspicions that it might have been the name. With all that aside, Anne truly developed a deep love for Sarah as she was dying.

Anne was eternally grateful for the kindness that Sarah had bestowed upon her, just as John had done that night. It only took that one night to cause Anne to open her heart to the man whom she swore she would resist like the devil, and just as she had done with John, Anne opened her heart to Sarah as she tended her grandmother with utmost care.

Anne passed in her sleep at the age of eighty-two. She was not buried in the family cemetery with Mary Cormac and the chancellor, as Johanna feared that her mother's grave may be reviled by the bitter hearts who believed what they wanted to believe about her. Rather, Johanna chose to bury her mother in an unmarked grave in the garden next to Ahyoka, for it was there that her mother loved to be, and it was the garden from where her adventure had begun, an adventure that led Anne to her true love, John Rackam. Nevertheless, Johanna had never even liked the cemetery anyway.

CPSIA information can be obtained at www.ICGtesting.com
Printed in the USA
LVOW042202130712

289989LV00002BA/1/P